WHITELEY WORLDS ISSUE 35

CONNOR WHITELEY

No part of this book may be reproduced in any form or by any electronic or mechanical means.
Including information storage, and retrieval systems, without written permission from the author except for the use of brief quotations in a book review.

This book is NOT legal, professional, medical, financial or any type of official advice.

Any questions about the book, rights licensing, or to contact the author, please email
connorwhiteley@connorwhiteley.net

Copyright © 2024 CONNOR WHITELEY

All rights reserved.

INTRODUCTION

This might be the last issue of Whiteley Worlds this summer, but I am so excited about it. There are a lot of fun, enthralling, gripping short stories and novellas to help us celebrate the end of summer, and provide perfect escapism this month.

There might be a lot of brilliant *Way Of The Odyssey* science fiction short stories, but they're fun, eye-opening and certainly set up critical events for the future. We kick off this issue with *Socially Criminal*, a brilliant reimagining of social rules and class divides in this sci-fi mystery short story.

Blackheart is an interesting, unsettling, surprising short story showing how the heart of this dark Imperium works. New and current fans of this series will love this new addition to the ever-growing series.

Communicating In Ultraspace, not only explains how communication works in the far future but it explains one of the darkest, deepest and most terrifying mysteries of the series. Readers flat out don't want to miss this stellar landmark short story.

Battle Doctrines is a suspenseful, tense space opera short story exploring the tactics and warfare methods of different fractions of the series. All set inside an urgent, unputdownable fight for survival.

In addition, I included one of my favourite *Agents of The Emperor* short stories in this issue as well. *Diving In Space* is a gripping space opera story, perfect for fans of USA Bestselling writer Kristine Kathryn Rusch's Diving series. You won't be disappointed by that story.

I have a lot of love for the different short stories in this great issue, but it is the novellas that I have so much love and excitement for. Since *The Assassination of Bettie English* was a blast to write and I flat out loved every second of it. The book focuses on an epic race against time and bullets as private investigator Bettie English struggles to stay alive as she uncovers a deadly conspiracy to kill her.

I'll always have a lot of love for that book.

Convergence Of Odysseys is the first novella in the *Way of The Odyssey* series and it was so much fun to write. It's gripping, explosive, vivid and ultimately, the setting is awe-inspiring. Since when the odysseys of fate finally make Ithane Veilwalker and Jerico Nelson meet on the world of Genesis, they quickly realise something far bigger and darker pulls the strings of fate.

If you want pure action-packed, magical science fiction escapism this summer, you NEED to read this stunning book.

I hope you enjoy it as much as I did writing it.

Finally, in this issue of Whiteley Worlds, we have *Damage, Healing, Love*. A wonderfully sweet, heart-warming, romantic gay university second chance romance. I loved writing this book because it was me playing around with the idea of "what if" I saw a certain person again, and it was amazing fun.

I love writing gay romance because they are so sweet, moving and emotional novellas that they provide me with a fun break from the explosive or dark nature of my other novellas.

If you enjoy gay romance then you're going to love this book.

Now we know all the fun, enthralling stories in this issue, let's turn over the page and start exploring some Whiteley Worlds.

AVAILABLE NOW AT ALL MAJOR BOOKSELLERS!

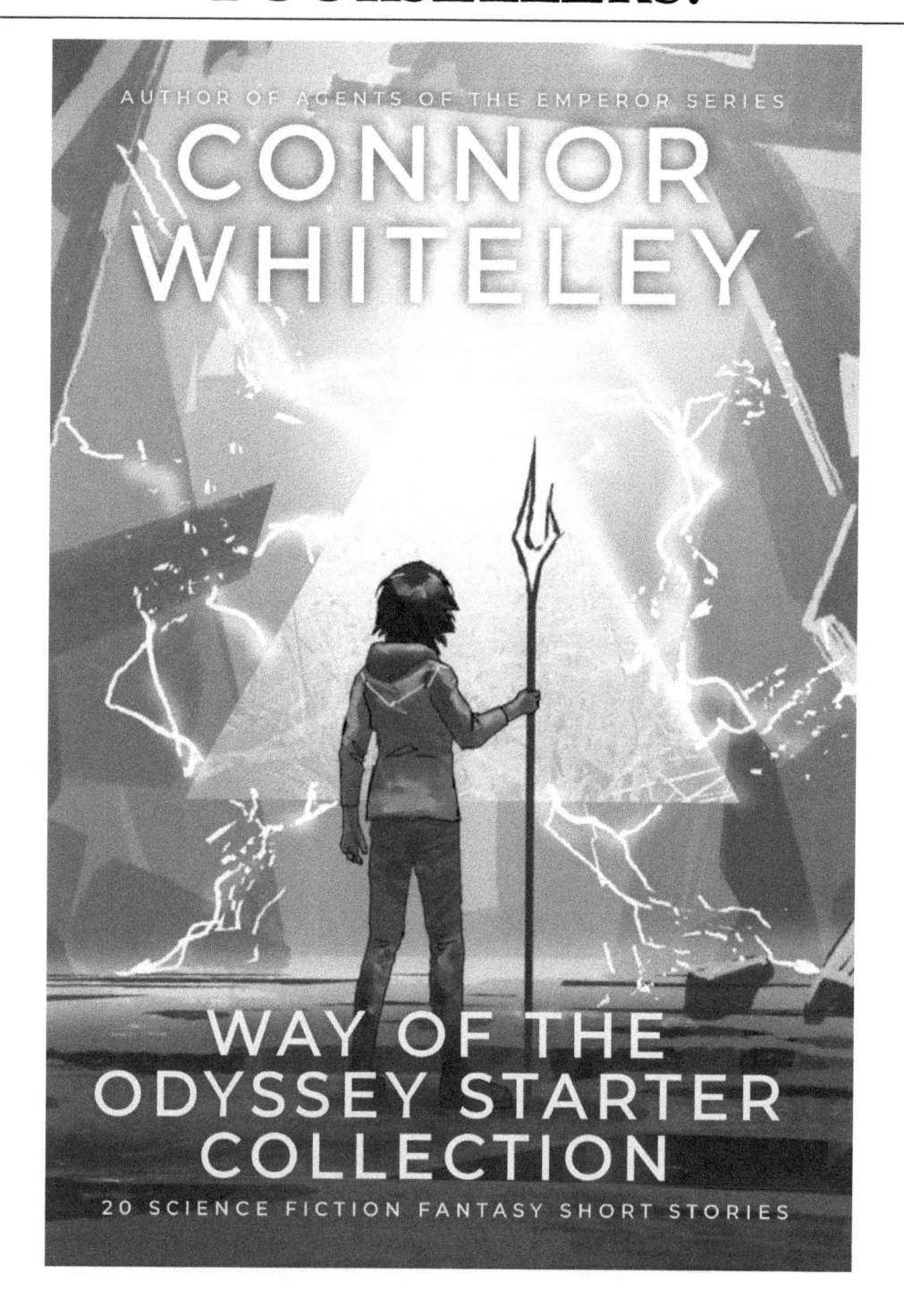

CONNOR WHITELEY

AUTHOR OF AGENTS OF THE EMPEROR SERIES

SOCIALLY CRIMINAL

A SCIENCE FICTION MYSTERY SHORT STORY

SOCIALLY CRIMINALLY

A Science Fiction Mystery Short Story

Justice Aisha Roar sat on her favourite cold, damp and sticky wooden bar stool in the messy Public House just off Main Street in the heart of the criminal underworld. The light was dark, scary and criminally good just how she liked it and the pub was thankfully filled with her favourite people tonight.

She sat towards the back like she always did and she pressed her black-armoured back against the sticky wooden walls that stunk of cheap alcohol, sex and sweat, just like how a good pub should smell. There were a few floating orbs of light swimming around against the dirty black ceiling providing just enough light, but it wasn't like anyone here actually wanted to see anyone's faces.

Everyone here was just here to drink, be merry and maybe have some random sex because it just felt good in the moment.

Aisha had always loved her time here and the constant background noise of people talking, laughing and shouting made her thinly smile. It was always great to be here after a long day of hunting down criminals and killing them because that was the law, but she always loved a good drink even more.

There was a brand-new wooden stage up at the front of the pub which Aisha really didn't like, because there was some hip-pop rubbish band from Earth playing there.

Aisha really didn't know what crime those fools had committed to end up in some junk bar like this one. The musicians were good, damn good so Aisha just couldn't understand whatsoever why these people wanted to play here.

They could easily get thousands of Rexes and then even more through tips if they played in the Spires, where the posh people lived. So maybe their crime was just stupidity and Aisha was half tempted to donate some of her money to them but she had already met her personal monthly quota of charity giving.

And she wouldn't want to get a foul reputation as a do-gooder. She actually shuddered at the very idea.

A cute young couple walked past her table, the woman looked okay wearing a very short black skirt, and the young man looked stunning in his tight jeans, shirt and boots. Hopefully both of them were in for a lucky night tonight, but Aisha was still alone.

Most of the Justices on the planet preferred to be alone because it was what their job required, each Justice was a law onto themselves and no one except the Glorious Rex himself on Earth could ever challenge their judgement.

It didn't make dating easy, it certainly made having a family impossible but Aisha still loved her job. It was her small way of helping to make the Imperium a better place with less freaks, criminals and alien scum in it.

"Lady Justice," a man said coming over to the table.

Aisha rolled her eyes. As much as she loved helping people, donating secretly to charities and making the Imperium a safer place, everyone knew never to disturb a Justice when they were drinking.

There might not have been a lot of social activity in the Imperium outside of work, watching fights and gambling, but drinking was a sacred activity of the Justices.

"I was hoping to have a moment of your time in exchange for this," the man said.

A small floating orb of light hovered over head and Aisha had a feeling that the owner of the pub was watching her, technically illegally but privacy was a joke these days.

Aisha focused on the small crystal glass of golden liquid and she instantly knew it was a very fine whiskey not found on this planet. That had to have cost the man a few thousand Rexes, so why was he giving it to her?

Aisha looked at the man and he was surprisingly young with smooth sexy features, a pretty face and his slim body looked amazing in his tight robes denoting he was from the local College.

Definitely a man that did not belong in the deepest, darkest depths of this planet.

"Are there not Justices at the Colleges? In the Spires? In your own family?" Aisha asked.

The floating orb of light dipped a little lower and if it dared to get much closer then Aisha would happily smash it. What could the owner of the pub do? Call the Justices?

"Of course but I require a more roguish touch for my problem and I know you have a very effective reputation for getting rid of people," the man said.

Aisha had to admit she loved how her reputation was finally taking shape but she really didn't want this young man thinking that Justices were dangerous, it was the criminals they hunted that they were the real danger. Then she just smiled because the constant indoctrination that all subjects of the Imperium went through should take care of that.

"Of course, if your target has committed a crime then they will die. That is the law. If they steal a slice of bread, they die. If they assault someone, they die. If they murder someone, they die," Aisha said.

The young man frowned a little. "My wedding application got denied recently and I want you to fix it,"

Aisha smiled. It was a great effective feature of the Imperium that in order for two people to get married the Rex had to personally approve it and even then they could only get married if it served the Imperium.

A lot of maths, statistics and problem-solving was used to calculate how great the marriage would impact the Imperium and most of the time marriages were accepted. It was important to the fabric of society that the rich only married the rich, doctors only married doctors and the poor only married the poor. It was critical to stop the corrupting influence of the lower classes from ruining the rich people that were actually going to make something of themselves.

Aisha wasn't always sure she agreed with but it was an interesting idea.

"The Rex made his decision, even a Justice cannot overrule them. What were the stated reasons?" Aisha asked.

"I cannot marry my girlfriend because I am a student and she is a military Commander two years older than me,"

Aisha nodded. That was strange and it meant that the girlfriend had to come from a military family to get promoted that quickly. But students and military types were always marrying.

Except when one thing was revealed.

"What are you studying in?" Aisha asked.

The man smiled and Aisha smiled too. He was clearly passionate about it, so it had to be something grand like the military, sciences, medicine or a whole host of other brilliant subjects.

"I'm studying game design," the man said.

Aisha just reached across the table, grabbed the man's whiskey and downed it in one.

There was nothing kind she could say to the man because game design was useless to helping the Imperium survived so he was a useless man. But it was clear as day that he loved the subject.

And Aisha had always respected passion.

"And I refused to take the propaganda module," the man said.

Out of instinct Aisha moved her hand down to her waist where her gun was but she stopped her. This young man wasn't a radical that was a danger to the Imperium. He was just a young man that wanted to marry his girlfriend.

He did not need to die no matter how many of her peers would have killed him for not helping the Imperium indoctrinate young minds through games.

That was actually a crime so technically she had to kill this young man but she wanted to learn more and help him.

And if she found more evidence of his crimes against the Imperium then she would sadly have to kill him.

"I've come to you because the personal reference on my marriage application lied about me," the man said.

Aisha leant forward. Now that was a much more serious crime.

"What's your name?" Aisha asked as she stood up and downed the rest of her drink in one.

"Joshua Laurie," he said.

Aisha grabbed him and took him out of the pub. "Well Joshua, take me to this liar and then we will see how he committed the most outrageous crime imaginable. They lied to the Glorious Rex himself,"

Aisha felt so excited as they left the pub because she was finally going to hunt down her criminal.

A criminal that might need the ultimate punishment.

***

Aisha was hardly surprised too much when Joshua led her down through the dirty, stinky and toxic narrow streets of the criminal underworld with her fingers tightly on the trigger of her gun.

Then Joshua led her into a very crawl and dirty metal chamber inside an abandoned building. The chamber itself was immense covered with black mouldy walls, puddles of stagnant water covered the floor as did streaks of brown dried blood.

Aisha just smiled as she watched two very attractive middle-aged men clearing up after the fight that had caused the streaks of blood, and judging by the sheer amount of holo-cigars, bullets and broken weapons there must have been a hell of a crowd here tonight.

There were only three social activities in all of the Imperium. There was drinking which Aisha loved, there was watching or taking part in fights or there was gambling. Aisha really didn't like the last two because she preferred fighting on the streets (illegal to all but Justices) and gambling was just stupid.

But judging by the chamber some people seriously loved watching a good fight.

"This is the man that lied on my application," Joshua said pointing to one of the two middle-aged men.

Aisha pointed her gun at him and just focused on how disgusting he looked in his dirty cloak, soaked-through boots and blackened teeth.

"Why the hell did you want this man on your wedding application?" Aisha asked.

"Because I'm his father," the man said.

Aisha just shook her head. There really was no ending to humanity's stupidity and it made no sense how this man working in the criminal underworld had managed to get a son into a local College. That should have been impossible.

Aisha made a note to herself to investigate the College tomorrow. There was no telling if Joshua's criminal family might have started corrupting the rich students of the College.

"Why did you lie dad on my application? I saw it and you said I was unfaithful to my girlfriend and I had donated to pro-Keres charities,"

Aisha pointed the gun at the son. The

Keres were foul alien abominations that wanted to destroy humanity and their way of life. It was an awful crime to help them.

"Relax Lady Justice, he did no such thing," the father said.

Aisha decided to put her gun away because these two people made no sense and their actions literally went against how the Imperium worked.

"How are you two even related? There are strict laws against poor degenerates going to College. How did you get in?" Aisha asked.

Joshua smiled. "My girlfriend pulled a few strings and got me into college. I rose up through the class quickly and effectively and now I'm on the Student Council,"

As much as Aisha wanted to be annoyed that a poor person had a position of power in the local College, she actually couldn't be annoyed. The man was clearly intelligent, kind and passionate and of course Aisha would never admit this to her peers but the Imperium needed more people like that.

And so many of the laws were just dumb social laws to control others that it was just so stupid.

Poor people needed to go to College, get educated and help the Imperium, because the rich people were hardly doing an amazing job.

The father came over to Aisha. "Please don't arrest me and my son. We're good people, I provide innocent workers with sanctioned entertainment and that is what my son wants to do. We want to be entertainers, not criminals,"

All of Aisha's instincts, training and textbooks were telling her to just kill these two people now because they were a theoretical threat to the Imperium, but they weren't.

They seriously weren't.

Aisha knew that the father just wanted to entertain people as did the son just through different methods, but there was still one important question left.

"Why didn't you want your son getting married?" Aisha asked.

The father looked at the ground focusing on a long streak of blood that looked impossible to clean.

"I wanted my son to marry who he actually loves. He doesn't love the military girl, they both only wanted sex from each other and they were both using each other,"

Aisha looked at Joshua. "Is this true?"

Joshua nodded like he was proud of it. "Yeah. She wanted to have sex with a poor degenerate for the thrill and I wanted to go to College. I wanted her as much as she wanted me but when her father started asking questions she wanted to get married to protect herself,"

"And you didn't?" Aisha asked.

Joshua nodded and Aisha had to admit it was nice when the father hugged his son, that was a rare sight these days in the Imperium. A very unfortunate day.

As Aisha just looked at the father and son she couldn't deny how badly the law said they both had to die. The father had lied to the Rex himself, the son had illegally gone to College and used a military girl for his own gain (a strange little law made that illegal) and even the girlfriend needed to die technically because she had been having sex outside her permissible social rank.

It was all so stupid and as much as it would end Aisha's life, career and drinking fund if anyone found out she simply lowered her gun and walked away.

There were no crimes here, not real ones anyway, and all these social crimes were all victimless but Aisha still had to investigate the College just in case.

But she really, really hoped that Joshua would find happiness because it was the very least that everyone deserved.

***

Aisha had loved stalking the long perfectly clean, refreshingly nutty-scented air of the local College as she had investigated for any sign of corruption amongst the local rich students, and thankfully there had been none. In fact they seemed to be even more dedicated and indoctrinated into the Imperial Cult that worshipped everything the Rex said as divine law.

That was brilliant for the sake of the Imperium.

As Aisha sat later that night at the back of the bar again resting her black armour against the wooden sticky walls and her hands wrapped around a wonderfully cold tankard of beer, she was really happy with herself.

Because by proving that the law was wrong about the strict social controls of the Imperium, maybe she could get them to be dropped as laws and then the Rex's plans for mass indoctrination could be even stronger, better and more effective so no one could ever question the righteousness of his rule.

Then maybe there would be less criminals and that meant more drinking time in this great pub. Aisha really did enjoy the constant sweet aromas of sweat, stale beer and sex, there was just nothing else like it.

And in a cold, unloving galaxy, Aisha knew that love was always needed and now Joshua was alive and free to find who he loved and hopefully Aisha could find someone to love her in the end.

She smiled at that, that really would be an amazing thing to have.

But until then would always be more criminals, more murders and thieves to find, investigate and kill and that seriously excited Aisha a lot more than she ever wanted to admit.

AVAILABLE NOW AT ALL MAJOR BOOKSELLERS!

AUTHOR OF AGENTS OF THE EMPEROR SERIES
CONNOR WHITELEY
ODYSSEY OF REBIRTH
A SCIENCE FICTION ADVENTURE NOVELLA

AVAILABLE NOW AT ALL MAJOR BOOKSELLERS!

AUTHOR OF AGENTS OF THE EMPEROR SERIES

CONNOR WHITELEY

CONVERGENCE OF ODYSSEYS

A SCIENCE FICTION ADVENTURE NOVELLA

DIVING IN SPACE

A SCIENCE FICTION SPACE OPERA SHORT STORY

CONNOR WHITELEY

AUTHOR OF AGENTS OF THE EMPEROR

DIVING IN SPACE
A Science Fiction Space Opera Short Story

Set against the stunning black oblivion of space, Diving Expert Marcus Joseph just looked into the perfectly calm, relaxing and exciting vastness of space out of the large floor-to-ceiling windows that were thankfully so common on all blade-like ships of the Great Human Empire.

A handful of bright red blade-like shuttles seemed to slowly float past the window as they passed the long blade-like space station of Omega-49 and the large red, green and blue planets in the Omega system just looked stunning.

The largest planet of the solar system looked very alluring with its constant hurricanes storming all over the planet, and yet somehow there were constantly moving but thriving colonies on the planet.

That was just yet another symbol of humanity's endless intelligence, engineering marvels and impressiveness. Marcus seriously loved how he got to travel all over the Empire seeing world after world and working in the place he loved.

He had always loved the sheer beauty and calmness of space ever since he was a child and went on his first-ever holiday to some planet that was well and truly dead now. Even then he had enjoyed the journey through space a hell of a lot more than the planet itself.

The planet might have been pretty but to Marcus, space was simply a perfect blend of magic, hope and endless possibilities and he was so glad that he finally got to work in space.

Omega-49 itself was a great accomplishment of Empire engineering and Marcus had worked on tons of space stations with his crew before performing dives on them to fix this and that but Omega-49 had to be the best.

There were tons of perks of the diving job like being out in space, getting paid a hell of a lot of money and more, but his second favourite perk after being out in space had to be staying in the most exclusive hotels as compensation.

A lot of people who arrived at Imega-49 never stayed longer than a few hours because it was just a waystation, but for people who needed to sort out paperwork before progressing down to any planet's surface they needed to stay in tiny cramped little hotel rooms.

Unless they had a lot of money and Marcus really loved it how him and his crew had been gifted the same rooms.

Marcus had been amazed how the air smelt so fresh and clean with hints of lavender, he had never smelt air that refreshing before, and the large open plan room itself with its own living room, kitchenette and massive bedroom was just amazing.

He partly wished his boyfriend hadn't been sent off on another diving job because the two of them certainly could have made excellent use of that massive bed. It would have been delightful.

"Good morning Mark," two women said behind him as they entered.

Marcus smiled at Jessica and Moncrieff, Monk for short, as they came into the large open-planned conference room with some "interesting" abstract art on the three metal walls of the room.

They were both wearing their white blouses, black trousers and black high heels as this was a business meeting and Marcus really hoped they were going to get a lot of money for this job. The rooms were expensive so hopefully the clients had money to burn, he meant spend on them.

Marcus gestured to the two girls they should take a seat on the large triangular conference table with light blue holograms showing streams of data to them. The data was going a little too quick for him to read it properly but it was something about the temperature and the other environmental systems.

"Good morning," a man said that Marcus had never seen before.

He was a large rich man with a large gut but as soon as he came and sat at the conference table the entire room started to smell of oranges, pecans and cranberries leaving the tangy, fruity taste of cranberry sauce form on Marcus's tongue.

The man certainly wasn't used to working with dive teams because he really should have given them more information before he hired them, but Marcus was getting to stay in a great hotel so he wasn't going to argue too much.

"I need you all to replace the environmental calibrator for us," the man said.

Marcus looked at the girls briefly and neither one of them seemed too impressed. That was the reaction he wanted, the problem with space stations was that all the environmental bits and pieces were always at the bottom.

And that created tons of problems with divers as it was so close to the communication wires, towers and metal pods that made getting lines tangled and ripping suits a very real danger.

The man smiled. "I am Hutch of Turning & Hutch InterSystem Hotels. I am going to be paying you ten thousand credits per minute to get the job done,"

Marcus looked at the girls again and they looked at him. None of them knew how to react because that was a great deal of money and it made no sense why he was offering that much for a simple fixing job.

"How many other dive teams have tried?" Monk asked.

Marcus nodded.

"Three teams. All died," Hutch said like it was nothing and it probably was nothing to him.

"Why don't you try bringing the space station onto a planet with low gravity for repairs?" Jessica asked.

"Because that would cost a lot of money and I would have to cancel guests. I cannot lose that much money and it is cheaper paying out to families because you died than cancelling guests' stays,"

Marcus just shook his head. He had always liked blunt business people but he was a business person.

"Is there anything else? Because I have to watch out for my people and this is too much of a risk," Marcus said.

Hutch nodded. "Of course but I have hired you because you are the best and in two hours the enviro-systems on the station will fail completely. And then ten minutes after that everyone will suffocate,"

Again he said that like it was nothing and Marcus just couldn't believe how cold he was being but there was probably no time for an evacuation and even if everyone did survive there would probably be too many people spreading the news about how deadly the hotel was.

Whatever happened Hutch and Turning as a company would fail after this unless Marcus and his crew helped them.

As much as Marcus didn't want to take the job because of how deadly it was, he really didn't want any of the innocent people on the station to suffocate either.

"Tell us what you want done," Marcus said.

***

With only an hour left before the enviro-systems failed completely, Marcus, Jessica and Monk were all in the large grey lifeless hangar of the space station that was closest to the enviro-systems that needed to be repaired.

Marcus had thankfully bought his own suits with him and with the high risk of suits being torn, he had decided to sacrifice speed and agility for protection. So he was wearing a slightly bulkier than normal bright orange suit with a thick plastic helmet around his face.

He hated the plastic helmets because he felt like a goldfish and the plastic messed with the technological readouts from his equipment because it was the only helmet he could have with good protection.

All he could hear over the loud hum of the space station's engines were the long, slow breaths coming from himself and it was almost deafening. That was another reason why he hated these plastic helmets, they really amplified the sound of his breathing.

Jessica stood proudly at the very edge of the hangar with her bright orange feet just over the edge and she had both her lines tightly in her hands.

Marcus grabbed his breathing line in his left hand and the icy cold line that attached him to the hangar, so if he slipped he wouldn't float off into space, in his right.

On normal jobs he would have a breathing line and would have used the technology that recycled his own breath and made it into oxygen but considering the dangers of the job he would have preferred a constant stream of oxygen.

The suit smelt fresh and clean and the hint of harsh cleaning chemicals filled with senses but Marcus forced himself not to focus on that as he slowly went over to Monk, allowing the two lines to slowly pass through his hands.

The job was simple enough and Marcus made sure that the small square suitcase filled with the replacement parts was tightly attached to his back. Again, he would have preferred something more flexible so the material could easily get unsnagged if it got caught but Hutch wasn't having any of it.

And he was the billpayer at the end of the day.

Marcus stood next to Jessica and her voice thankfully echoed in his ear so at least their communications were working.

"You ready boss?" Jessica asked.

Marcus nodded. "Remember we have to do the job slowly and carefully. Do you read us Monk?"

"Yes boss, your signs are good and I'll bring the lines in if you get into trouble," she said.

Marcus felt so relieved that Monk was the person staying behind making sure that if anything was to go wrong she could react and help them, or bring in their unconscious bodies if needed.

Hopefully she wouldn't be needed at all.

"Let's go," Marcus said and a second later Jessica nodded.

The first part of the dive was always the most exciting as Marcus stepped out through the thin film-like shield that separated the hangar and the cold void of space and as his suit hummed to life the icy cold sensation of being in space was gone.

But Marcus still loved how freeing it was, he loved being out in space and it was just magical being able to float around without gravity for a few moments until his suit's abilities activated.

As Marcus felt his hands warm up so the mag-lock technology was activated, he slowly turned himself around making sure his lines weren't going to get caught on anything and he smiled as they were so close to the immense white blade-like dip of the space station.

The dip was only a few tens of metres away from them and Marcus just gasped and smiled like a schoolboy when he realise all the thousands of kilometres of the sheer white space station above them. They really were like ants crawling over a planet.

Marcus used the mag-lock technology to slowly pull himself towards the white metal hull of the space station and thankfully there weren't any immediate signs of danger. No rough pieces of metal, no rods that shot out and no space traffic to interfere with them.

Marcus made sure that Jessica was okay and she seemed to be just fine.

They both started climbing down the space station making sure they did it quick enough because of the threat of everyone dying but slowly enough that they didn't miss any real dangers.

"What needs changing again?" Jessica asked.

"The environmental calibrator. It should be on the outside of the enviro-system stuff so it shouldn't be hard to get to," Marcus said.

They both continued down the side of the space station but Marcus hissed when he saw the bottom of the station and it was clear now why so many people had died trying to do this.

The dips of all space stations were meant to be smooth without things shooting out of them and any risks to divers, but this space station was very much the exception to the rule.

The very bottom of the space station had to be easily the size of a small parking lot but it was covered in immense icy grey rods used for communication signals and the station had clearly been attacked at some point judging from the sharp burnt pieces of metal.

It was going to be next to impossible to get through all of his without getting a line caught.

Marcus could just about see the small black metal box in the middle of the dip so that had to be the environmental calibrator that they needed to change.

Marcus slowly went down to and floated just in front of the communication signal rods, using the mag-lock technology of his suit to stop him going off into space.

"What you see down there?" Jessica asked, and Marcus realised that she was right above him.

"I'm wondering can we hold onto the signal rods and use them to pull us towards the calibrator," Marcus said.

"Negative," Monk said. "Communication rods are far too delicate for that and this space station has thousands of incoming and outgoing messages each second. If you touch a rod then you risk entire messages getting destroyed,"

Marcus rolled his eyes. Of course he couldn't do things the easy way.

"And I take it I can't use my mag-lock technology too much because the interference it would cause with the rods." Marcus said.

"Confirmed," Monk said, "and Hutch wants me to tell you that they're trying to communicate with the planets about getting help to the station before the systems fail,"

Marcus had no idea why they didn't just do that earlier but Hutch wasn't his concern for now, saving all of these people was.

Jessica eased her way down next to him and Marcus wanted to remind her how risky that was because one false move would get their lines tangled together but he trusted her.

"How about I push you over to the calibrator and you use your mag-lock tech for one second to get you over there?" Jessica said.

It wasn't the worse plan that Marcus had ever heard because it wasn't ideal. They could get their lines tackled, the push might make him go off course and he could cut his suit perhaps on one of the rods.

But it was the best idea they had for now.

"Okay," Marcus said.

He moved his body so he was perfectly streamlined and he reached towards just below the dip of the space station so he wouldn't hit any of the communication rods.

He felt Jessica grab his feet and she pushed him.

Marcus floated towards the bottom of the station and he loved it. He was flying through space.

He felt something pull on his line.

A yellow warning light flashed into his helmet.

His line connecting him to the space station was caught.

Marcus hit a communication rod and he felt their weak metal structure wrap around him. He was trapped but grateful that the suit hadn't ripped for now.

Yellow warning lights flashed around his head highlighting ten pressure points that could rip at any moment.

"It wasn't me I promise," Jessica said.

Marcus carefully moved his head just enough to see that his attachment line had wrapped itself around the edge of the communication rod. Damn that.

"Boss you okay? The station's communication system has gone dark," Monk said. "We cannot get any support now,"

Marcus rolled his eyes. That was the last thing that he wanted to hear.

"Jess," Marcus said, "with the communication system down you think I could use meg-lock tech now?"

He had no idea if it would work but he seriously hoped so.

"No, because these rods are too weak. Any use of mag-lock tech could rip and destroy them,"

"Damn it!" Marcus shouted. He just wanted something to go right.

Then he remembered how mag-lock technology worked two ways. It could bring a person closer to a metal object but it could also push them away from one.

Marcus reversed the technology in his hands and activated the tech in his feet to and he managed to push himself off the rods.

Then he disconnected his line attaching him to the ship and he carefully climbed the line to where it was wrapped around and he unwrapped it.

His heart pounded in his chest as he finished unwrapping it because one false move and he would have been sent off into space.

Then Marcus carefully swung himself over the dip of the space station and he used his mag-lock tech to pull himself down.

Jessica laughed in his ear in happiness and Marcus was surprised that the fix was simple as swapping one black small suitcase that was what housed the calibrator with the fixed one and his communicators between him, Monk and Jessica filled with static.

Jessica fled the scene and Marcus didn't understand why and he couldn't ask her.

Her head popped over the lip of the space station and she waved him to follow her which he did.

A moment later he felt the strange heat and light energy zap behind him as the calibrator got connected into the enviro-systems and started performing tasks Marcus had no idea about.

He was a diver, not an engineer and he was more than glad he had managed to save the lives of all the wonderful innocent people on the station with the help of some even better friends.

***

Marcus supposed he really shouldn't have been surprised the next morning (Earth time of course) when the large blue blade-like warships of the Arbiters turned up, stormed the hotel and arrested Hutch for risking the lives of everyone onboard. At least Hutch had already paid them in full with a little bonus on top which certainly made the delightful breakfast of steamed red rice, smoked Beast meat and boiled Lava eggs even more delicious considering this entire breakfast probably cost a few thousand.

Marcus sat at a large circular table with Jessica and Monk chomping away at their own great-looking breakfasts, all whilst the constant talking, chattering and laughter of the hotel guests in their wide-ranging states of dress became mere background noise.

Marcus had really enjoyed this ship, the dive was always thrilling and everything about his job he loved more than life itself. And it was even better that he had his two best friends in the whole Empire right next to him.

Monk's freshly fried fish smelt heavenly as she sliced it up and carefully wrapped each piece around her fork before taking a careful mouthful like the food here was more dangerous than the dive.

"What's the next job boss?" Monk asked after a mouthful.

Jessica leant forward so she was on the edge of her seat. Damn, Marcus really couldn't have asked for better friends that were just as passionate about this job as he was.

Marcus shrugged. "I checked out a bunch of contracts last night and if we travel back to the Sol System, I hear there's a space station that might would need repairing in a year's time. We should be able to get there in time,"

Jessica raised her tall blade-like glass of "orange" juice from a world he couldn't pronounce and they all cheered each other.

"To a job well done and to many a thousand more," Marcus said before sipping his bitter coffee that was just right.

The two girls nodded and Marcus was so looking forward to meeting back up with his boyfriend on the way to Sol and he couldn't wait to get back out into the icy cold void of space once more. But as the girls started laughing about one of Hutch's oddities, Marcus just grinned because he was going to have to wait for about a year, but he couldn't think of better company for that year than the two women at the table.

They really were the best of friends and Marcus loved that.

AVAILABLE NOW AT ALL MAJOR BOOKSELLERS!

AUTHOR OF AGENTS OF THE EMPEROR
CONNOR WHITELEY
A CRASH COURSE PROBLEM
A SCIENCE FICTION SOLARPUNK SHORT STORY

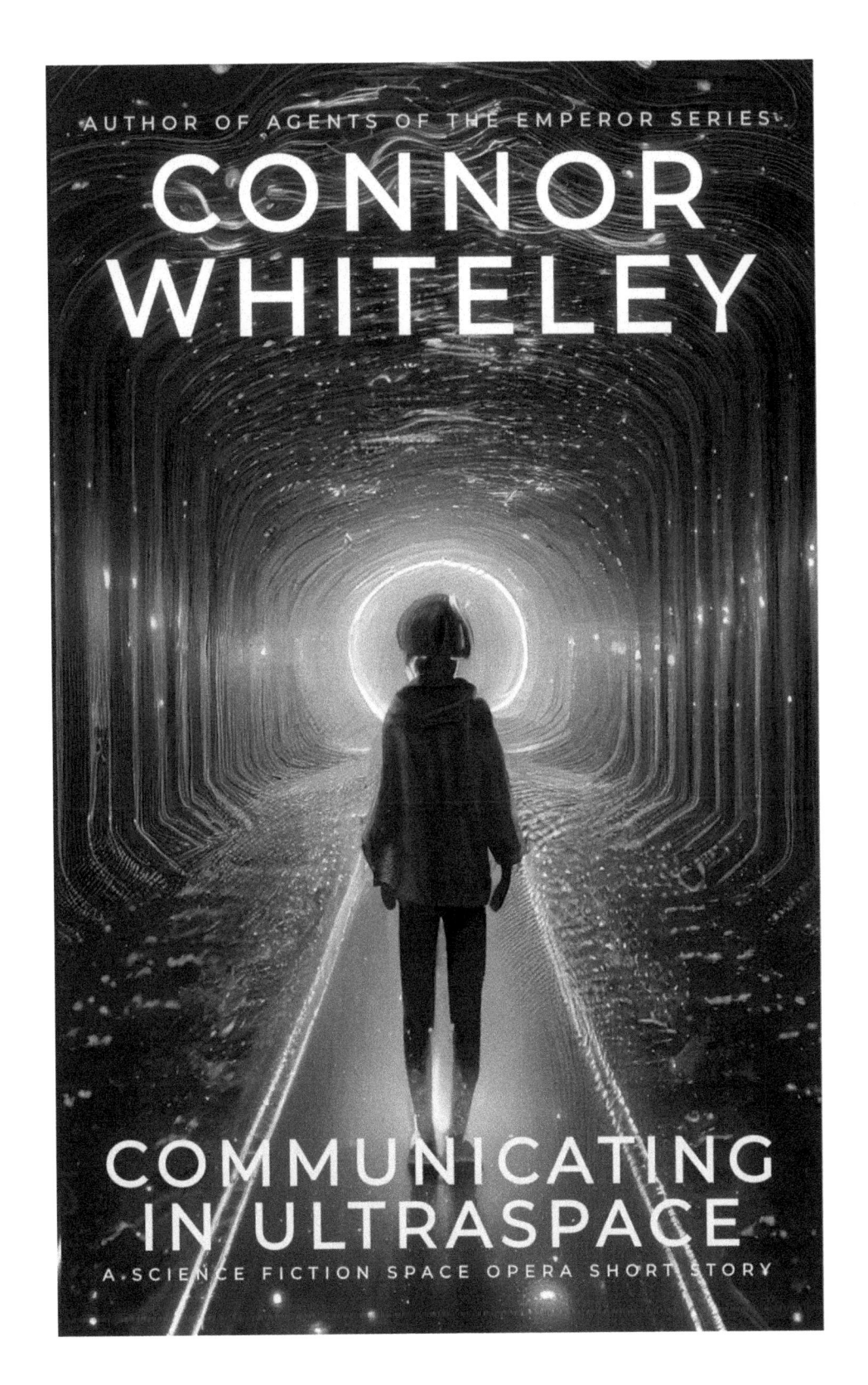

AUTHOR OF AGENTS OF THE EMPEROR SERIES
CONNOR WHITELEY

COMMUNICATING IN ULTRASPACE
A SCIENCE FICTION SPACE OPERA SHORT STORY

COMMUNICATING IN ULTRASPACE
A Science Fiction Space Opera Short Story

COMMUNICATING IN ULTRASPACE

This was the day he died.

Chief Communication Officer Grayson Jones sat on a large grey metal table that was surprisingly smooth, shiny and very relaxing oddly enough. It was almost strange for a table in his little metal boxroom of a break room to be so relaxing and well-maintained. Normally when he worked on ships the breakrooms were so dilapidated that they were just flat out disgusting.

Thankfully everything about the brand-new black circular ship imaginatively called the *Communication* was up to date, clean and perfectly maintained. Grayson had already been on the ship for two weeks and he had yet to find a single problem with the ship.

The only problem with the ship was that it was the smooth walls of the break room were just so plain and dull. Grayson wanted to splash some colour on the walls and maybe hang a few pictures. A nice red, blue or orange might have looked nice and it would be a nice reminder of his homeworld.

Grayson really liked that idea as he wrapped his rough hand around his coffee mug, the sharp bitter taste of it was one of the highlights of living on the ships. And it helped to provide a brief distraction against the overwhelming aromas of roasted peaches, sweat and salted peanuts that clung to everything in the corridor amongst the ship.

He didn't know why the environmental systems were so obsessed with the smell, they could have been faulty, but it was rather nice at first before getting old real quick.

At least the job was simple enough, he was just in charge of making sure all the equipment ran smoothly so all the nearby Imperial forces could route their communications through his station, before the ship blasted the messages off through Ultraspace towards their destination.

Ultraspace was amazing and Grayson really loved learning about it at university. It was just stunning how humanity had managed to create or tap into an intergalactic network of tunnels that allowed for faster-than-light travel.

It was simply brilliant.

And the only thing Grayson needed to do was keep it all working otherwise he absolutely hated to imagine what would happen if he failed. Battle orders might not be read or sent, distress calls might not be heard and vital intelligence might not be known about aliens and terrorists.

If Grayson failed then he sadly knew a lot of good people could die and there was no way he was ever allowing himself to have that on his conscious. He didn't volunteer for five years in the Peace Corps to allow innocent people to die.

"We have a problem," a woman said as a large circular door opened with an annoying screaming sound that almost made Grayson jump.

He looked at the Chief of Engineering, a beautiful woman called Mary wearing a very attractive pink blouse, trousers and white trainers.

But if she was coming to him then it had to be bad.

"What happened this time?" Grayson asked grinning.

"The Ultraspace generator died," Mary said plainly.

Grayson just shook his head. Of all the damn things that could possibly go wrong, he seriously didn't want this to be the problem.

Without their Ultraspace generator then the ship couldn't run away or travel through the network basically increasing their travel time by a factor of 100 and that meant the Ultraspace Communicator would fail sooner or later too.

Grayson had sadly worked too many jobs where the failing of the Ultraspace generator wasn't seen as the first sign of an Ultraspace shutdown on the ship so when the damn aliens attacked. There was no way of escape or call for help.

Those people always died.

"And there's ten Keres ships two systems over. The great benefits of invading their territory," Mary said.

Grayson seriously didn't want to attract the attention of the foul alien beasts with their awful magic. He wanted to escape in short order and he hardly agreed with Mary about space being the Keres' domain. The stars belonged to humanity and only humanity.

"I presume you've tried turning it on and off?" Grayson asked.

Mary playfully hit him over the head. "I didn't come to you to get mocked. This is a communicator error, the Ultraspace Communicator is *telling* the Generator to shut down,"

Grayson leant forward. He had heard a hell of a lot of things in his decades of service as a soldier fighting the Keres and then even more as a communication specialist. He had never heard of pieces of the ship *telling* each other what to do.

He wasn't even sure if the Keres's magic could do such things to Imperial ships.

"Take me there immediately please," Grayson said.

He was surprised at how hesitant Mary was to let him go but she nodded after a few seconds and smiled.

"You're going to need an environmental suit. It's pretty nasty in there,"

Grayson hated it how his stomach twisted into a painful knot as he realised that things were going to get a hell of a lot worse before they could ever get better.

***

Grayson had always hated damn environmental suits. He hated their bright red appearance that made him look like a tomato, he hated how his movements were so slow and controlled and he hated how it was always just damn impossible to see out of them.

Even now as he slowly went into the environmentally sealed Ultraspace chamber, an immense black metal chamber with two huge metal tanks containing strange complex technology allowing them to tap into Ultraspace whenever they wanted, Grayson realised just how bad this all actually was.

He had been in chambers like this all over the Imperium and they never changed much but they were always clean, smelt sweet and they always left the taste of lemon drizzle cake on his tongue just like how his father used to make it when he was a child.

But this chamber was simply disgusting with the smell and taste of harsh chemicals, toxic radiation and death filling his senses. His suit's warning systems were already starting to flare to life and no one else knew this but Grayson knew there was a rip in Ultraspace.

He had read about Ultraspace rips plenty of times and they were always kept under wraps and a strange type of radiation always leaked into the ships and sometimes something worse leaked through with them.

He didn't know what the reports said about the so-called creatures that leaked through the rips but people died and then became ghosts of a fashion. Grayson had no intention of dying today so he looked around for a weapon but there weren't any.

He had thought he was going to die plenty of times in battle, on ships or getting involved in beer brawls. Normally he didn't care about dying as long as it was in service but for some reason he just felt closer to Death than even before.

As Grayson went towards the two metal tanks he could have sworn that he heard laughter and people wanting him to do something. It was like a corrupting chant in the back of his mind urging him to do something dangerous.

He felt the urge to remove his helmet so

he could breathe more freely and not have to listen to the constant groan of his breathing but he couldn't.

He had to stay alive or everyone else on the ship might die too.

Grayson took out a smaller scanner that he had picked up on the way over here and he started scanning the chamber and surprisingly enough the Ultraspace Generator was working perfectly.

In fact, everything was apparently working perfectly, or it was working well enough not to register.

Grayson looked at Mary and just frowned as she had completely removed her environmental suit, her eyes had sunken in on themselves and her feet were now ghostly.

He shook his head as he realised that the rip had corrupted her and she had come to get him because he was the only one that could stop the corruption.

"Death is the ruler of the Network not humanity," Mary said. "Humanity might have wiped out my creations of the Keres but we will rise again,"

Grayson broke out into a fighting position. He had no idea what the hell had corrupted Mary but it was clearly insane.

Sure humanity wanted to obliterate the aliens but they weren't dead yet sadly. So this corrupting creature had to be something to do with their strange alien mythology and abominable magic.

This creature had to die.

The creature infecting Mary just grinned and kept looking at him up and down like he was a piece of meat ready for the slaughter.

Grayson tried to think harder about what had happened to the surviving members of the ships where rips had occurred. He couldn't remember. He knew he had to close the rip but he didn't know how.

He didn't even know how the rips occurred in the first place.

"I see your mind human. You fear me. And just know that Death grows stronger so your Network will die like your race,"

Mary charged.

Her fingers became swords.

She slashed them.

Grayson rolled to one side.

He couldn't move.

His suit wasn't flexible enough.

He was stuck.

He felt Mary slashed his back.

Grayson screamed as radiation poured into him.

His lungs roared as toxic chemicals filled them.

He screamed as his body turned cancerous.

Every single cell felt like it was fire and then his world went black.

But he knew that he had died for sure.

***

Grayson hated how ghostly, light and strange he felt as he woke up on the bright white floor of an Ultraspace Tunnel. It felt so weird to be inside a tunnel and yet not blinded by its intense white sterile light with a few white circular ships zooming overhead.

The air was unfortunately cold, icy and bitter and Grayson really didn't like how the air smelt of damp, but he just couldn't understand why he was inside a tunnel and not dead-dead.

He looked down at his legs, arms and chest and he bit his lip as he realised that he was like a ghost. He wasn't completely see-through but he might as well have been.

When he turned around Grayson shook his head as he saw a tear the size of his hand behind him, he went out to touch it but crippling pain filled him. He knew that the rip lead to his ship but he was dead so he could never return.

A strange suckling and humming and buzzing sound came from behind him.

Grayson turned around and he wanted to swear as he saw a very thin shadowy black figure like the Grim Reaper carrying his scythes that Grayson just knew was dripping his own blood.

The figure didn't smile or anything, or maybe he was because Grayson couldn't see his face but the figure was immensely tall, easily five times the height of him. And yet Grayson had no idea what he was.

"I told you I get more and more powerful each day human," the figure said.

"What are you?" Grayson asked. "I don't know you. I don't know who you are. You are nothing to me,"

Grayson guessed that made the Figure smile.

"I am one of the Gods that you claim don't exist. The Keres called me The Destroyer but I prefer the term The Obliterator. Now you have served in your military. You know what I can do?"

Grayson looked to the bright white floor for a moment and he did sort of remember the strange heretical beliefs of the Keres. They believed in a Dark and Light group of gods with The Destroyer being the creator of their Death Magic but they were just myths.

Myths created by a strange doomed dying pathetic race of aliens that humanity would hopefully slaughter one day.

The figure echoed. "Humans are so stupid. You doubt I exist but I feed on your thoughts, your dreams, your ambitions every single time you travel through my network. Do you think it was an accident that your Rex found the Network?"

Grayson nodded.

"Of course not. I grow stronger with more of my Dark Gods are being found and soon I will be free of this prison and soon the galaxy shall burn once again with my rage,"

"Again?" Grayson asked.

The Figure laughed even more. "It is amazing humans can even begin to imagine the grandeur and complexities of the galaxy but I will not tell you anymore. So how about we make a deal?"

Grayson really didn't know what to do about this figure, he was clearly evil, deranged and hellbent on destroying humanity but he could also be a weapon against the Keres. And any weapon against the Keres was a good friend to Grayson.

"Whatever you want," Grayson said.

The Figure laughed as he stretched out a palm without fingers and black energy shot out of them.

The tendrils of black magic swirled, twirled and whirled around Grayson and he screamed in agony for a brief moment as the magic turned him to ash.

But whilst he knew that humanity was ultimately doomed if they didn't learn how to work with the Keres instead of facing them because of the sheer power of the servants of The Destroyer, he knew that his life, knowledge and power was being exchanged for sealing up the rip.

So his friends, crew and ship were now safe and Grayson smiled as he finally became just another white light in the tunnels because he had done his mission, and that would have to be enough for now.

And at least he died in service. Just like he always wanted.

AVAILABLE NOW AT ALL MAJOR BOOKSELLERS!

AVAILABLE NOW AT ALL MAJOR BOOKSELLERS!

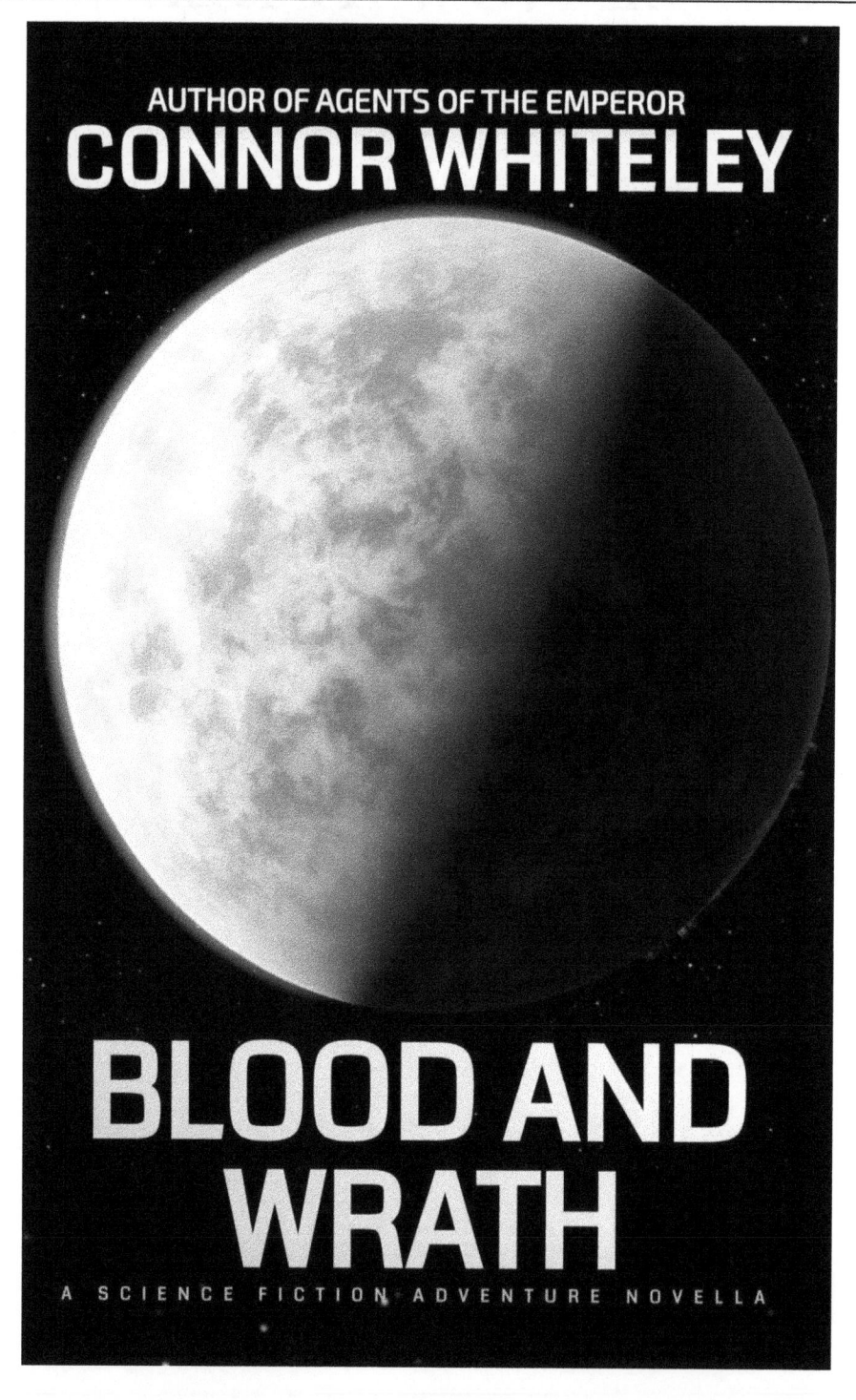

AUTHOR OF AGENTS OF THE EMPEROR
CONNOR WHITELEY

BLOOD AND WRATH

A SCIENCE FICTION ADVENTURE NOVELLA

AUTHOR OF AGENTS OF THE EMPEROR SERIES

CONNOR WHITELEY

BLACKHEART

A SCIENCE FICTION FAR FUTURE SHORT STORY

BLACKHEART
A Science Fiction Far Future Short Story

Brother meets brother.

Being Imperial Regent has a hell of a lot of great, amazing and rather delightful benefits that I, Jack Blackheart, certainly enjoy most of the time. Especially, as I stood on the very top of the immense black metal Imperial Fortress with the icy cold wing slowly rubbing my cheeks dry.

I had always enjoyed the Fortress way too much actually. It was such a beacon of the Rex's immense power, authority and sheer brutality with its huge black 8-point star design that stretched on for thousands of miles in all directions and upwards even more.

It was next to impossible to look down below and see the charred black stone ground that so many soldiers walked over every day, because it was their duty to the Rex. I actually wanted to know if they did this out of choice but I doubted I could ever get a reliable answer.

The part of the fortress I was standing on had to be my favourite. I was north towards the largest city on Earth and it might have been miles upon miles away but it still looked great with its fiery spires reaching up into space and so many little beautiful lights of ships, shuttles and fighters buzzing around the city like bees.

The wind might have been icy cold scented with wonderful hints of jasmine, lavender and peanuts leaving the good taste of nature on my tongue but I honestly could have stayed out here for hours.

And that city was so damn beautiful.

On cold dark nights like this, it was something to behold and it just reminded me how great humanity could be. When I first joined the Rex, I was so filled with hope about the Imperium.

Of course back then I believe, I believed the Imperium was a force for good, change and the betterment of everyone. But that was a lie, probably the biggest lie in human history because the Imperium was all about control these days.

I was probably the most free person in the Imperium because I was the Rex's right and left hand but even I felt the imposing stare of security cameras from time to time. So I just admired the sheer beauty of the nearby city and just dreamed for a single moment that the people in the city might be free, laughing and smiling with each other.

Footsteps came up behind me and I dared to imagine it was someone to save me.

I just had to smile at that idea because whenever I visited a place in the Imperium, I always donated Rexes, food and machinery to the local population just so they might have a better life, and maybe I could continue to believe in that small, small moment that the Imperium was a force for good once again.

I often argued with myself about leaving, running away and just abandoning the Rex to his crazy delusions of control and power but I didn't want to.

As stupid as it sounded this was still my home, the Rex had found me when I was a late teenager on the streets and starving so he bought me in, gave me food and shelter.

And I served him, happily at first and now I just press on because the work can be great at times.

"You're up late tonight, Lord Regent,"

I recognised the voice instantly. It was a deep female voice so I turned around and grinned at my old friend Perrigin, or Perry for short, in a great-looking blue dress, military boots and small gun in her hand. She still looked beautiful.

She was meant to be in charge of forcing the various Planetary Governors in the Imperium to the Rex's Will but she was so good at it that most of them didn't notice they were being manipulated. And most of the time Perry was just too much fun to be around.

But she looked serious tonight.

"I never knew you had a brother," Perry said not daring to look at me.

I frowned at her. I hadn't even thought of my brother for four decades, he had abandoned me when the Rex's forces invaded our settlement and killed our parents. It was the reason why I was on the streets and it was awful.

My brother had been a good man, a hard worker and a good fighter but whilst all the other men and women in our settlement rushed to fight the invaders. My brother ran. I screamed out his name. He ran even faster.

"Why?" I asked.

Perry shrugged. "I have a new prisoner to enjoy and he claims to be your brother,"

I had to nod at that. It was a hell of a story and I still didn't understand why the Rex "gifted" prisoners to Perry. I know that her mother was an expert interrogator but I doubted she had passed on the knowledge to Perry.

"You want me to talk to him then?" I asked, really hoping she would say no so I could continue to enjoy the view.

"Yes because if this is your brother then I want to know why he was sneaking about trying to assassinate the Rex," Perry said frowning.

A lump caught in my throat as I realised that if this was truly my brother then he was a dead man. As much as I too wanted the Rex dead, I certainly wasn't stupid enough to try.

He was too smart, too well protected and too damn paranoid to ever allow an assassin within two miles of him. Let alone allow an assassin into his Fortress.

"Take me to him," I said.

Perry hugged me, grabbed me by the hand and she dragged me towards the prisoner.

This wasn't going to end well I knew that for sure.

***

One of the many foundational lies the Imperium is built on is that the Imperium is a type of democracy where the millions upon millions of planetary governors vote amongst themselves for who should have critical roles. Like the people in charge of the military, policing, security and so on.

It's all a lie because the Rex controls everything and every single bit of freedom a person believes they have is a carefully crafted lie by the Rex himself.

I was starting to understand that now.

I followed Perry into a massive stone domed chamber with rough grey walls and it was barely large enough to swing a cat inside, and as soon as I stepped inside the temperature dropped so much my breath formed thick columns of vapour.

It was a horrible feeling seeing the hairs on my arms shoot up like defences and small crystals of ice formed on me. The chamber looked like it was meant to be warm and cosy but nothing could be further from the truth.

There were no white-armoured guards or soldiers in the chamber like I had seen in their thousands all over the Fortress. There was only a single man in the chamber with his cheeks and eyes swollen so much that I couldn't tell if this was my brother or not.

Sure the man had the same long raven black hair as my brother but it was burnt and ripped out in places, probably thanks to Perry.

The man's fingers were bleeding and shooting off in weird angles and I really didn't care to look at the rest of him.

I didn't have a cast-iron stomach like Perry clearly did.

My stomach twisted into a painful knot just looking at him so I focused on a small chipped spot on the domed wall behind him instead.

"You came then," he said in a course loving voice that my brother always used on me because he really did love me back in the day.

The lump from earlier returned stronger to my throat. I just couldn't believe this was my brother. The big brother that had taught me how to hack into a holo-system. The big brother that had cooked my dinners when our parents had to work late. The big brother that had loved me every moment of every day.

He was here and he was suffering.

"I came because it is my duty to the Rex," I said out of instinct.

My brother grinned. "Do you remember my name brother?"

I nodded. "Jason,"

Perry smiled as she took out a massive dagger. "This dagger is way too clean for my liking so please tell me, who are you working for?"

I forced myself not to look in horror at my friend. She shouldn't be doing this, this was wrong on so many levels.

"I would rather die than tell you Rex scum," Jason said.

Perry laughed. She went to thrust the dagger into him but I grabbed her wrist.

Her eyes widened as we both realised what the hell I had just done and I seriously hoped that Perry was going to break her orders and training by not killing me immediately.

"I will get the information from him," I said hoping to buy myself some time. "If he still doesn't give me the information then you can flay him alive if you care,"

I didn't want that to happen but I wanted more time.

Perry nodded so I went down and knelt in front of my brother's twisted tortured form.

"Did you ever find a boyfriend?" I asked smiling. That was actually what I hoped had happened to him over the years, I hoped my big brother had found love, happiness and joy.

He frowned and looked at Perry. "She killed him two years ago,"

I nodded. "I'm sorry,"

At least that ruled out any romantic links being the people helping him but I didn't know what I was hoping to achieve by getting the information from him.

He was going to die unless I could magically come up with an idea to save the both of us. I was clever. I just doubted I was that clever.

"I won't tell you who's helping me," Jason said.

"But they'll kill you if you don't,"

"They're going to kill me anyway," he said and I knew he was lying.

"Then I can promise you they'll kill you faster and less painfully," I said looking at Perry.

She rolled her eyes like I had just taken the fun out of her playtime but she nodded.

I was about to take Jason's hands but then I realised how mutilated they were and how tortured the rest of his body was. I didn't dare touch him in case it caused him crippling pain.

"Please. You protected me a lot during school and my childhood. Let me repay the favour by helping you now," I said.

He shook his head. "Why do you work for them?"

And before I realised it I was replying out of instinct. "Because the Rex is the only one that can help humanity not descend into chaos, hatred and anarchy. He is the difference between freedom and chaos and control and safety,"

Jason laughed. "I will not tell you who helped me because there was no one. I don't work with the Keres and their magic, I don't work with the Enlightened Republic and I don't work with anyone else,"

I almost believed him because humanity hated the foul alien Keres with their freakish magic with a passion. I had met people from the independent and so-called free people of the Enlightened Republic and my brother didn't have the arrogance of them, but my brother had lied.

He had admitted he worked with people because Perry had killed his boyfriend two years ago.

"You worked with your boyfriend so who are you working with?" I asked. "I am Imperial Regent, I designed and reviewed the security plans of this Fortress myself almost daily. Unless you had inside help, it is impossible for you to do this,"

Then I looked at Perry and I frowned.

I reached for a weapon I normally carried but I was having it cleaned tonight as I was meeting the Rex tomorrow.

When I looked at Perry again she had a dagger pointed at me and I just shook my head. She was a traitorous bastard and then she clicked her fingers.

Jason screamed in agony as his bones, muscles and skin were ripped apart and reforged into the image of Jason's real form. He was tall, muscular and attractive like a university jock that all the girls gushed over. He looked perfect.

But I just couldn't believe that Perry had magic or something. I knew as Imperial Regent that it was a lie that no human could produce magic but the numbers were like 1 in every one trillion.

I had no idea that Perry had magic before now.

"So why this?" I asked.

"Because I knew you were a fake," Jason said. "My brother was a good man, he hated the Rex and he never would have attacked a woman trying to help me kill him. You have changed. You are one of his puppets,"

I shook my head and noticed there was a small red flashing light behind them and I sort of felt like I needed to make them confess.

It was a strange sensation but as soon as I thought about it I realised I was right. Yet if there was help coming to stop these assassins then I just wanted to make sure I didn't die in the process.

And the Rex's help was always conditional on me being loyal to him. If I showed any sign of weakness here then he would allow these two to kill me.

Before killing them himself.

"This isn't delusion Jason. This is just the truth. The truth is the Rex is the only person who could save humanity and that's a good person," I said not even forcing out the words.

Jason took a dagger out from his back. "I'm disappointed that you allowed yourself to believe in these lies,"

I shook my head. I had to find out what their plan was.

"And why you Perry?" I asked. "You were always good to the Rex and he rewarded you,"

"Because everything is a lie and everything will burn!" Perry shouted.

She charged at me.

I jumped back.

She swung again.

I punched her.

Jason tackled me.

Pinning me against the wall.

He whacked me round the face.

Forcing his blade against my throat.

"Why do this?" I asked. "What do you intend to achieve? Make us a democratic republic?"

"I would never allow us to become like the Enlightened Republic but Truth must happen," Perry said.

And then I realised exactly what had happened to her. My good friend Perry had simply allowed herself to think too much about reality, she questioned all the lies and propaganda and the foundations the Imperium was built on.

As Imperial Regent I often created the foundational lies and considered them, it was possible to know what was fact and what was fiction these days but reality was a lie.

Of course over the years it had destroyed my mental health, I had been on the brink so many times of just wanting to annihilate it all because I just wanted the truth.

I had never jumped off the edge. Clearly Perry had.

I looked my brother dead in the eye. He didn't want to do this. He looked vulnerable.

I punched him.

He fell backwards.

I jumped forward.

Grabbing the dagger.

Snatching it out of his hand.

He charged at me.

I thrusted the blade into his chest.

Perry charged at me.

Screaming in emotional agony.

She wasn't focusing.

She swung her blade.

I ducked.

She rushed past me.

I leapt up.

Stabbing her in the back.

And as the Rex's personal white-armoured bodyguards stormed in, I just shook my head as I stared at the corpse of my dear big brother and I truly realised that these two were always going to die tonight.

Because every single freedom a person thought they had was a simple lie created by the Rex.

This was all a test and one I feared for my life that I had passed. I hoped.

***

The next morning I was standing at my most favourite spot on the immense stone fortress walls staring at the beautiful city in the distance. The bright morning was surprisingly warm, calm and the sun was strongly beaming down on me like a spotlight. The air was wonderfully fresh with hints of jasmine, lavender and pecans filling the air and I was so glad to be alive.

Last night might as well have been a blur for all the good that happened to me. The bodyguards had stormed in and chopped up the corpses to make sure my dear brother and Perry were well and truly dead and then the chunks were taken away.

I was left alone in the room for a few moments before I confidently walked out and I almost jumped out of my own skin at the imposing sight of the Rex in his jet-black, twisted, terrifying armour.

He didn't say anything to me. He only grinned, smiled and nodded like he had been proven right about me and maybe he had.

I had always believed that I was different to the rest of the Fortress, I believed that I was playing a long game against the Rex but maybe I wasn't anything that I thought I was. Maybe I really had become the lies, deceit and carefully crafted mould of what I was meant to be by the Rex's design.

And now I was thinking about it, maybe that wasn't a bad thing. Sure the Rex was a master of manipulation but he trusted me, wanted me to live and I was already the second most powerful person in the entire Imperium so maybe, just maybe I should start acting like it.

Of course I wouldn't take the galaxy for myself but maybe I could have all the power I desired and I could become something, someone completely different to the little boy who had lost his brother and parents.

Maybe I could become something far greater but simply allowing the Rex to remain in power for a little while longer, because there was a simple truth that everyone, even people as *smart* as the Rex, forgets and that is that every ruler falls in the end.

Every King, Emperor and Regent in human history has fallen at some point and when one of them falls there is something, someone to replace them.

And I'm fully determined to make sure when the Rex falls that I am the person to replace him and history will remember my name and there is a single word that will echo across the centuries as the person who took over the Imperium after the evil Rex had fallen.

I just smiled and allowed the warm sun to embrace me lovingly as I realised just how great the future could be, and I was really looking forward to how everyone would remember the simple name *Blackheart* in the bitter end.

AVAILABLE NOW AT ALL MAJOR BOOKSELLERS!

AUTHOR OF AGENTS OF THE EMPEROR SERIES

CONNOR WHITELEY

BATTLE DOCTRINES

A SCIENCE FICTION SPACE OPERA SHORT STORY

BATTLE DOCTRINES
A Science Fiction Space Opera Short Story

Ship Mistress Olivia Flapper stood on her raised metal platform in the middle of her white spherical bridge on her great warship *Rex's Hammer*. She had always wanted to be a Ship Mistress, a great leader of the Imperium's war efforts and now after so many years of service, fighting and political workings she was finally one of them.

The bridge was still brand-new to Olivia but it was as wonderful as she ever could have imagined. She really liked the spherical shape of the walls, its smooth white metal was a little too shiny in places but she would sort it all out in time.

Her small raised platform was only big enough for her to stand on which was absolutely perfect, especially as Olivia wasn't a fan of the constant smells of body odour, sweat and blood that seemed to pour off her command crew like rain from a duck. It wasn't exactly pleasant.

At least the small bright golden orbs of light bounced around the bridge, bouncing from one wall to another and back again.

Sometimes when Olivia was alone (which wasn't as often as she would have liked) she just stared at the little orbs. Sometimes they were happier, freer and more content with life than she was.

As much as Olivia loved her new position, her service to the Rex and her life, she just felt like there was more to life than always searching for the next promotion and intensely studying the next battle doctrine that old men with no military experience had created.

The circular warship hummed loudly and Olivia looked down at her command crew, all twenty of them, as they were hunched over their large bulky metal computer screens having to have computations by hand, having to calculate their trajectory by hand and having to inform different departments of the warship by hand.

This certainly wasn't the most modern ship she had ever been on but it was customary for all brand-new Ship Masters and Mistresses to get put on the lowest ships first of all. Apparently it was so they could develop their skills, but Olivia knew it was because the new ones were the most likely to die so it was cheaper to put them on poorer ships before "gifting" them the more expensive warships.

She wasn't really a fan of that rule.

Olivia waved at her command crew as they walked about or did their work wearing their long white robes denoting their position and their newness to the role. It was a shame that Olivia was surrounded by newbies judging by their bright white robes without a single speck of dirt on them.

Either they were so new that they had only graduated from the academy in the past two days or the environmental systems were *so* good that they seriously purified the air.

Judging by the rest of the ship, Olivia fully believed it was the former.

"Ship Mistress, we're detecting three enemy ships incoming. Within firing distance in five minutes," a very short man said with a balding head.

Olivia nodded slowly and her hands tightened around the cold metal railings of her raised platform. She had been sent here on this mission to deliver bombs to a faraway planet to help Imperial forces annihilate a rogue cult of Dark Keres, but clearly the enemy didn't want these bombs delivered.

She had no idea what separated the Dark Keres to the rest of their foul, magic freaks of their Keres species. The Treaty of Defeat was such a weak little treaty that might have meant the awful Keres species was starving itself to death but the Dark Keres were awful.

Unlike the normal Keres, these so-called Dark Keres actually had a spine and they were fighting back against the righteousness of humanity. It was humanity's Rex-given right to rule the stars, purge entire species and claim all the planets they wanted.

And it was the Keres's duty to die or at least join humanity as slaves as so many of their foul kind had.

Olivia focused on the icy coldness of space dead away from them as two large holographic screens appeared showing Olivia the endless blackness of space with no nearby planets, imperial forces or stars close by.

They were alone.

Olivia really didn't want to fight these Dark Keres because they might have been breaking the law time after time but they were just trying to do what they could to survive.

Humanity was constantly doing questionable things to make sure it survived, so maybe the Keres' weren't so different from them after all.

"Battle Doctrine Mistress," a very tall woman said.

Olivia bit her lip as she couldn't even see the foul enemy ships yet, she didn't know what Dark Keres ships looked like but she was going to have to proceed as her training suggested she should.

"Advancement Battle Doctrine," Olivia said.

As the bridge became a hive of activity with her command crew running round like headless chickens, she had to admit it wasn't her favourite Doctrine.

The Advancement Doctrine was sadly all about travelling quickly through space to make sure the enemy couldn't catch up with them. It meant deactivating the weapon systems to give the engines more power but hopefully it would still work.

Olivia really wanted to see the enemy but she just couldn't.

The Keres were masters of their magic and it was so damn annoying that they were probably using it to cloak their ships. For all Olivia knew they could be right next to them.

"How did you know the Keres were here in the first place?" Olivia asked.

None of the command crew were paying attention to her as the warship hummed, banged and vibrated as the engines were given more power. She hated this.

Olivia had fought the Keres plenty of times and whilst the Dark Keres might be different to the rest of their race, she was still willing to bet that they used the same or similar tactics.

The Keres were waiting to ambush them and she feared that the Advancement Doctrine was exactly what they wanted.

"We found them on the edge of the system for a brief second before they cloaked themselves," a woman said as she rushed past.

Olivia nodded but it made no sense. The Keres knew that they couldn't outgun, beat or destroy an Imperial warship because they were so weak, so why in the Rex's fine name did they reveal themselves?

Unless it was all part of a plan.

It was moments like this that just made Olivia want to jump into Ultraspace and zoom through the galaxy at light speed regardless of how apparently dangerous that was with the bombs.

She just wanted to keep her crew alive, and herself of course.

"Scan the surrounding area," Olivia said.

Only one man looked up at her but he shrugged as he ran the scan and then shook his head at her.

Olivia's heart pounded in her chest. She was used to dealing with impossible humans, impossible tasks and impossible crew members. She wasn't used to dealing with impossible aliens.

She didn't want her crew to die. She didn't want to fail. She had to deliver the bombs to the planet over ten hours away.

Then Olivia realised that sometimes the Keres did a little trick where they magically project their ships into space to make the Imperium believe they were in one location when they were actually in another.

The enemy was a lot closer than Olivia ever wanted to admit.

Then Olivia felt her skin turn icy cold and she had only ever had that reaction once. Seconds before the Keres attacked her in the most violent way possible.

"Invasion Doctrine!" Olivia shouted.

But it was too late.

The ship jerked.

Throwing Olivia across the bridge.

Other crew members smashed around her.

Bodies shattering.

Streaks of blood painting the walls.

Alarms screamed overhead.

Flashing lights exploded on.

Olivia forced herself up. She forced herself towards her raised platform.

Her body screamed in protest but she accessed her private hologram.

She saw thousands of victims all over the ship from the impact. A bomb had hit their starboard side but their shields were intact and their anti-magic systems were okay.

At least the Keres couldn't teleport or board them for now.

The two massive holograms that showed her the darkness of space earlier now showed three immense dagger-like warships with blood red crystal hulls appear next to her.

Olivia couldn't believe that the damn Dark Keres were right next to them. That was the last thing she wanted.

She had to somehow figure out a way to keep herself and her crew alive and how to get the bombs to the battlefleet.

For the briefest of moments Olivia supposed she could activate the bombs right now and just kill them all and the Keres warships next to her. But she didn't want to use the No Hope Doctrine just yet.

She wouldn't dare give the alien abominations some reward for their attack. Olivia was going to win no matter what it took.

"Mistress," a voice said but Olivia didn't bother to see who it was. "The Keres want to contact us. They're requesting we surrender to them,"

Olivia shook her head. These damn aliens were never going to get her to surrender.

Olivia forced herself upright and she gripped the metal railings of her raised platform and frowned at the two holographic screens showing the enemy warships.

"We need to activate the weapon systems immediately," Olivia said.

"It will do us no good. The enemy are on the starboard side and our weapons on that side are destroyed," a man said.

Olivia couldn't believe how damn infuriating these aliens were. And the man was right sadly.

A loud humming of pure magical energy crackled around her and Olivia rolled her eyes as the damn anti-magic systems were failing. It wouldn't be too long now until the Keres invaded and slaughtered them all like the beasts they were.

Olivia opened a ship-wide communication channel. "All forces this is the Ship Mistress enact the Containment Doctrine immediately. Do not allow a witch to live,"

Olivia just shook her head even more as her command crew all bit their lower lip. They all knew this was bad because if the anti-magic generators collapsed then the Keres would easily rip into reality and stalk the holy halls of their warship.

And they would kill human after human until they all died.

The Containment Doctrine was simple but useless. A simple hell mary to throw into the air to buy Olivia some more time.

"What about the engines?" Olivia asked.

A young woman from the crew stepped forward. "Contained by Keres. They're using our magic to immobilise them. I could undo the magic but it would take time,"

"How much?"

"Ten minutes," she said.

The air crackled and murderous screams echoed around the ship.

"Do it," Olivia said to the woman before turning to her crew. "Connect me to Keres ships. I'll buy us some time. Weapons won't free us here. Words might,"

Olivia could literally feel the tension in the bridge now and she wanted to slice it with a sword but she had to focus and remain strong. Some Keres creatures only needed eye contact to use their magic.

Olivia had to focus and not allow the abominations to use their magic on her.

Moments later a very tall, thin elf-like woman appeared in blue holographic form with very long golden black hair that flowed around her like angelic wings.

"You must hand over your weapons please my friend," the woman said. "My forces want to unleash their Death Magic on you but I am buying you time,"

Olivia grinned. The woman's voice was very elegant, lyrical and perfect but she was just stupid. Olivia was a Ship Mistress of the Imperium, she did not listen to the lies and deceits and corruption that aliens spread.

And she wasn't going to give them anything.

As soon as the engines were free once more she was going to escape and jump into Ultraspace and to hell with the consequences.

"I will not give you a damn thing alien. These bombs will reach the planet and they will be dropped on your kind and then humanity will rule the stars," Olivia said.

She wasn't exactly sure if she believed it and she didn't know if the Keres on the planet deserved to die but she wanted to act tough at least.

Olivia noticed the female Keres was looking at someone else probably behind the hologram then the female Keres nodded.

"Then you leave me no choice and I know your workers are trying to free the engines," she said.

The entire command crew went still but Olivia waved them to continue.

"Let me show you just a touch of our Death Magic," the woman said before uttering strange twisted words in a tongue Olivia didn't understand or care to listen to.

Olivia cut the transmission but when she looked back at her command crew they were all wide-eyed with terror as they stared back at their computer screens.

Olivia climbed down and looked at the silent ghostly pictures of their friends, fellow crew members and even loved ones turn to black crystal before shattering into dust.

"Two percent of the crew is dead," someone said but Olivia didn't care who.

"Are the engines free?" Olivia asked.

"Almost," a woman said.

Olivia climbed back up to her raised platform and contacted the Keres warships again.

"Did you like my gift? I know the Goddess of Souls was particularly happy," the female

Keres said.

Olivia's hands formed fists. She seriously didn't care for the strange alien mythology of the Keres.

The air charged with magic energy and Olivia felt the icy coldness of the Keres's foul touch around her. They were within striking distance.

She just had to buy her crew a little more time.

"Does your Goddess love Keres souls?" Olivia asked.

The female Keres laughed. "Souls are souls my dear. I'll let you meet her now. Because now you die!"

An alien claw formed in the air.

Slashing at Olivia.

She stumbled back.

The claw chased her.

Olivia leapt off her platform.

She smashed onto the floor.

The claw lashed at her.

Olivia rolled forward.

Another claw appeared in front of her.

Olivia jumped to one side.

She hit a table.

The two claws flew at her.

The ship jerked.

The engines were free.

"Into Ultraspace!" Olivia shouted.

The entire ship screamed in protest.

The Keres were trying to anchor them into reality.

Olivia whipped out her pistol.

She shot the two claws.

They disappeared.

The warship zoomed off into Ultraspace and all Olivia could think about was how badly she didn't want the bombs to explode.

***

Olivia absolutely had to admit that the next hour was the longest one of her entire life, each second she was half-expecting one of her crew to shout that the bombs were overheating or somehow having a reaction to Ultraspace travel.

Thankfully they weren't.

Olivia just smiled as she leant against the warm metal railings of her raised platform and watched as the streaks of purple light from the Ultraspace network tunnel (she really didn't know how it worked) zoomed past her.

Then with a quiet thud the tunnel disappeared and Olivia was so damn happy that she was alive and that her crew were okay. Then the entire ship hummed a little as an Imperial network connected to her ship and took control of the bombs.

For a small moment Olivia thought that the Dark Keres had followed her but everyone knew that the Keres were too dumb to use Ultraspace and they stuck with their clearly inferior Nexus System of their own magical creation.

Olivia didn't know how it worked and she didn't want to know. The Keres were dumb, end of story.

And as she watched on the two massive holograms the Imperial fleet zooming around an orange green planet with Keres ships trying to flee, she grinned as the bombs rushed towards the planet ready to be used exactly where they were needed most.

Olivia still wasn't sure if this was just, needed or even right but she hadn't examined the facts of the battle and in all fairness it hadn't mattered.

As much as she didn't like to admit it, the

military wasn't designed to produce thinkers, it was designed to produce soldiers that could pick up a gun and march to the beat of the Rex's eternal war machine so humanity could be kept safe, secured and all the enemies could be killed.

The laughter, cheering and even some happy dances filled the bridge as the command crew and everyone else on the ship was so happy to be alive and Olivia was definitely going to join them later on.

She might have doomed a lot of aliens to death but she had helped to protect humanity, her crew and the future of the Imperium. That was certainly a job very well.

And with thousands of other battlefields spread out across the galaxy, Olivia was really excited about flying away from here and seeing what other great adventures, herself, her crew and her great lower warship could travel to.

Then maybe, just maybe Olivia could finally get a promotion and get a real warship because as she had survived this adventure Olivia was fairly sure she could survive anything.

And that was a great realisation to have and that was all thanks to her battle doctrines.

AVAILABLE NOW AT ALL MAJOR BOOKSELLERS!

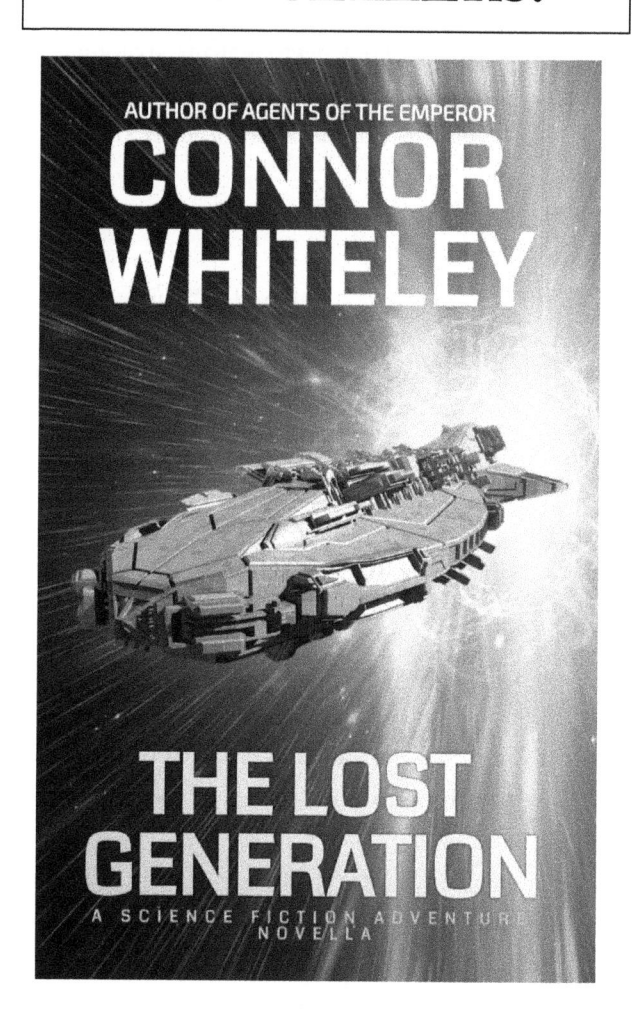

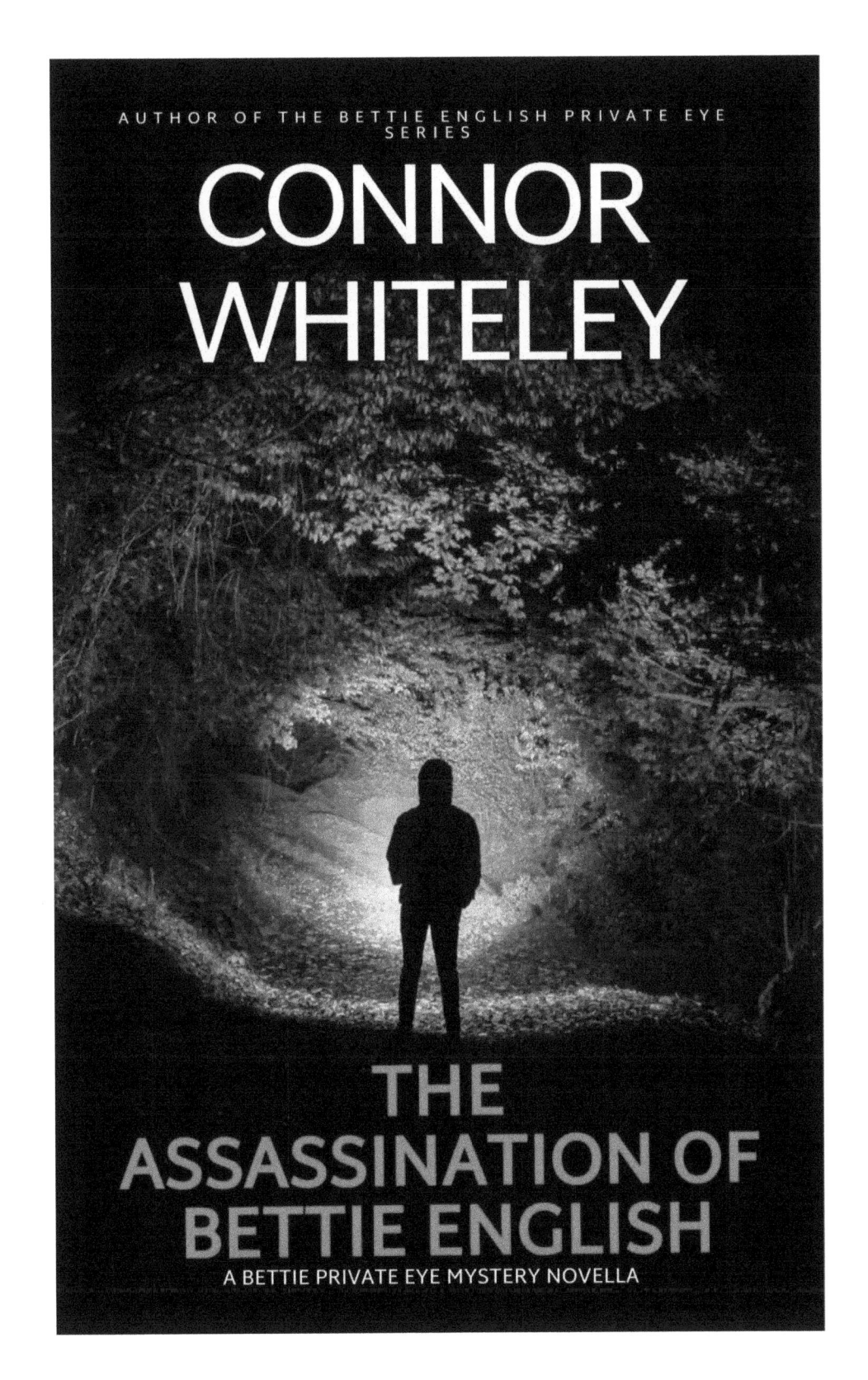

AUTHOR OF THE BETTIE ENGLISH PRIVATE EYE SERIES

CONNOR WHITELEY

THE ASSASSINATION OF BETTIE ENGLISH

A BETTIE PRIVATE EYE MYSTERY NOVELLA

THE ASSASSINATION OF BETTIE ENGLISH
A Bettie Private Eye Mystery Novella

CHAPTER 1
15th August 2023
Canterbury, England

This was the day she learnt her cases had deadly consequences because Thomas Birch was about to die.

Private Eye Bettie English was so glad to be alive as she walked down the long cobblestoned high street of Canterbury. She had always liked how wide, open and wonderful the high street was with its weird little roman buildings and city wall still visible a thousand years on.

There were delightful coffee shops, sweet bakeries and banks hiding in its ancient buildings made in the last century or two, and large shopping outlets in immense glass buildings that just somehow worked in amongst the ancient stone.

Bettie loved how Canterbury was always a strange mixture of new and old and that was certainly true for the students. Large crowds of young university students walked up and down the high street like raging rivers.

Bettie focused on the students from all different backgrounds, classes and ages walking about laughing with their friends and just having a good time.

She smiled at a young couple as they walked past hand-in-hand. The woman was wearing a very tasteful blue dress and the man wearing a cute white t-shirt. They looked good together.

Bettie was really glad to see everyone was okay. She knew it was precious to have small peaceful moments between cases and business work (she was the President of the British Private Eye Federation too) to enjoy normal life.

Bettie felt great to be alive as she continued towards her office just above the high street. She had finally secured extra funding for a brilliant new programme that would allow medical students, especially poor students, to get post-mortem experience before they graduated allowing them to have better skills employers wanted, and Bettie just couldn't be happier.

She was doing what she loved, and she was helping innocent, wonderful people.

Her assistant Thomas Birch wearing a very expensive navy suit walked next to her. And Bettie really liked having Thomas with her, he was calm, collected and what he lacked in the detective department he more than made up for it in his business sense.

Bettie was surprised how many great ideas Thomas had come up with lately about ways to increase membership and convince more people to become private eyes. And it was brilliant that Thomas was going to become a dad in nine months' time.

"Morning," Thomas said to someone as they walked past and he waved at a baby in a pram.

Bettie really looked forward to getting home to see her own two little monsters, Harrison and Elizabeth. She didn't leave them too often but she was determined to still be a private eye and do President stuff one day a week.

And every week for a single day Bettie hated being away from her 11-month-old twins but she couldn't imagine being anything else but a private eye. She loved her job and she loved helping people even more.

"We'll drop these files off at my office then I think we can just go home," Bettie said knowing Thomas wanted to see his girlfriend so badly.

"Thanks," he said looking forward to seeing the woman he loved. "What tips have you got for being a dad?"

Bettie laughed as she glided through a gang of tourists. "You're going to be a dad in nine months. Believe me you have time just relax and enjoy the pregnancy,"

"Did Graham?"

Bettie had absolutely no idea if her boyfriend, Detective Graham Adams, *enjoyed* the pregnancy. She knew that he loved her and the babies with all his heart but they were always working during the pregnancy and having fun on their cases. She had no idea what a normal non-private-eye pregnancy looked like.

"He loved every second of it," Bettie said

knowing it was basically the truth.

"Good," Thomas said grinning like a little schoolboy. Bettie knew he was going to be an amazing dad.

"Here we are," Bettie said pointing to her office up ahead. She wasn't sure why she hadn't bought Thomas here before but at least he now got to see how she started off her private eye career.

It exploded.

Flaming bricks rained down.

People screamed.

People cried in agony.

People burnt alive.

Glass popped.

Glass shattered.

Slicing into flesh.

Bettie looked at Thomas.

His head exploded.

Bettie screamed.

Bullets screamed towards her.

Bettie scanned the area.

Five black armoured men raced towards her.

Firing as they went.

Bullets smashed into the cobblestones.

Bettie ran in the opposite direction.

Bullets smashed into innocent people.

Chests exploded.

Blood sprayed up Bettie's face.

She kept running.

She took out her phone.

It exploded.

Cars screamed towards her.

Three black SUVs without number plates raced towards Bettie.

They jerked to one side.

More black armoured men leapt out.

They fired.

Not at Bettie.

At people chasing her.

A black car door opened. A hand gestured Bettie inside.

A bullet sliced into her arm.

Bettie legged it.

Diving into the SUVs.

The SUVs raced away.

Bettie just hoped she hadn't traded one killer for another.

CHAPTER 2
15th August 2023
Canterbury, England

Detective Graham Adams was so looking forward to when his beautiful, sexy girlfriend Bettie got home. He sat on their wonderfully soft black sofa in their large living room with the bright golden sunlight of the late morning shining through the windows. Graham loved how the living room was the perfect suntrap because it was just heaven.

He was more than grateful that they had decided to repaint the living room two weeks ago because the bright white walls just reflected the sunlight a little too much and it was blinding. Not exactly relaxing.

Graham really liked the cream-coloured walls that made the living room feel bright and airy without it being too blinding.

The large blue rug on the floor was covered in baby toy walkers, blocks and all the other toys that Harrison and Elizabeth just loved throwing about. He seriously loved it that they were walking now and they were even more of a nightmare together than they had been at 10 months old.

Graham smiled at Harrison and Elizabeth

as they walked about holding each other's hand going toy to toy, inspecting each one like whatever they choose would be the only toy they could play with for a while.

They were both wearing a matching blue baby-grow and Graham wasn't sure if he liked them always wearing matching things but he couldn't deny they didn't look damn cute together.

He just loved his kids and so did Bettie. She couldn't wait for her to get back and then she could watch, laugh and play with the kids like he had been doing all morning.

That definitely had to be the best thing about being a floater detective with Kent Police so he wasn't tied down to any one single department. And when no police department had work for him (or wanted him for being an incorruptible cop) he got stay at home and he was paid minimum wage. Graham just donated it to charity anyway, the advantages of having a millionaire girlfriend.

Graham was a cop because he got to help people, not because it paid well. It had never paid well.

A kitchen timer beeped a few times and the entire house smelt wonderful with hints of garlic, rosemary and lemon as the joint of lamb that their nephew Sean was cooking for a surprise lunch for Bettie was almost finished.

Graham enjoyed the mutterings and random words Harrison and Elizabeth were saying as they decided to play with a small blue walker that they were slightly too big for now but the kids loved it, so Graham hardly had the heart to get rid of it.

Sean and his boyfriend Harry were in the kitchen talking about random university stuff that Graham really didn't understand. He didn't do engineering at university so he wasn't really sure what the lovers were talking about, he was just glad they were happy.

Graham's phone buzzed.

It was probably Bettie saying that she was late, wasn't coming home til later or something like that. Graham loved her more than anything in the entire world but she was a nightmare at times.

He looked at his phone and the world changed.

Protocol R.

Graham knew the text message was a coded message from Bettie or someone they trusted. It meant the Russians were after them and they needed to get to safety now.

"Shit," Graham said already up. "Procotol R!"

Sean and Harry immediately stopped in the kitchen and they rushed out passing Graham rubber gloves.

He put them on and Sean's tasteful pink highlights in his blond hair went wild as he rushed to put them on.

The gloves were to make sure they didn't touch any nerve agents in case the Russians had already attacked the house or where about to.

Sean and Harry rushed upstairs. The kids still didn't know anything was wrong.

Graham ripped the cushions off the sofa and grabbed the large black suitcase underneath filled with clothes, baby toys and everything they needed.

Sean and Harry rushed down a minute later with their own to-go bags.

Someone pounded on the door.

They had all practised this so many times.

Harry and Sean grabbed the kids gently and took them out into the kitchen.

Graham picked up the black heavy crowbar that was also under the sofa. He went over to the door.

It exploded open.

A black armoured woman stormed in.

Graham swung it.

The woman screamed it smashed her hands.

She punched Graham.

He fell to the ground.

The woman whipped out a pistol.

Graham threw the crowbar at her.

The woman dived to one side.

Graham leapt up.

He jumped on her.

She punched him.

Knocking him off.

She climbed on top of him.

Grabbing his neck.

Graham felt she was about to tense.

A bullet screamed through the air.

Her corpse collapsed off him.

Graham grabbed her pistol aiming it at the door.

Agent Daniels MI5 stormed in wearing a tight black suit and nodded at Graham.

Harry and Sean ran towards them with the kids and to-go bags.

None of them were messing about.

The backdoor smashed open. More Russians were coming in.

Graham grabbed his to-go suitcase and everyone dashed into Agent Daniels' car.

He just hoped that Bettie was okay and knew to follow the plan to the letter.

Or all of them were going to die.

CHAPTER 3
15th August 2023
Canterbury, England

Alina Vagin sat inside the stupidly hot interior of her little black car as she watched foul Graham Adams, those two gay abominations and intelligence officer Daniels drive away in their Land Rover.

The street was awful even by English standards. Alina had no idea why the English were obsessed with silly flowers, cars and other decorative items on their front garden or whatever they called it.

These people and every single English person as a whole were beyond dumb but at least sooner or later they would be ruled by China or Russia.

Alina couldn't believe her first assassin had been so silly to be killed by someone as weak, pathetic and English as Graham Adams. He was not a man, he was a weak little boy compared to the might of mother Russia and soon the silly English family would learn of the power of Russia.

She had always hated how silly the English were and how vain they were for daring to call themselves "Great" Britain. There was nothing great how this dying country but that was why missions like this were always so much fun.

The British were clueless and so easy to manipulate because they thought themselves as God's gift to the world but the world was changing. China was growing more and more powerful and Alina was just waiting for Russia to join them.

The West was dying and without Bettie English and Graham Adams the West would die even quicker.

Alina started her engine and looked

forward to finally putting a bullet in Graham's and Bettie's stupid English heads.

CHAPTER 4
15th August 2023
Canterbury, England

Bettie hated it as the SUV sped away and she quickly did her seatbelt up. She had no idea what the hell was happening, who was trying to kill her and who the hell she was with now.

The windows were blacked out. The car was racing along and there was no light on in the car.

After a few moments the car slowed down a little but not by much and Bettie forced herself to focus on everything around her. The seats felt cold, fresh and leather so this was clearly a high-end model of SUVs similar to those that the Federation use.

These SUVs were probably top of the line with bullet proof glass and other top-end features, in fact she realised this felt exactly the same as a Federation vehicle but no one in the Federation was armed.

And they wouldn't grab her like this. They would at least have a light on in the car.

The air smelt strong of fire smoke which was strange because there wasn't a fire. It wasn't even gun smoke or anything like it but it smelt exactly the same as smoke from a bonfire.

Bettie noticed there was another smell to under it, something similar to strawberry jam or tea. Bettie realised it was both she smelt smoke, tea and strawberry jam.

There was only one person in the entire world that had her tea the Russian way with jam, would have the firepower for a *rescue* operation and be willing to save her.

"Penelope Bishop I presume," Bettie said.

A moment later three bright golden lights flared to life in the car and Bettie just grinned as she stared at a very tall blond woman wearing a long white dress with a China cup of black tea in her hand.

Next to Penelope was a very small China jug of milk, a pot of custard and strawberry jam. Bettie had no idea why the Russians got their tea like that but she liked it.

Bettie had to admit that the very last person she ever expected to see was the Russian Foreign Minister who she had sadly worked with on a case last year to stop cryptocurrency from being sent to Russia to invalidate all the western sanctions on Russia for their foul invasion of Ukraine.

Bettie was more than happy to stop Russia but she was less pleased Penelope had managed to wipe out her opponents in the process and ended up with a powerful position in the Kerelim.

"Jumping into a random car when being shot at, is that smart?" Penelope asked grinning as she stirred her tea.

"What other choice did I have?" Bettie asked perfectly straight and looking forward to the weird power play that always happened between them.

"I don't know leap over the cars," Penelope said admitting how much she enjoyed this power play. "But I will confess I don't know. It is good to see you Miss English?"

"Tell me Foreign Minister, why are five Russians trying to kill me? And I presume you have infiltrated UK security services enough to know that Protocol R has been established,"

Bettie said.

Bettie knew it wasn't a question because as much as she hated Penelope for being such a Russian puppet and she was always scheming against the UK, Bettie couldn't deny that Penelope was damn smart.

"Of course," Penelope said as the car jerked to one side. "I know the Federation setup an alert in a number of eastern European and UK intelligence networks as soon as one of them learnt you're a target that Protocol gets triggered,"

Bettie smiled. "You don't know what the Protocol is though, do you?"

Bettie loved it as Penelope frowned and took a massive sip of her tea.

"Of course not even my powers are limited,"

"Good," Bettie said. "The Protocol sends an alert to mine, Graham's and Agents Daniels' phones preparing us for a Russian attack. We need to stop and leave whenever we are and meet at a safehouse in Kent. And we wear rubber gloves to protect against nerve agents,"

Penelope laughed. "Clever,"

Bettie leant forward and looked at the delicious looking custard next to Penelope. She really wanted to try some later.

"Now you need to tell me why you're here. I know you aren't going to kill me,"

Penelope smiled. "Really? How do you know I'm not delivering you to the Russian assassins right now? How do you know I'm not buying my time? Maybe I want information before I kill you?"

Bettie shrugged. "Because I know you like me too much and as much as we both hate each other's politics and country we respect each other. I know from your political speeches in Belarus, China and Argentina that you value *respect* too much to kill me,"

"Fine," Penelope said pouring Bettie a cup of tea. "You want to know the truth. The truth is the Russian President bless her heart learnt of our actions last March that costed Russia millions in cryptocurrency,"

Bettie bit her lower lip.

"Of course I blamed you exclusively and she believed me. That money would have helped us complete our special military operation in Ukraine already so now she wants to kill you,"

Bettie nodded. It made sense. "Don't you dare call the murder of innocent Ukrainians a military operation. It is murder plain and simple,"

"Of course it is but I am the Foreign Minister,"

Bettie hated her sometimes.

"Anyway the truth is I don't want you to die because if you die it is the end of the world as we know it. And the start of World War Three,"

Bettie gasped as she realised that very much might be the case.

CHAPTER 5
15th August 2023
Canterbury, England

As soon as Graham bordered Daniels's Land Rover they started off down the road with little two-storey houses lining it with red, black and green cars outside. Graham was glad to see his neighbours weren't on the street but everything else just looked so normal, so calm, so relaxed.

There were red roses shining in people's

front garden, white lilies danced the warm summer breeze and tomato plants bore bright red fruit ready to be chomped on. Graham just focused on the road ahead as Daniels calmly drove onwards.

It almost seemed stupid that Daniels was driving so calmly but the theory was that if Russian vehicles were patrolling the area, they shouldn't have known what Daniels was driving so driving normally was the best way to go undetected.

Graham turned around and was glad to see Elizabeth and Harrison quietly playing and talking to Sean and Harry. Those two never failed to amaze Graham, they were just so calm, put together and great in situations like this.

Graham wiped his hands on his blue jeans and forced himself to take long deep breaths of the pine-scented air coming from Daniels's air fresher. It was a silly smell to have after everything that had just happened but it was relaxing. Exactly what Graham needed just now.

He wasn't sure why the Russians were attacking now and why the Protocol had been activated. Graham knew that Bettie had setup 26 different Protocols when she first became President of the British Private Eye Federation.

And she had always expected never to use them and Graham hadn't either. They had only committed them to memory, practised them in secret and got Sean and Harry involved (because they had been living with them ever since they had been viciously attacked last year) just in case Russians or any other group attacked them.

Graham couldn't believe this was actually happening.

"Everyone got rid of their phones?" Daniels asked.

"Yes," everyone said.

"Both of ours were thrown on our bed," Sean said.

Graham nodded. He had just left his on the living room floor. All of their phones were heavily encrypted so even if the attackers took them as "evidence" they wouldn't be able to crack them.

"Good," Daniels said pulling onto the motorway.

Graham felt his stomach flip at the idea of what was happening but he was looking forward to getting to Bettie and once they were together then everything would be okay.

Together they were unstoppable and Graham had to focus on that.

"What happened on your end?" Graham asked.

Daniels smiled. "MI5 went batshit at the Russians as soon as a mole told us about an Assassination Order has been given for Bettie English with the extreme caveat at the kids, Sean and Harry are *not* to be killed,"

Graham was so relieved at that.

"And it's signed by the President herself," Daniels said.

Graham was even more relieved because whoever these assassins were, he doubted they were stupid enough to try and kill those three. Because the assassins would all die if the Russian President found out she was disobeyed.

Then Graham realised he was easy pickings still. And oddly enough he was rather excited by that idea.

"As soon as MI5 and 6 were informed," Daniels said, "we set to work and sadly Alpha-

6 with Beta-5 have been hired to do the assassinations,"

Graham gulped. He had read tons of news reports recently about massive assassinations, acts of mass murder and kidnapping from those two groups in Russia, Ukraine and tons of small African countries that Russia had a *vested* interest in.

These ten assassins were the best of the best.

"It gets worse," Daniels said. "We've found out that Bettie's death would be the start of World War Three,"

Graham shook his head. "How? I love her and I would be destroyed if she died but how would her death cause a world war?"

"Order 20 and 66," Daniels said.

Graham nodded. Those were the blackmail articles that the Federation had on every single government, institution and politician all over the world since they were created in 1916 by the UK liberal government of the day.

Graham knew the articles were designed to protect the Federation in case any government tried to attack them or any members for unjust reasons but Graham understood the articles could be used to destroy any country if needed.

There was enough damage in those articles to expose the corruption in every single facet of public life. And Graham had heard Bettie mention that if the public knew every single corrupt thing the UK Government had done since 1918 then no one would trust a government.

Any government.

"The thinking at MI5 is if Bettie is assassinated by the Russians, the UK Government because it is spineless wouldn't do anything,"

"Causing the entire private eye community," Graham said, "to become outraged and pressure the new President to release the articles,"

"And once released," Sean said, "the articles would destroy any trust the West has in each other, the people would turn on governments and NATO would never be triggered,"

Graham gasped. He hadn't realised that the articles also covered all the top-secret ops each western "friendly" nation ran against each other too. Like the UK stealing from the USA and vice versa.

And NATO Article 5, the legal mechanism for making NATO fight as one united blade against Russia and China, could only be agreed if all member states agreed to it.

"So Russia and China could just walk all over the west," Sean said.

Graham nodded. "It's a perfect plan. Did the Russians intent for this to happen or is this an added bonus?"

Daniels flicked on an indicator and moved into another lane.

"They hadn't even clocked it and the articles would destroy Russian-Chinese relations too," Daniels said. "But one name did turn up in the assassination order in a very unexpected way,"

"Who?" Graham asked.

"Penelope Bishop is a target of opportunity,"

Graham hadn't heard that foul name for ages and his stomach flipped as he realised if she was involved then no one was safe at all.

Graham was about to ask another

question but he clocked two black SUVs racing towards them coming up their rear.

They had company.

And they had a long way to go until safety.

CHAPTER 6
15th August 2023
Canterbury, England

Bettie couldn't believe what she was hearing as Penelope finished telling her everything she knew, everything she had learnt and everything she had predicted could happen if the assassination actually worked.

She couldn't deny that she was hardly surprised about the predictions as she leant back into the cold, refreshing leather seats of the SUVs, and she focused on the steaming cup of Russian Canavan tea in Penelope's hand.

Bettie felt the SUV jerk a little as they went over a speedbump and the sweet aromas of smoke, strawberry jam and vanilla custard filled the air as Bettie focused back on Penelope.

She had already known that the membership of the Federation loved her and her entire job as President had been to gather their support, get them to like her and really make sure that she gave her members everything they needed. Thankfully they all loved her.

But Bettie also knew there were darker sides to that love and there were certain corners or elements within the Federation that half-worshipped her. They were definitely the sort of people to get in power, use the articles to get revenge and then be damned with the consequences.

Penelope smiled. "Where's this safe house you want to go to?"

Bettie couldn't understand why Penelope was allowing her to decide where to go. She would have expected Penelope to take her to some Russian gang base or something.

"I need to drive," Bettie said. "I don't really know how to describe the route unless I'm driving,"

"Wow," Penelope said. "The English are as pathetic as always. I am trying to help you and I know my men will not allow you to drive their SUV,"

Something exploded.

The SUV jerked sharply.

Bettie slammed into the door.

Penelope dropped her cup.

Bright golden sunlight streamed through the windows.

A motorbike was next to them.

The driver wore all black. It was a woman. She aimed her assault rifle.

She fired.

Bettie jumped but the windows stopped the bullets. For now.

The SUV flew towards the motorbike.

Smashing into it.

Deafening cracking of bones echoed around the SUV.

Bettie just looked at Penelope.

Bettie fell backwards as the backing of the car seats fell away.

She looked up and saw she was leaning in the driver's compartment. A massive muscular Russian woman frowned at her as she drove.

Penelope helped Bettie back up.

Bettie spun around.

The lead vehicle was gone. Probably exploded.

"You were tracked," Bettie said. "I don't have my phone or anything. what aren't you telling me?"

Penelope laughed as she took out a Glock from under her seat. "I am no longer working for the Russian government,"

"Why?"

"Because believe it or not Miss English," Penelope said. "It was the only way to make sure the assassins didn't kill your children, Harry or Sean. We love killing gays but even I have a heart,"

Bettie was shocked as the SUV hooked a right and she realised they were entering the motorway. The exact same motorway needed to go to the safehouse.

"You already know the safe house don't you?" Bettie asked.

The SUV banged.

Bettie screamed as she saw the rubber casing of a front wheel roll away.

The rear vehicle exploded.

And the SUV Bettie was in shot forward.

Bettie climbed forward into the front passenger seat. She couldn't talk to Penelope right now.

She just needed to be safe.

"Let go," Bettie said grabbing the wheel.

Another SUV smashed into the back of them.

Bettie heard people jumping on the roof.

Penelope prepared her gun.

She fired through the roof.

Corpses splattered onto the road.

Bettie grabbed the wheel.

The woman let her.

Bettie went sharply to the left.

Tons of cars ahead were stopping.

There was traffic.

Bettie went onto the hard shoulder.

Bright orange signs lit up ahead.

There was road works on the hard shoulder.

The Russian woman went to grab the wheel.

Bettie slapped her hands away.

Bettie went straight.

Smashing into the road signs.

Potholes vibrated the entire SUV.

Bettie saw motorbikes follow them.

The potholes knocked them off.

Bettie kept driving.

A massive patch of wet tarmac was ahead.

Bettie went straight.

The SUV smashed into the tarmac.

It started sinking.

Bettie ordered the woman to hit the floor with the accelerator.

Bullets smashed into the SUV.

The windows shattered.

The SUV started moving again.

Bettie kept steering.

She re-joined the main motorway with all the other drivers staying well away from her and all that Bettie wanted was to see her family.

Yet she knew they would be somewhere along the motorway by this time.

She just hoped they were having better luck.

And hopefully no one was going to die.

CHAPTER 7
15th August 2023
Canterbury, England

Graham was so glad beautiful Harrison and Elizabeth were peacefully snoring away in the back of the Land Rover as he watched the two black cars come up towards them.

He knew they didn't have a lot of time left

and Graham expected that because it was a Tuesday morning there would be traffic up ahead. If they stopped for even a moment then they were going to die or at least be captured to lure out Bettie.

It was so damn stupid of the Russians to do such a thing and as soon as Graham found Penelope Bishop he was going to punch her. He didn't know how she was involved but she just was.

Hell she was probably the person behind all of this and she was probably the person hunting down Bettie. The dumb woman.

Graham went to open a window but he noticed that the two black cars behind them were keeping their distance back. They were waiting for the ideal time to strike this wasn't good at all.

Graham noticed in the distance a large group of white, orange and blue lorries were slowing down so chances were traffic was starting to build up.

"Take the next exit," Graham said pointing to a slip road away.

Daniels didn't even argue he did it and Graham was more than grateful for that. He had never been hunted before but he was a cop first and foremost he had an idea about what to do in these sort of situations.

The Land Rover pulled out onto the slip road and Graham noticed the black cars were following them. Graham knew this slip road would take them to a roundabout and then there were two options. There was a long and very quiet country lane they could take to the safehouse or they could take the longer but busier main road through a town.

"I'm taking the country lane," Daniels said approaching the roundabout.

Graham nodded. It wasn't ideal but Daniels was the MI5 intelligence officer so maybe he knew best.

He noticed that Daniels was speeding up more and more towards the roundabout. It looked clear but there was a large hedge ahead that cut off their view.

They were approaching the roundabout.

A massive artic lorry appeared behind the hedge.

Daniels slammed on the brakes.

The two Russian cars sped up.

The article lorry kept going.

"Gun," Graham said.

Daniels smashed his fist on the dashboard.

A Glock jumped out of the ceiling.

Graham picked it up. Undid the window, aimed and fired.

He wasn't brave enough to look at the black cars and aim properly.

He just needed to slow them down.

Graham was really grateful for the firearm training now.

The artic lorry finished going around.

Daniels shot forward.

The Land Rover jerked.

Graham jumped.

Dropping the gun as they raced away.

"That was close," Daniels said racing round the roundabout.

They dived down the country lane and Graham gripped the door handle tightly as Daniels sped down the little country lane.

"Just pop the gun in the glove compartment for now," Daniels said.

Graham just did up his window again. He couldn't believe he had been so stupid and allowed the gun to fall out of his hand.

That was beyond bad and he doubted

Daniels had another gun just lying about in his car. This was turning into an absolute nightmare.

"Where's the gun?" Daniels asked.

"I dropped it," Graham said.

"Wow," Daniels said. "Wow. That is… bad,"

"Sorry," Graham said checking the mirrors to see if they were being followed. He didn't doubt that the Russians had already hacked their way into the local traffic cameras so it was only a matter of time before they were found again.

"Make sure you don't destroy this one yet but under your seat is a burner phone. Turn on and call the Federation," Daniels said.

Graham did as he was told and called the only woman in the Federation he could trust right now. He called the de-facto deputy President Fran and told her everything.

"I'll notify the membership," Fran said. "I'll contact the home office, MI5 and counterterrorism whilst I'm there. But Graham make sure you tell no one where you are,"

Graham couldn't understand why.

"We found a security breach two hours ago. Every single scrap of information the Federation has minus Article 20 and 66 was being fed directly to the Russians in Moscow,"

"Shit," Graham said.

"Everything is secured now but I don't know who you can trust right now. I even think I might be targeted. Just be careful and for God sake make sure Bettie's protected,"

Graham didn't know what to make of that and he really wasn't sure if she should tell Fran about Penelope Bishop but he just needed some support right now.

"What's the police situation like and what happened to Penelope Bishop?" Graham asked.

"That damn woman's back?" Fran asked over the phone. "Damn her but I guess the police are aware of the situation but they're clueless. Ten police officers have been killed and the army's being called in,"

Graham shook his head. This was turning into a full-blown diplomatic crisis and all because the Russians were pissed at Bettie.

Graham noticed they were approaching a crossroads. He turned around and was glad that Daniels had bought two little car seats for the twins that were completely enclosed.

He hadn't noticed that earlier but he was more than glad they were there and Sean and Harry had already placed the kids inside them.

"I love you all," Graham said.

Two black cars smashed into them at the crossroads.

One each side.

Graham's head smashed into Daniels's.

His world turned black.

CHAPTER 8
15th August 2023
Canterbury, England

Bettie still wasn't impressed at all with the entire damn situation as she continued sitting on the passenger front seat with the muscular Russian woman who was clearly refusing to talk to her kept driving whilst listening to Bettie's directions as best as she could give them.

The roads were mainly quiet with only a few red, blue and white cars gently passing them as Bettie had ordered the Russian woman to keep to the speed limit. It was the best way to not draw attention to themselves and thankfully there were other black big cars on the road too.

Bettie didn't like having to keep her head low at times because all the windows were shattered now. At least she hadn't sliced herself on any of the glass but she wasn't a fan of the loud howl whipping through the car.

The scent of car fumes, sweat and even a little wee filled the air as it whipped through the entire car. And Bettie was so looking forward to getting to the safehouse in the middle of nowhere.

Once at the safehouse Bettie could finally stop and think about her next move and hopefully find the family and man she loved more than anything else in the entire world.

She really hoped they were okay.

Bettie felt Penelope leant closer. "I didn't expect Alpha and Beta units to hire local criminals to help kill you,"

Bettie had no idea if that was meant to make her feel better or not. Then she realised exactly what ten Russian special forces members Penelope was talking about.

She hadn't told Graham about this at all but the Federation had had intel lately from private eyes on cases in eastern Europe that told her those ten members of elite Russian units were abandoning Ukraine and coming towards the UK.

It was only now she realised why. They had new orders to kill her and thankfully not innocent Ukrainians.

After this Bettie was so donating millions of her own money to the Ukrainian government. She was going to do anything to piss off the Russians even more. If she was still alive that was.

"What's your plan?" Bettie asked.

Penelope smiled. "The first plan is to keep you alive and of course I have my own plans in the background,"

"I don't believe you quit your job in the Russian government to save my nephew, his boyfriend and my children,"

Penelope frowned and Bettie looked at her.

"You think I wouldn't do everything in my power to protect children?" Penelope asked but Bettie wasn't buying it.

"What about all the children Russia is kidnapping in Ukraine?" Bettie asked.

Penelope's hands formed fists. "That wasn't my decision,"

"And yet you defend and spread lies about your government,"

"And you actually think the UK and West are so innocent," Penelope said. "We can debate ideology all day Bettie but I would much rather keep you alive for now,"

Bettie supposed she had a point so she focused back on the road and told the driver to take the next exit and hopefully once they were down the country lane they would be a lot closer to the safehouse.

The smell of a gun being fired made Bettie tense but then she realised it was a recent firing so maybe Graham had been through here lately. She really hoped he was okay.

The Russian woman slowed down as they approached the roundabout and Bettie hated that there was a large green hedge blocking their view.

Then the driver stopped and pulled a gun on Penelope.

"Sorry boss but business is business," she said in a thick Russian accent. "The President sends her regards,"

Bettie lunged forward.

Grabbing the gun.

Pointing it upwards.

The Russian fired.

Bettie punched her in the face.

The Russian slapped Bettie.

She fixed the gun on Bettie.

She fired.

Bettie ducked.

The bullet missed.

Bettie jumped on the Russian.

Penelope aimed her gun.

Bettie leapt off the woman.

Penelope fired.

Blood rushed off the headwound.

Bettie undid the woman's seatbelt and pushed her corpse off the seat and out of the car.

"You saved me?" Penelope asked.

"Maybe you aren't lying about quitting your job but I know there's more to the story," Bettie said. "Especially as I doubt the Russian President would have you of all people killed without good reason,"

Penelope grinned. "You know me Bettie I am always scheming, have a plan and everything else,"

Bettie nodded as she slipped into the driver's seat and went round the roundabout down the country lane.

Penelope fixed the gun on Bettie. "Which is why I need you to help me prove my allegiance to Mother Russia,"

"For fuck sake," Bettie said.

She seriously hoped things couldn't get any worse but she knew they would. Things were going to get a hell of a lot worse before they got better.

CHAPTER 9
15th August 2023

Unknown Location, England

When Graham finally woke he hissed in pain as he felt the burning hot black tarmac he was resting on was far away from the car and he couldn't hear anything. The warm summer breeze made the branches of the massive oak trees that lined the road smash into each other and Graham was glad to be alive.

He quickly checked himself mentally to make sure nothing was broken and besides from the warm trickles of blood going down his face he knew nothing else was damaged or broken.

Graham forced himself up and frowned at the smashed-up wreckage of Daniels' Land Rover.

Both sides were caved in from where the two Russian cars had smashed into him. All the doors were open and even the boot was too.

Graham went over to the Land Rover and four heavily armed women in full body armour stepped out from the crossroads and Graham just frowned at them.

He checked the backseat and was glad to see Sean, Harry and the two babies were still in the back unharmed. Graham was even happier when he heard Harrison and Elizabeth were snoring loudly.

That just melted his heart, trust his kids to not be awoken by a car crash. Typical.

"You," a Russian woman said pushing an assault rifle in his face. "Coming with us,"

"No," Graham said. "Not until you tell me what all this is about,"

Graham realised he had the phone he used

to call Fran in his pocket so it was risky but he dialled 999 and hoped beyond hope the cops could trace the call.

"I am Detective Graham Adams of Kent Police," he said, "you are committing a criminal offence threatening a police officer,"

Graham had said that more for the 999 operator more than the Russians but it might get them to make a mistake.

"You are no threat to us," the Russian said.

"Enough of this," two other women said aiming their rifles at Sean and Harry. "Come with us or they will die,"

"They are not on the assassination order," the Russian with the rifle in Graham's face said.

"Be dammed with the President and her orders. She ordered us into Ukraine and I lost my boyfriend, my brothers and parents to those Ukrainian Nazis. Be damned if she kills me too,"

Graham looked at Sean and Harry and mouthed *where's Daniels?*

They both shrugged and Graham felt a wave of happiness wash over him, at least there was a slice of hope. Graham just needed to keep the Russians talking and being divided long enough.

"Damn the President?" the other Russians asked fixing their rifles on those two women.

"We all know it is true," they said.

Graham hissed as bullets roared through the air cutting down those two women like the foul dogs they were.

The last two remaining women focused their rifles on Graham. "In the car now,"

Graham shook his head.

"We are allowed to kill you," one woman said.

"And if you kill me then the entire Western world will come after you,"

"Those spineless idiots," the women said laughing. "Yeah I'm really scared of those sissies,"

Graham watched Daniel pick up two rifles from the dead women and shot the women in the head.

Two corpses dropped to the ground.

Graham picked up a rifle and threw another one to Sean. He knew he didn't have tactical training but he had loved Call of Duty as a kid so Graham hoped he had learnt something.

The sound of another car coming down the road made Graham and Daniels aim their rifles at the incoming black SUV.

The SUV started honking and it took Graham a moment to realise it to morse code for SOS. Bettie was driving and she was in trouble.

The SUV stopped a few metres from them and both beautiful Bettie and damn Penelope Bishop stepped out. Graham couldn't see Penelope's weapon but he knew she had one.

Graham and Daniels fixed their weapons on her immediately and she grinned. Bettie quickly walked over to them.

She raced into the backseat probably to make sure her little angels were okay. Graham loved how great of a mother she was.

Then Bettie quickly caught them up on everything that had happened. Graham wasn't happy that Thomas Birch was dead, he was a good man and would have made a great father.

"Why do you need us to prove your allegiance?" Graham asked Penelope.

"Because someone in the Russian government sold top-secret information to the

Chinese," Penelope said, "and because I was on a diplomatic visit to the region at the time. They believe I did it,"

"How can we help?" Bettie asked Elizabeth and Harrison who looked like this was fun and games.

Penelope smiled. "I have no idea but if you all want to stay alive I suggest we get cracking,"

Graham nodded at Sean as he popped out of the smashed Land Rover and pointed his weapon at Penelope so he could talk to Bettie in private.

Graham kissed Bettie's soft wonderful lips and he was so damn happy she was alive and okay. She was beautiful.

"What do you think?" Graham asked.

"That Penelope Bishop of all people doesn't have a backup plan and she's using us more, that is a massive underestimation of her. But equally we do need to find who trying to kill me and we might as well help Penelope too,"

Graham wasn't sure he wanted to help a woman like Penelope but she had saved the woman he loved, she didn't really have to do that. So Graham was willing to help Penelope for a little while and she would know a lot more about Alpha and Beta-6 including how to stop them from killing Bettie.

They weren't that far from the safehouse but Graham was more concerned about who knew else about the safehouse.

The Russians seemed to know everything for now so Graham destroyed his burner phone and got everyone in Penelope's SUV.

And just hoped beyond hope he wasn't going to regret this.

CHAPTER 10
15th August 2023
Canterbury, England

Alina just grinned as she stood at the very edge of the narrow country road watching Bettie and her idiot family drive off towards their so-called safehouse. She enjoyed the silly coolness of the breeze brushing her cheeks but the weather explained why the English were just sissies.

Alina had been bought up in the icy coldness of the Russian mountains and she had been killing since she was nine years old, not that the weak English would ever know what that was like and that was exactly why the English would fall in time. They were the weakness of the entire West.

Alina watched as the little black SUV was out of sight before she allowed herself to step out onto the narrow country road. There was so much green here and somewhere in the local area had to be the safehouse they were entering or heading too.

She knew that Bettie was too arrogant to think for a moment there was a tracking device installed on Penelope's SUV that she had secretly placed herself. And there was a reason why Graham Adams was in the middle of the road.

Alina had had to slice open his shoe and implant a small tracking device that he wouldn't notice until it was way too late. The English were so dumb.

And as for Penelope Bishop Alina was so looking forward to ending that traitor once and for all.

Alina laughed and just waited for the trackers to reveal the location of her sissy little pray. And once nighttime fell they could finally have some fun.

And finally Bettie English would be dead.

CHAPTER 11
15th August 2023
Unknown Location, England

As Bettie slowly drove the SUV up the private road with thick dense oak trees lining it, she knew she had triggered over a hundred different security systems. She had once hired former CIA, SAS and MI5 officers to try and infiltrate the local woodland undetected and all of them had failed.

Bettie was more than pleased about that because at least she knew she was going to be safe.

The private road was narrow and the thick oak branches veiled the sky so only thin slivers of golden sunlight dared to light up the private road. It was perfect to counter enemy satellite coverage but Bettie had to admit she was way out of her element here.

She was a private eye not an intelligence officer or anything and this was probably her most dangerous case ever. She just hoped everything was going to be okay.

The SUV hit the gravel driveway and the sound of crunching gravel echoed around the woodland, another great security feature to alert them to danger once inside.

Bettie grinned at the large cottage in the middle of a gravel clearing. The cottage had beautiful white walls, bullet-proof windows and there was only a single entrance and exit. Even that was made from solid three-inch steel.

Bettie stopped the car and got out. She took the kids off Sean and kissed them softly on the cheek, she had never meant to put any of her family through this but she was glad they were okay.

Everyone else grabbed their to-go bag and Penelope scanned the area with her Glock making sure no one was going to jump out at them.

"What is this place?" Penelope asked. "I've searched all the properties you, the Federation and other people connected to you have. This isn't one of them,"

Bettie smiled. "That's because this is property that doesn't exist on any official record, government, Federation or otherwise. The house was gifted to us in the darkest days of World War One when the Federation was first founded,"

Everyone nodded and Bettie loved everyone was listening to her.

"This was actually where the Federation first met and they planned attacks and infiltration missions for the UK Government back in 1916 to 1918. After the war and the liberal Government was voted out, no one else knew we had to so this Federation had always had this secret base. Just in case,"

A loud banging sound made Bettie smile as the front door opened and Harrison just gave Penelope a look of horror as she aimed her gun at the man coming out the doorway.

Bettie went over to her oldest friend Mr Harley Nelson the second-ever President of the British Private Eye Federation. He was a tall man with a large muscular body and he might have been in his eighties but Bettie knew he could fight as good as any twenty-year-old if the situation called for it.

"Protocol R you said?" Harley asked grinning. "Ah you bought me a gift in the form of Penelope Bishop,"

Penelope seemed a little annoyed she had no idea who this man was. Bettie had no problem with her being annoyed.

"Sorry to crash your house like this," Bettie said, "but it's an emergency. Alpha-6 and Beta-6 are coming after us and they want to kill me,"

Harley spat at Penelope. "Damn Russians and your stupid ideas and games,"

Bettie watched as Penelope smiled and Bettie supposed Penelope liked being challenged.

"Can we trust her?" Harley asked looking at Penelope like she was a trained assassin which all Bettie knew she could be.

"For now," Graham said.

Bettie nodded. "Is the house prepared?"

"As soon as I got the Protocol R notification I've been preparing for this moment. The Russians will find us at some point and then we need to be prepared,"

Graham stepped forward. "How long?"

Bettie had no idea why Harley sniffed the air but it made her smile.

"Tomorrow night they will attack. I can promise you that,"

Penelope placed her gun away. "Some time you and me will get along alright,"

Harley laughed as he gestured the others to come in. "I doubt that very much lassie. I don't mix with your kind,"

"Then by the end of this, let's hope our blood doesn't mix together," Penelope said storming into the house.

Bettie kissed Elizabeth and Harrison on the lips and she was looking forward to finally working this all out, finding out who was after her and most importantly what Penelope was truly after.

Bettie knew Penelope wasn't helping her out of the goodness of her heart and she wasn't buying the whole allegiance idea. So what was really going on?

And Bettie just hoped it wasn't going to kill her or anyone else she loved.

CHAPTER 12
15th August 2023
Unknown Location, England

Graham was really pleased with the "interesting" look inside of the cottage as Harley and Bettie led them inside. Graham had expected the inside to be nicely decorated, perfectly intact and filled with weapons to help them defend themselves against the Russian attack that was bound to happen.

Instead Graham just shook his head and stared at the naked wooden floorboards covered in dust, the entire cottage was made up of a single massive downstairs room with a dusty red sofa, chair and dining table.

Nothing in the entire house was clean and the entire place just looked dodgy as hell. He certainly wasn't allowing the kids to walk or stumble around here, this was awful.

There were a few steps down towards the sofas and Graham wasn't even sure he trusted the stairs and judging by the look on everyone else's faces, they completely agreed.

Graham hated the awful smell of dust, mould and rotting meat that clung to the air like a fungi infection. Graham hated this entire house and he was even willing to bet there was more of a chance of him dying in here then the Russians killing him.

"You seriously don't think I would bring us here without a trick do you?" Bettie asked.

Graham shrugged. He knew Bettie was full of wonderful surprises but he supposed even she could have her moments (or days) of madness.

Bettie nodded at Harley and he clapped his hands rapidly and a large chunk of the floor rose up and Graham saw a long silver staircase lead down into the basement. He followed as Bettie and Harley went down.

As soon as they were at the bottom of the staircase, Bettie put the kids down and Graham smiled as they just crawled a few metres from Bettie but stopped like they were terrified to go any further.

He couldn't blame them.

The basement was an immense single room with a ceiling metres high and walls all made from solid steel with all sorts of weapons lining the further wall from knives to assault rifles to pistols, another two walls were covered in bookcases and files, and Graham really liked the last wall because it was covered in laptops and technology.

Exactly what he wanted.

Graham liked the jet-black sofas and coffee table arranged next to a kitchen area and he was happy that Bettie had this place. Everything seemed to be okay and Graham actually believed for a moment that they could win this fight.

Sean and Harry went over to the technology wall and picked up a tablet each, Penelope looked like she wanted to inspect the weaponry but Graham just looked at her. That was the last place he was allowing her to go.

Instead everyone went over to the sofas and Graham hugged the woman he loved as Sean and Harry sat next to him and Harrison and Elizabeth played by Graham's feet with the toys he had bought them.

"We all know why we are here," Bettie said. "We are here to find and stop the ten people that were hired to kill me and I hope Penelope here can tell us more,"

Penelope leant back on her own sofa like she owned the place and grinned.

"Thank you Miss English. Let me just say that Alpha-6 and Beta-6 are the best of the best and even I haven't been able to beat them in a sparring much,"

"And that's an achievement?" Harley asked.

"Come at me old man," Penelope said. "See how quickly I kill you,"

Graham had a feeling Harley wouldn't be as easy to kill as Penelope believed.

"Anyway there are twelve people sent to kill you Bettie but as we saw on the motorway they have resorted to hiring local criminals too to kill you," Penelope said. "I have never ever seen both teams being hired for the same job,"

Graham was surprised for a moment to see that Penelope was actually surprised and maybe even a little upset about that detail. But knowing her she was probably just concerned about Bettie not being able to help her with her own games.

Graham was determined to figure out what the hell her endgame was.

"How many have we killed so far?" Graham asked.

Penelope laughed. "From everything you've all said, there's the four people you killed at the crossroads. There is the person Daniels killed when he collected you and that's it,"

Graham rolled his eyes. He was hoping to be a little better so far than leaving seven highly trained Russian assassins alive.

"And it is only the seven of us," Graham said knowing that Daniels was outside checking the perimeter.

Penelope and Harley laughed together. "Seven?"

Graham nodded but he noticed Bettie was also smiling.

"Graham," Bettie said. "These are Russian assassins, Penelope, Daniels and Harley can take them on but we need to be extra clever if we want to do something,"

Graham leant forward as soon as he realised that Bettie wanted to be evil.

"What you thinking?" Sean asked.

"I know if we engage these assassins in hand-to-hand combat we die," Bettie said. "But we can still be good at long range,"

"Sure," Penelope said holding her arms in the air. "Give a kid a gun and enough bullets eventually they're gonna kill something,"

Harrison and Elizabeth just looked at her.

"Sorry I didn't mean it," Penelope said.

Graham blew his kids a kiss each as they went back to playing with their toys.

"My real concern is the Master," Penelope said. "The President would never ever trust her best assets to go to the UK, do a mission without a backup plan in place to get them out,"

Graham rolled his eyes. That was sadly common sense.

"We have to find the Master because he or she would know exactly what's happening with the mission," Penelope said.

"And I presume," Harley said, "it would be someone in the President's inner circle,"

"So kill them and scare the President?" Bettie asked.

Penelope bit her lip. "For a change you are exactly right,"

Sean and Harry passed everyone a tablet or laptop. Graham took a laptop and couldn't believe how excited he was that they were going to be researching the highest levels of the Russian government.

The very worst of all governments.

CHAPTER 13
15th August 2023
Unknown Location, England

A few hours later Bettie stretched and just allowed the immense black sofa to just take her weight and claim her. She had always loved how soft, comfortable and perfectly supportive these sofas were and she had missed this place.

She hadn't been at all in 2023 and even before that she had only visited three times as President and only then to drop off some stuff. It was a weird place but Bettie loved how quiet, peaceful and isolated it was.

And even with Penelope here, it was nice seeing Sean, Harry and Graham just working away wanting to save her. Harley was making everyone a cup of English Breakfast tea even though it was way past breakfast and approaching dinner time.

But Harley had probably just made everyone English tea to annoy Penelope.

Bettie liked the sweet hints of mint, vanilla and strawberry that filled the air from a small tray of shortbread biscuits and sweet treats that Harley bought over before he bought the tea.

As soon as he placed the tray down Bettie leant forward, grabbed a knife and covered a shortbread biscuit in a thick layer of custard. She loved it and it was the first thing she had eaten all day and it tasted amazing.

Penelope gave the biscuits and sweet treats a sceptical look as if they were poisoned so Bettie laughed.

"You can put it in your tea if you want," Bettie said.

"No she cannot," Harley said truly offended. "This is *English* tea I am about to serve and you want *her* of all people to add Russian stuff and drink it how Russians do. The very same people that are trying to kill you,"

"I would rather not fight over something as simple as tea," Bettie said smiling.

"I'm sorry," Harley said bringing over everyone's tea. "I just worry about Bettie,"

"Thank you," Bettie said. "And has anyone found something?"

Everyone shook their heads.

"Everyone in the President's top inner circle has been sanctioned by every single western nation so if they come here they're in trouble," Graham said.

"And your weak little governments have issued arrest warrants for them too in spite of diplomatic immunity," Penelope said.

Bettie had no idea how that would work if the UK tried to arrest anyone with diplomatic immunity but she would love to see them try.

But Bettie understood the point clear enough, the Master couldn't be anyone of the inner circle of the President.

"Wait," Bettie said looking at Penelope.

Harley whipped out a gun pointing it at Penelope.

"What if you're the Master?" Bettie asked.

Penelope laughed. "Really you think I would actually want you dead,"

"You know I respect you," Bettie said.

"You know I have at least the smallest amount of wanting to work with you, you could use your relationship with me to lure me out,"

Penelope gestured around her. "I think I've done that very well,"

Bettie stood up and Graham gently grabbed the kids and made them play behind the sofas, like they actually cared.

"You could have been lurking and waiting to see what's happened to me, where I was going to be and then you could create a fake Master to lurk me into a trap," Bettie said.

"I admit," Penelope said, "that I am that intelligent but I didn't. I didn't betray you, want you dead or anything but there is a bargain going on,"

Bettie looked at Harley and she really wanted him to lower the weapon because she knew Penelope was telling the truth but thankfully her safety was his top priority.

"When that information was sold to the Chinese, the reason why they thought it was me was because two million US dollars appeared in my bank accounts. You know the ones not sanctioned yet because the West is useless,"

Bettie just wanted to hit her.

"And they knew I have, I have a husband that defected about a decade ago and I killed him but they don't care,"

Bettie folded her arms and went a little closer to Penelope. "Your plans are actually unravelling. I always presumed you wanted to be President of Russia but you can't do that can you?"

Penelope frowned. "I would have been a good President you know, I at least want to work with the west a little, just a little though, and that was always my end goal of my schemes, my power plays and my killings,"

"What went wrong?"

"You," Penelope said. "You're too good at your job so when you thankfully took down that cryptocurrency company and wiped out the money of my opponents. I failed to realise the President had a lot of money in that company. She found out I was the one behind helping you and now, yeah she wants me dead,"

"And you aren't allowed in Russia anymore?" Sean asked.

Daniels came back down the stairs shaking his head. "This is an impressive place but the Russians are doing a grid search. I've heard three commercial drones overhead so sooner or later they will come for us,"

"No I am not allowed in Russia as of this morning so I fled and now," Penelope said staring into Bettie's eyes, "I promise I will do whatever it takes to keep you and everyone in this room alive,"

Bettie nodded her thanks. "I believe you but I don't believe you don't have another plan up your sleeve,"

"Then you Miss English are probably the smartest woman, no person on the planet," Penelope said gesturing a cheers as she drank her tea. "Disgusting English tea passed me the custard,"

Bettie laughed as she passed over the custard but she noticed that Graham was looking at her. She couldn't blame him if the Russians were conducting a grid search then they really didn't have long left to set up, prepare and make a final stand.

A stand that she was determined to win.

CHAPTER 14
15th August 2023
Canterbury, England

Graham so badly wanted Penelope to be gone, dead and defeated because he just knew she was up to something very, very bad. Even if the Russians did want to kill her Graham refused to believe that she wasn't planning something, if anything that little detail only made her even more dangerous.

Graham kissed Bettie on the head as she snuggled into him and they all turned their attention to the upcoming battle. He was guessing they had until very late tonight or even tomorrow morning because it was impossible for the Russians to find them right now.

Just flat out impossible.

Graham watched Daniels, Harley and Penelope sit on the same sofa together and it was funny seeing the look of horror on their faces whenever someone else moved. Almost like they were expecting each other to attack.

"We have shotguns so we can saw down the barrels," Harley said, "making them more powerful,"

"We can also cut open the shotgun cartridges," Sean said, "get the black powder, put some screws in lightbulbs and make them explode when someone turns on the lights,"

Graham had no idea if he should be concerned or grateful Sean knew that little trick.

"The house is from 1910s," Penelope said. "You English were hardly ever master builders. Cut up some of the floorboards to weaken them then as soon as a bastard stands on them they'll go through the floor,"

Graham was about to say something when he felt two little hands tap his foot. He had been sitting with his right leg over his left for ages now but he looked at it and saw that Harrison was playing with his foot.

Harrison had never ever done that before and when Elizabeth half-crawled, half-walked over she started to do the same.

"What are you doing to daddy's shoe?" Graham asked.

"Shiny thing," Harrison said laughing like a little kid having the best time of his life.

Graham had no idea what the kids were talking about. He was wearing his black soled shoes like he always did, there was nothing shiny on the bottom.

"Let daddy have a look," Graham said taking off his shoe and Harrison looked like he was about to cry.

"Daddy," he said.

Sean went over to him. "Come on buddy I know you like bouncing with Uncle Harry,"

Penelope let out a long disgusted sound, Graham shot her a warning look.

Graham turned over his shoe and realised the kids were on to something. Bettie sat up perfectly straight and as he bent his shoe a little he noticed a small bullet-shaped tracking device was inside.

"Damn," Bettie said. "That's how they knew to start a grid search,"

"And," Daniels said, "if Penelope's driver was a traitor then I doubt she wouldn't have put a tracking device on the SUV,"

"I'm sorry Bettie," Graham said.

Bettie waved him silent. "It's fine but we have a lot to do now,"

Graham nodded as he placed the shiny tracking device on the floor and Bettie had to grab Elizabeth to stop her from going for the shiny object.

He stomped on the tracker.

"As soon as the sun sets they will attack," Penelope said. "That gives us three hours to prepare, fortify and… say our goodbyes,"

Graham wondered if she was joking for a moment but Penelope wasn't in the slightest. Graham had seen the same look of fear, desperation and terror on the face of fallen cops and other people he cared about when they realised they were going to die.

Harley got up and grabbed two huge machine guns off the wall and smiled.

"Then let's give the Russians hell," he said.

Graham looked at everyone he loved in his room, minus Penelope, they were all such amazing people that were perfect, wonderful and if he was going to die here today then Graham was glad he was going to be surrounded by friends.

But he knew he wasn't dying today.

Only the Russians were.

He hoped.

CHAPTER 15
15th August 2023
Unknown Location, England

Alina was surprised the foolish English had managed to find the tracking device, they were normally way too dumb and stupid and weak for such an intelligent thing. Not that it mattered, Alina was more than glad she had the final location of Bettie English and now her mission could be completed.

Alina sat around a roaring, crackling fire with her seven remaining assassins. They were all strong, muscular Russian men and women that were so much better than the English.

All these men and women had been in

countless battles, fought in the Russian army for close to a decade each and they had killed every single nazi they had come across in Ukraine. Russia would win the Ukraine special military operation and then they would conquer the rest of Europe.

No one could stop the might of the Motherland.

Alina reached down on the ground and picked up her own assault rifle, Soviet issue so it was clearly superior to everything the English could throw at them.

She lifted the weapon, checked the sight and smiled. It was going to be an exciting night for all of them.

And there was only one single thing the President was wrong about, the assassination order had been explicit in not hurting Sean, Harry, Bettie's kids and Penelope to some extent. But Alina couldn't exist taking Sean and Harry with them, forcing them against their will to take up arms for the Russian army in Ukraine.

That would be a glorious way to kill them and make them serve the motherland. Alina grinned in excitement and because Bettie's kids would not have a mother or father then they would need to be bought up in the motherland and given a righteous education.

Alina grinned at the new plan and she couldn't wait until sunset.

Because Bettie English was finally going to die.

CHAPTER 16
15th August 2023
Unknown Location, England

Over the next three hours, Bettie flat out couldn't believe how much fun it had been preparing the house and making sure that everything was ready for their uninvited guests.

As much as she didn't know how to fight despite her self-defence classes and more, she knew that their plan was as perfect as it was going to be.

Bettie fully intended that once the Russians had gotten through the steel front door that narrow corridor would be a perfect kill site so Penelope and Daniels were going to be firing their assault rifles until they were empty at the incoming enemy.

If the Russians survived that Bettie was really looking forward to Sean's brilliant idea happening because as soon as the Russians made it into the large single living room Bettie would turn on the lights.

Causing a massive explosion and high-speed screws to rain down on the enemy. Distracting them long enough for Harley to go out and attack.

Bettie's stomach twisted at the idea of the Russians surviving that because if the Russians used the silver stairs to come down to the steel room then Bettie had managed to saw off the shotgun barrels so she at least had a high-powered close-range weapon.

As well as the other pistols she had grabbed.

"That is it then," Bettie said.

It was only minutes until sunset and everyone was in position, Bettie stood next to Graham as a small section of the weapon wall opened up to reveal a large steel room with.

"The room is beyond bomb-proof and only you can open it," Bettie said to Sean and Harry as they placed baby toys, baby milk and everything else from the kids' to-go bags inside.

"The room has oxygen recyclers and everything you need to live in there forever. It is a nuclear bunker. But don't come out for the next two days unless you hear me say *I hate Graham,*" Bettie said grinning.

Bettie hated saying all of this but it was the only way to keep the kids safe whilst all this happened.

Bettie knelt down on the floor and hugged Harrison and Elizabeth tight even as the kids protested because they wanted to play and they didn't know what was happening.

"Mummy loves you both so much okay. You're going to go on a little adventure with Uncle Sean and Harry okay," Bettie said kissing her babies and forcing herself not to cry.

After a few moments she forced herself to let go so Graham could also say his goodbyes to the kids just in case.

Bettie grabbed Sean and hugged him so damn tight she wondered if she was going to crack a rib. "You are so amazing, I love you and just keep being the amazing person you are,"

Sean kissed her. "You won't die Auntie,"

Bettie forced away tears as she kissed her nephew in case this was the last ever time she was going to be able to do that.

Graham said his goodbyes to Sean and Bettie hugged Harry.

"You might not be from our family by blood but by God are you an English," Bettie said hugging Harry. "And for God sake marry Sean already,"

Harry laughed. "You're the most amazing woman I've ever met Miss English,"

Bettie hugged both Sean and Harry. "And if anything does happen look after our kids for us. The Wills and everything legally is done, just love them like your own,"

Sean and Harry slowly nodded and they picked up the kids and took them into the nuclear bunker.

And the moment that thick heavy metal door slammed shut Bettie collapsed to her knees as she realised that honestly could have been the last time she ever saw her children, nephew and his wonderful boyfriend.

She heard Graham crying next to her but Bettie forced herself not to join him. The only way they were going to see their kids again was if they survived this.

She had come up with a good plan but now she just needed to make sure everyone followed it.

And they all got out of this alive.

CHAPTER 17
15th August 2023
Unknown Location, England

Harley had fought in wars, gun fights and battles against all sort of foul criminals and Russians but he knew this would be his last. His duty was to protect the President of the Federation and he was gladly going to die in the process. Especially if it meant allowing wonderful Bettie to see her family again.

He stood in the far corner of the huge single living room in the pitch darkness just waiting for the Russians to storm in the front door and Daniels and awful Penelope could attack.

Harley had to admit Bettie's plan was perfect and she might not have had military experience but she clearly had a brilliant mind.

He checked his assault rifle and aimed his night vision scope towards Penelope and

Daniels but he could have sworn he could hear a loud whooshing sound.

Like that of a rocket launcher.

The wall next to him exploded.

Throwing Harley to the other side of the room.

His ears rang.

He couldn't hear.

He tried to find his rifle.

Harley had lost it in the explosion.

Smoke bombs flew into the living room.

Smoke veiled the room.

He couldn't see. Couldn't feel. Couldn't react.

Harley saw shapes moving in the smoke.

He searched the floor.

He found his rifle.

He leapt up.

The front door exploded open.

Four Russians stormed in through the explosion opening.

Harley fired.

Penelope and Daniels fired at the narrow corridor.

Smoke burnt at Harley's eyes.

He couldn't see. He was firing blind.

A bullet smashed into right leg.

He knelt to the ground.

Another bullet smashed into his other leg.

Harley couldn't believe this was happening. The plan had been so perfect.

A Russian screamed as he went through a floor board.

Harley aimed at that direction.

A Russian screamed.

One dead.

Three bullets slammed into Harley's body.

His rifle flew out of his hand.

The smoke started to clear.

The Russians stormed over to him.

Shooting as they went.

Harley's felt his blood flood out of his body.

He couldn't die yet. He had to protect Bettie. His entire life had been about protecting Bettie.

He had to activate a defense procedure only he knew about.

"Activation 999!" Harley shouted.

Machine guns dropped from the ceiling.

Firing at everything in the living room.

Penelope and Daniels swore.

The Russians screamed.

The guns jammed.

The Russians stormed over to Harley and snapped his neck.

He had died protecting the woman he loved as a daughter.

CHAPTER 18
15th August 2023
Unknown Location, England

Daniels flat out couldn't believe how damn crazy Harley had been to install such an overpowered and ultimately useless thing as those machine guns in the ceiling. It was even worse that they actually jammed.

He felt agonising pain pulse up his leg from the endless damn bullet wounds from the stupid Russians and machine guns in the ceiling as he rested against the ancient wooden walls of the cottage.

Daniels sat in the narrow corridor and he couldn't understand the Russians weren't pouring in to finish them off.

He couldn't deny that Bettie's plan was perfect but it depended on the Russians coming through the front door. And Daniels had forgotten the stupid bastards never followed the rules.

Daniels hated the attackers.

He knew that Harley was dead and from what he could see Harley had killed one Russian and another three had been killed by the machine guns so maybe they weren't that useless after all.

There were still three assassins left and Daniels wasn't sure if that was good or bad.

"You okay?" Penelope asked coming over to him.

Daniels nodded and forced himself up but he couldn't put too much weight on his right leg. It was too bloody shot up. He hated this and he just wanted to make sure Bettie was okay.

Daniels leant on Penelope and they both scanned the area with their assault rifles as they moved over to the silver staircase. For Bettie Daniels was more than willing to die or get injured. He just had to make sure she was okay.

"Stop!" a woman shouted in Russian.

Daniels frowned as three heavily armoured Russians stormed in and focused their AK-47s on him and Penelope. He couldn't understand why Penelope was smiling but he hoped she had a plan.

"Low your weapons," the woman said again in Russian. "Penelope Bishop you are a traitor to the motherland,"

Penelope shook her head. "We both know whoever your leader is stole the information and framed me,"

Daniels was surprised the Russians didn't even say anything.

"The information wasn't stolen was it?" Daniels asked. "The damn Russians only did that to cover it up, the President gave the information to the Chinese and framed you to get rid of you,"

The Russians laughed and Penelope swore.

The Russians fired.

Penelope threw Daniels to one side.

Daniels landed with a thud.

He whipped up his assault rifle.

Firing.

The bullets screamed through the air.

Two bullets smashed into the floor around Daniels.

Click went the trigger. Click. Click. Click.

The Russians laughed as they came over to him and Daniels couldn't see Penelope. She hoped that she was with Bettie and everything was going to be okay.

He couldn't fail Bettie. She was amazing and the world depended on Bettie English more than they ever knew, hell more than Bettie could ever know.

Daniels swung his leg around.

But as soon as his injured leg smashed into the enemy he screamed out in agony as the leg bone broke.

"Nice try Officer Daniels," a Russian man said in perfect English.

"Enjoy your sleep,"

"Bettie! They're-" Daniels shouted as the Russians whacked him over the head with the butt of their rifles.

Now the assassins were going to kill Bettie.

CHAPTER 19
15th August 2023
Unknown Location, England

Penelope hardly felt bad for abandoning poor, old, silly Officer Daniels to his fate at the hands of the assassins. She actually didn't mind the guy, he was fun to play intelligence games with, he was fun to challenge and he was one of the few things stopping Russia from completely controlling UK "democracy".

She laughed to herself as she silently travelled through the thick oak forest and she didn't mind the calming refreshing tang of the damp nightly air. She was looking even more forward to finally meeting Alina Vagin.

Of course she had never told Bettie about who the Master was because that just wasn't fun. And Bettie needed to learn. Granted Penelope would never have allowed any real harm to come to Bettie because she was a good person and maybe one of the only tolerable English people on the planet.

Yet Bettie had served her purpose in drawing out Alina into the open and as the sound of crackling flames got louder, Penelope just grinned because she was in complete control here.

Alina might have been Federal Security Service but she was dumb, arrogant and pathetic at heart. She was so blinded in her devotion to the President that she had never learnt the skills of learning what was best for oneself. Like knowing when to betray your country.

But that was normal considering Alina was the President's daughter, not for much longer though.

Penelope stepped out into the small clearing where Alina was grinning at the crackling fire like a crazy person.

She kneecapped her and as Alina screamed out in pain, Penelope just smiled because it felt so good to hurt this bitch of a woman.

Alina started crying and Penelope kicked her in the head so she was on the floor. Then Penelope simply took her weapons away and wrapped her hands around her throat.

"Ah sweet Alina," Penelope said, "I need to know where the money is. I know your sweet little mother would not have sent you all this way without millions of dollars, a weapon cache and maybe even a small boat for your escape,"

Alina started swearing in Russian.

Penelope snapped Alina's nose. "Play nicely and I will give you a quick death,"

"You will be hunted for the rest of your life," Alina said.

Penelope laughed. It was amazing that every single person on the planet except Bettie English always underestimated her without fail. It was remarkable really.

"Not if I make the English take credit for it and well, I know they will not do that but I know it is what Russia will believe. Tell me,"

Alina frowned. "I am dead anyway,"

Penelope nodded. "Fair point but at least if I kill you I will snap your neck and you will not have to face British Interrogation and the torture they pretend to never do,"

"Never," Alina said.

Penelope just snapped her neck. Alina had always been a little shit so Penelope simply searched Alina's pocket, found her smartphone and used her fingerprints to unlock it.

Penelope was almost surprised that all the millions, location of the cache and weapons and more were all on the phone. Then again Alina had never really been that clever.

So the only job now was to make sure the body was discovered by Bettie, get Alina's money, cache and other things and finally Penelope could begin her criminal life on the run from the Russians that hated her and the Western world. All of them wanted her dead but Penelope was looking forward to building a criminal empire that was focused on destroying Russia once and for all.

And it was all because dear sweet Bettie had done her job perfectly. Penelope wanted to make sure she was okay and alive but she had more pressing concerns.

And Penelope would just send her a card. That's what the silly English did to the people they loved so that's what Penelope would do.

CHAPTER 20
15th August 2023
Unknown Location, England

Sean hugged little Elizabeth and Harrison as the two little kids started falling asleep in his arms as he heard the muffled sounds of bullets flying, explosions and shouts echoed outside the bunker. He absolutely hated all of this, he hated his family being in trouble, his family being attacked and he hated that he wasn't outside helping them.

He couldn't deny that the bunker was perfectly comfortable with its cold metal walls, enough food and water to last them for years and an Xbox console connected to a range of computer screens.

Beautiful, sexy Harry was leaning against the edge of the computer terminal studying the computer screens and Sean couldn't deny his boyfriend had a great ass. But it was what Harry was looking at that really interested him.

It was clear that Bettie's plan had failed which was strange considering how perfectly brilliant Bettie was, and Sean hated seeing how Harley was dead and everything was failing.

He knew sooner or later the Russians would be right outside and they would attack Bettie and Graham.

Sean just couldn't handle the thought of something happening to the auntie and uncle that had given him and Harry so much after the attack last June. They had to do something.

"Come on babe," Sean said. "We study Advanced Technological Engineering we should be able to figure something out,"

Harrison looked like he was stirring a little so Sean gently bounced the cute twins in his arms.

"Like what?" Harry asked.

Sean looked around the bunker. "Well we know we're the only people that can open the bunker, there's probably a bunch of wires and stuff in these computers,"

Sean had to admit he wasn't really sure what he wanted but he just wanted some hope.

"You want to build something," Harry said loving his boyfriend's hope, "but let's just remember Bettie could have put anyone in here. Including herself she wanted us in here,"

Sean smiled. He loved his boyfriend, he was so damn clever.

Sean stood up and bounced the kids in his hands a little more. Bettie would have put something in the bunker for them to use. They both already had an assault rifle and pistol each but that wasn't enough.

Then Sean noticed the Xbox.

"Turn on the console," Sean said.

As soon as Harry turned on the console, the face of the old Federation's President David Osborne appeared. Sean hated the man with a passion considering he was a sexist pig that assaulted women and was now locked away forever but maybe he had something useful to say.

"If you are in the bunker then something bad has happened," David said. "And whoever is President at the time must be dead so I trust they wanted you in here to save the day. There is a panel behind these computer screens. I hope this helps. The Federation Protects,"

Sean couldn't believe that David hadn't been that clear but he gently placed Harrison and Elizabeth on a pile of blankets on the far side of the bunker far away from the door as they both snored away.

Sean and Harry went over to the computer screens and Sean grinned when a small panel opened revealing a suitcase full of electronic parts, a black commercial drone and some kind of gun with armour-piercing bullets.

There was an audio player too so Sean pressed play.

"I have no idea if this will ever get used," Bettie said, "but Sean has just started applying for unis to some engineering stuff so I hope there's enough pieces for him to do something with in case the worse happens. The Federation Protects,"

Sean was surprised that Bettie had made this bundle of stuff back in late 2018. He knew she planned like no tomorrow but this was something else.

"We can build a shooting drone," Harry said. "Remember Mr Lambs' drone lecture three months ago,"

Sean didn't have the heart to tell his boyfriend he had been a little distracted at that lecture because of Harry's new jeans, shirt and very sexy aftershave.

"Of course," Sean said.

"Liar," Harry said grinning. "But given a little time we can rig the drone to carry the gun, fire whenever we want and more,"

Sean looked up at the computer screen smoke was filling the silver staircase.

"We have to hurry," Sean said.

He just hoped for the sake of his aunt, his family and the world that they do it in time.

CHAPTER 21
15th August 2023
Unknown Location, England

Graham's heart thundered in his chest as he looked up from behind the large black sofa him and Bettie were hiding behind. They were both aiming their assault rifles at the top of the silver staircase and they both had knives, swords and shotguns next to them if needed.

Graham had no idea how to fight in hand-to-hand combat so he was really hoping they were never going to be needed. He just hoped beyond hope that Bettie was going to be okay and they were both going to make it out alive.

But if he needed to Graham was more than happy to sacrifice his life for Bettie. The woman he loved more than anything else on the entire planet.

Smoke bombs smashed down the staircase.

The staircase exploded.

Graham fired.

Bettie fired.

They emptied their weapons. Graham tried to reload but his hands were shaking.

He heard three sets of footsteps touch down on the steel floor.

Graham threw his assault rifle forward.

He grabbed his shotgun.

He fired.

Bettie did the same.

Then he looked up and noticed that the Russians were simply leaning against the wall waiting for him and Bettie to finish whatever amateur shooting they were doing.

Graham aimed his shotgun but noticed there were three little red dots on his chest and he wasn't wearing body armour. He knew the Russians were going to kill him but if he played along for now then there was a chance that Bettie could find a moment and escape.

The Russians stormed over and surrounded him and Bettie. Graham just stared into the soft beautiful eyes of the woman he loved.

"We're going to be okay," Graham said.

"Call in Alina," one of the assassins said. "She wants to kill Miss English herself,"

"Then the damn woman should have been here," another Russian said.

"She is the President's daughter. The President would kill us all if she learnt her daughter was on a mission," the final Russian said.

Graham couldn't believe he finally knew exactly who was behind the assassination attempts and he was firmly going to kill the damn woman. He didn't care if the security services wanted her for political leverage or whatever other political bullshit they wanted.

Alina had tried to murder the woman he loved. He wasn't allowing her to get away with it no matter how valuable she was to the UK government.

Graham looked at Bettie and noticed she was holding a dagger very close to her chest. He needed to buy her time.

The Russian punched Bettie and grabbed the knife. "Clever little bitch,"

Graham forced himself not to react but he needed something to focus on, something to help and then he realised the Russians responded to power and wealth maybe that was the way to save Bettie.

"How many millions would it take for you three to not kill us?" Graham asked his voice firm.

All three Russians fixed their guns on Graham.

"She betrayed the motherland. President English could have saved Russia from the evil sanctions of your corrupt nations but she chose to stop that company from saving us. Russians are starving, Russians are suffering all because you Westerners believe Ukrainian Nazis over us,"

"You know the Ukrainians are not Nazis," Graham said firmly.

The assassins shrugged. "Whatever they are they are enemies of Russia and they will all end up with bullets in their head either way,"

Bettie jumped forward.

Tackling a Russian to the ground.

Graham went to help.

A Russian punched him in the head.

Another Russian got Bettie in a headlock.

"I cannot reach the damn woman. Alina isn't coming," another one said.

"Then let's just kill her,"

Graham watched as the Russian's muscles tensed around Bettie's neck.

He screamed out for them to stop.

They laughed.

Everyone stopped as soon as they heard the whooshing of the nuclear bunker door opening.

Graham couldn't believe Sean had opened the door.

The crazy young man.

But Graham just couldn't understand why Bettie was grinning.

CHAPTER 22
15th August 2023
Unknown Location, England

As the bunker door opened Bettie's stomach twisted into a painful knot and she instantly remembered she had hidden a bag of stuff for Sean and Harry behind the computer screens. It was only now she remembered it.

She hoped beyond hope that Sean and Harry had found it and had put it to good use.

Bettie struggled against the man who held her in a headlock as all of them focused on the bunker door.

A moment later a large black drone zoomed out of the bunker with a rifle attached. Bettie just hoped the boys were good at shooting.

The drone fired.

The man holding Bettie hissed. The bullet smashed into his shoulder.

Bettie leapt backwards.

The man released her.

The drone fired.

A Russian's head exploded.

Bettie climbed on top of the man that held her.

She grabbed a sword on the ground.

Ramming it into his head.

The man moved.

Going for his gun.

Bettie twisted the sword inside his head.

The man screamed as his skull cracked.

Bettie leapt up with a pistol.

Her, Graham and the drone focused on the last remaining Russian.

The Russian whipped out a detonator and unveiled a suicide vest.

They all fired.

The woman never stood a chance at killing them all.

As soon as it was over she turned to look at the door of the bunker and moments later she laughed as Harrison and Elizabeth raced out of there with Sean and Harry chasing after them.

Bettie laughed and hugged the man she loved. Life was finally back to normal but she knew nothing was done just yet.

She wanted to find this Alina woman and kill her and then Russia was going to answer for all of this.

CHAPTER 23
16th August 2023
London, England

Over the next twelve hours, Graham supposed he shouldn't have been that surprised to find Alina's body outside clearly tortured and roughed up before someone (Penelope) had snapped her neck. And as much as he didn't understand at the time why Alina's phone was missing, he was glad that Daniels had told him on the way to the hospital that the phone probably contained all the money and location of weapons and more that Alina had.

Graham was still surprised that Penelope's entire motive for helping them had been money-related. It was a shame because he was almost, almost starting to like her and respect her. But clearly she was only interested in herself and not helping Bettie to stay alive.

As Graham sat in a very comfortable red

leather chair in a government office with rather interesting (tasteless) brown oak walls, ancient first edition books lining the room and a huge ancient desk in front of him. Graham was glad him and Bettie were here.

Graham was impressed with some of the books on the shelves. There were first editions of all the best-known fiction and nonfiction writers from Dickens to The Art of War and more. He doubted anyone looked at or read these books judging by the dust on them, but whoever created this range of books originally had great taste.

The large window behind the desk gave Graham a great view of London with Big Ben, the Houses of Parliament and the Shard all in clear view, and it seemed that in-between pacing around Bettie was also enjoying the view.

Graham enjoyed the sweet scents of oranges, cloves and caramel in the air that came from an air freshener on the desk. It made the great taste of toffee apples form on his tongue and Graham knew this meeting was going to go well.

The office belonged to the UK Home Secretary but Graham was more than grateful she wasn't coming because she was just a foul, awful woman so instead the foreign secretary was meant to be here later with representatives from MI5 and MI6.

All to confront the Russian ambassador that was coming.

A moment later the large white door to the office opened and Graham stood up as three very tall men wearing black suits walked in frowning and another shorter man stormed in smiling wearing something Graham could only describe as a fake Russian military uniform.

The ambassador clearly wanted to make a statement but Graham knew Bettie was not going to tolerate that for one minute.

The Ambassador took a seat, the Foreign Secretary and person from the security services stood opposite the ambassador. Graham and Bettie stood to one side.

Graham smiled as the man from the security services threw a thick file at the Ambassador.

The ambassador grinned as he saw photos of the dead Russians.

"You conducted an illegal operation on UK soil without our consent and you tried to assassinate Bettie English," the Foreign Secretary said.

"These," the man from the security services said, "are transactions, flight details and emails confirming the assassination was ordered by the President herself,"

Graham gripped Bettie's hand.

The ambassador looked at Bettie and Graham. "You are both okay like I predicted. I tried to tell her it is stupid and now we've made an enemy of the British Private Eye Federation but she, what's the English phrase, *bat crap crazy?*"

Graham took a step closer to him. "So you admit this?"

"Of course," the ambassador said. "There's nothing you can do about it. You can keep sanctioning Russia as much as you want but unlike you're dying economy Russia can weather the storm,"

Graham hated the ambassador.

"We could arrest me, oh but I have diplomatic immunity. All the attackers are dead and you cannot arrest the Russian President because that means you invading Russia.

Which the West are too weak to do and come on, World War Two taught the world that you can invade Russia but you can never hold it,"

The ambassador stood up but Graham gripped his wrist tightly. "If you ever come after my family again I will kill you and every single Russian in your government from the lowest pencil pusher to the President herself,"

The ambassador laughed. "Oh you English never fail to realise what's truly going on. We knew the assassination had the potential to cause World War Three and it would have worked. Lines are being drawn and that is the greatest thing about the Motherland and China,"

"What?" the Foreign Secretary asked.

"We don't have democracy," the ambassador said. "All the major Western powers have elections in 2024 and once the USA president gets changed then Russia will win every single war in existence because he will pull out of NATO and we all know NATO is useless without the US."

Graham frowned because that was the major flaw of NATO, the only thing that stopped Russia and China from invading Europe and other tiny member nations. In theory Russia could invade all of Europe but unless the US and Canada agreed to trigger Article 5 of NATO. NATO forces couldn't be used to support the weaker NATO members that didn't have much of an army to defend themselves with.

Graham shook his head as he realised just how right Russia was to some extent. Given time Russia had the potential to conquer the world with China's help.

Bettie just grinned. "But you forget that you have made an enemy of the Federation,"

The ambassador frowned. "And what could a woman like you do to Russia?"

Graham hugged Bettie proudly as she folded her arms.

"I stopped your plans twice now I can do it a third time,"

The ambassador stood, went over to the door and laughed. "You know what they say Miss English or at least you weak English people do, three time's the charm,"

The ambassador allowed himself to be escorted out of the building and the Foreign Secretary and the man from the security services walked out muttering to each other about how bad the situation was.

Graham couldn't agree more but that was well and truly tomorrow's problem because Russia only responded to strength and Bettie, the wonderful woman he loved, had just shown Russia not to mess with her ever again.

So life was thankfully back to normal and Graham was so looking forward to going home, spending time with his family and just kissing the beautiful woman he loved and had come so close to losing.

CHAPTER 24
17th August 2023
Canterbury, England

Bettie had absolutely loved the past day with sexy Graham just fussing over her, getting her everything she needed and just being extra tender in bed. It had been so fun going out for a picnic with the kids, Sean and Harry as well and Bettie really did love her life.

Her entire family was so wonderful, supportive and great that Bettie had been scared to go out without them earlier to double-check on the funeral arrangements for Thomas Birch. But she had managed and everything had been more than fine.

Bettie stood in front of a massive crowd of all her members (or at least the majority of them) as they all wore their best black suits, black shoes and black dresses. No one was really smiling at her but Bettie knew they were all happy that she was still alive.

She had gotten a hell of a lot of hugs earlier from almost all her members and they all said their congratulations on being alive and Bettie had kissed them on the cheek. Her membership loved her and Bettie really, really appreciated that.

They were all sitting in an immense white stone hall with breathtaking masonry work giving the hall such depth, texture and interest that Bettie had inspected every inch of the amazing ceiling and walls when she first got here.

But she knew she was just distracting herself because she didn't want to look at the light-tanned coffin standing next to her right now.

Everyone was focusing on Bettie waiting for her to make a speech or something. Thomas's girlfriend and friends and family had given him a great eulogy and said some of the kindest words she had ever heard directed at herself and poor Thomas.

And now as President of the Federation she had meant to say something. Bettie really hated this, she was a private eye, a mother and a girlfriend to amazing people. She did not speak on behalf of the dead, at least directly.

"Thomas Birch," Bettie said surprised that everyone was hooked on her every word, "wasn't just my assistant. He was my friend, a person I could confide in and he was always there for me when I needed him most,"

Bettie took a deep breath of the sage-scented air.

"If I could do anything that would bring him back I so would," Bettie said. "He was so excited about being a father, getting to spend more time with his girlfriend and he so badly wanted to marry you,"

Bettie smiled at the girlfriend and was relieved that she was smiling too. Bettie had already agreed to send her £25,000 a year which was what Thomas earned until the child was 18 so at least the girlfriend wouldn't struggle financially.

"But Thomas would have wanted us to continue with our duty. He was never much of a private eye, by God was he awful at that,"

Everyone laughed. It was hardly a secret how bad of a private eye he was.

"And yet he wanted to work in the Federation and he hounded me as soon as I was appointed President. He wanted so badly to work for this amazing organisation I damn well respect that. So I want to finish this speech by thanking Thomas for everything and encouraging all of us to be more like Thomas and fight for the Federation we want to make. So we can continue improving lives, helping people and solving crime,"

Bettie bowed slightly but no one else moved.

"The Federation Protects!" everyone shouted at her.

Bettie smiled and forced the tears she had been hiding for so long not to come out because the membership wasn't saying that to be kind, nice or because it was tradition. They were saying it because they wanted Bettie to know that they would always love, protect and cherish her.

"And I you," Bettie said as the membership started to go out and round to the pub next door for the wake.

Bettie was about to join Graham, Harry and Sean by the exit (because the kids were at Bettie's mum's today) when her phone rang.

It was a blocked number so it could only have been Penelope Bishop.

"You were smart enough to work out I had killed Alina," Penelope said, "and you informed the Russians about that detail. You are far more clever than I expected,"

"I thought we didn't underestimate each other," Bettie said smiling at Graham.

"I clearly have more to learn as you English people say but that was a nice speech I will admit,"

Bettie looked around.

"Relax Miss English I am not in your sorry excuse of a country. The beaches of Syria are nice at this time of year and with my new resources I will look forward to building my criminal empire,"

"Thank you for saving me," Bettie said meaning every word of it.

"No problem," Penelope said her voice wobbling. "Until we meet again Miss English,"

"I look forward to it,"

"As do I,"

Bettie cut the line and as she just grinned at Sean, Harry and Graham. They were her family, her loved ones, her everything, and everything was finally back to normal. As Bettie went over to them hugged them all and started to head over to the pub for a very good wake, she realised that yes her cases did have consequences.

AVAILABLE NOW AT ALL MAJOR BOOKSELLERS!

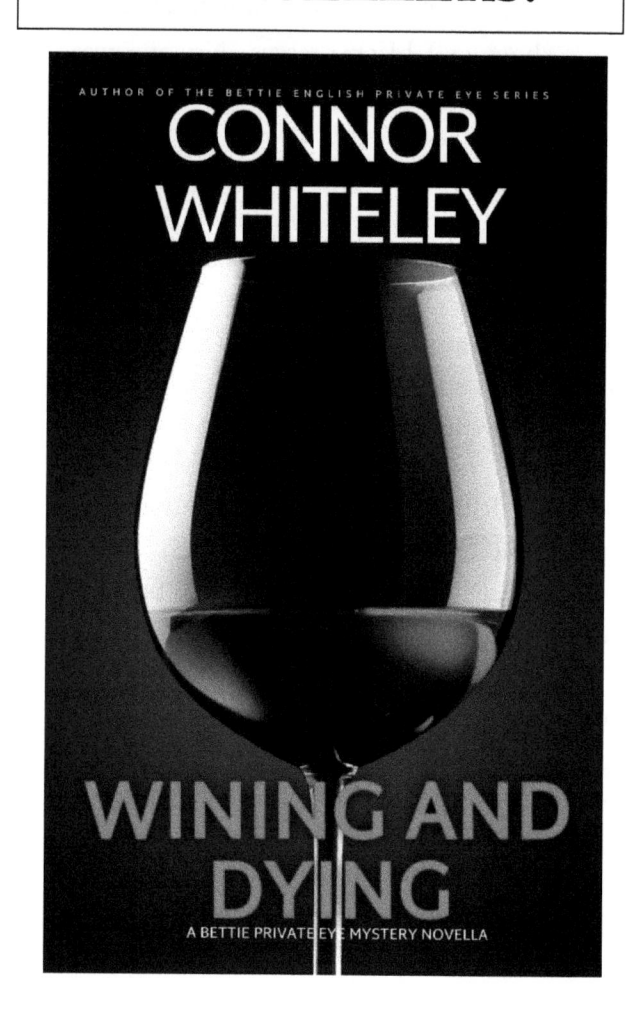

CONNOR WHITELEY

AUTHOR OF AGENTS OF THE EMPEROR SERIES

CONVERGENCE OF ODYSSEYS

A SCIENCE FICTION ADVENTURE NOVELLA

CONVERGENCE OF ODYSSEYS
A Science Fiction Adventure Novella

CHAPTER 1

When the *Lady Of Light* dropped out of Ultraspace, it entered a battle.

The long blade-like warship jerked, vibrated and moaned softly as I, Ithane Veilwalker, stood on the massive oval bridge watching the situation unfold. Loud flashing warning lights and alarms sounded overhead to warn the rest of our fleet what was happening, and everyone was preparing for battle stations.

We were about to go to war.

I leant on the lovely warm back of my purple crystal command throne as I focused on what was happening in the void outside. Thousands upon thousands of immense white pods that looked like white peas from this distance darted, swirled and zoomed through the void like their lives depended on it. Then even more white warships appeared to be approaching us.

I didn't know what the Imperium wanted but the very fact that my fellow humans were here wasn't a good sign. Especially as black smoky, shadowy blade-like warships were also swarming the Imperial warships.

The entire void was a firework display of explosions, laser fire and death. Imperial warships shattered like glass and the black smoky warships of the Dark Keres exploded too and screamed out bloody murder as the Death God roared out in pleasure of consuming the souls of his followers and those of his enemies.

I flat out hated that the Dark Keres were too. Unlike my fleet that was a beautiful mixture of Keres and humans with me being a human that was brought back to life by the Goddess of Life Genetrix to serve her. The Dark Keres had sold their souls to the Death God Geneitor, a foul divine being that only wanted to consume all life in the universe and probably any universes beyond this one if such things existed.

"Battle Stations," a human male said to my left as everyone just got on with their duty.

The *Lady Of Light* continued to hum, vibrate and jerk as we were fired upon. And the foul aroma of death, burnt ozone and gunpowder filled my senses as my psychic abilities tapped into what was happening here. We were all here for a single purpose.

It didn't matter if the living soul was human, Keres or Dark Keres and it definitely didn't matter what fraction they served. We were all here for the soul purpose of something we didn't even understand.

Every living creature was having their fate and their odyssey spun and twisted and ended by a thousand different factors all pulled by Geneitor or Genetrix. They were the masters of fate and sometimes I really did feel like a puppet, but those two divine beings had led all of us here.

And I just didn't understand why.

I had been on a mission to recover one of the Soulstones, crystals that contained the souls of the 5 lesser gods of Genetrix and Geneitor, and these Soulstones were the key to resurrecting both of them. Apparently a human male had it and he was meant to be heading here.

I just didn't understand why the others were here. It made no sense.

"Brace!" a woman shouted.

I looked up and saw an immense missile scream through the void towards us.

"Have a little faith Captain," I said holding out my hand and allowing bright white tendrils of magical energy to zoom out of it.

The magic atomised the missile instantly but I had to sit down after that stunt. I wasn't used to destroying something that powerful so easily.

I sat on my delightfully warm command throne and clicked my fingers so streams upon streams of data revealed themselves. I started reading it and it was as bad as I feared.

"Have you looked at the Mother World?"

I looked up and weakly smiled at the tall female Keres standing to my left. She was as beautiful, extremely thin and elf-like as the rest of her kind but I could tell she was scared. Because this battle wasn't just happening around any world in the galaxy, this was happening around the most holy world to the Keres.

Genesis, the mother world of their kind.

I forced myself to look past my holographic data readouts, past the exploding ships and fighters in the void and I weakly smiled at Genesis. An immense green world covered in the most beautiful forests I had ever seen and I had seen photos of the planet from Imperial and Keres archives and it was sensational.

It was the most beautiful planet in the galaxy.

Yet this time it was burning.

I stood up as I noticed entire continents were ablaze sending immense black columns of choking, toxic smoke high into the atmosphere. This was one of the most outrageous sights I had ever seen and this wasn't just a physical insult against the natural beauty in the galaxy. This was an attack against the mind, spirit and history of the entire Keres race.

That explained why the Imperium wanted to annihilate it.

"The Motherworld is lost," I said standing up to face the entire bridge.

CHAPTER 2

Commander Jerico Nelson flat out couldn't believe what the hell he had let himself get involved in for the sake of honouring the dying wish of a dead friend. He hadn't really minded the same dead friend "gifting" him the necklace that was meant to combine the so-called soul of a God (what rubbish) but he didn't want to get involved with a war over a planet by three different sides.

Jerico shook his head as he leant against the cold, perfectly smooth brown bark of an almost straight tree with thousands of little branches shooting off in all directions. Jerico had never seen small diamond-shaped leaves before that glittered in the orange, yellow and red light coming from the flames sweeping across the entire planet.

Jerico knelt down on the cool muddy ground on the edge of the cliff and just shook his head as he saw the raging inferno that was devouring the valley below him. It must have been a good two kilometres down to the valley floor but Jerico could only watch as trees, plants and Keres were devoured by the dancing flames.

He flat out didn't believe in all this rubbish about the Keres Gods and Goddesses but he couldn't deny something wasn't natural about those flames. They were surely too big, too controlled and it looked like they were dancing too much for them to be natural.

The sound of the roaring, crackling, popping flames was deafening and Jerico was so looking forward to getting off this planet. Jerico loved how beautiful it had been a day or two ago but it was monstrous now.

He wasn't even sure what had happened. He had arrived yesterday to try and find out more about this Ithane Veilwalker woman but no one seemed to know her and then Imperial and Dark Keres ships had appeared at the exact same moment. It wasn't right, it wasn't natural and Jerico couldn't help but feel like something much larger was going on here.

An explosion overhead made Jerico reach for his sniper rifle and machine gun as he saw fresh explosions light up the smoky black sky. He wasn't sure but Jerico could have sworn these were new explosions that were slightly different to the explosions he had been watching for hours.

Maybe there were new players or ships or even armies here. He really hoped that wasn't true, he didn't want anyone else to die and he was sure this world was going to become his tomb.

Jerico smiled as the necklace containing the so-called Keres God of Hope Spero pulsed bright white and sent warmth into him. Jerico supposed he was going to miss this necklace and its weird abilities when he met this Ithane woman but he had to honour his dead friend.

"Arms up," a woman's voice said to him.

Jerico rolled his eyes and slowly turned around to see a female Keres standing behind him. She was definitely from this planet with her smooth beautiful skin, extremely thin, unnatural humanoid features and long blond hair that crackled with golden magical energy.

"I am a friend of the Keres," Jerico said not sure if she was going to believe him.

"Impossible. No human is a friend of ours. Look at what you have done to our world," the woman said.

Jerico frowned as the air crackled with black magical energy and he really didn't want her to kill him. He had to complete his mission.

"I'm looking for Ithane Veilwalker. Do you know her? I'm meant to give something to her, can I show you?" Jerico said.

The woman hesitated but after the longest moments of his life, she nodded and Jerico revealed the still-glowing necklace to her.

She smiled and the air stopped crackling immediately, but Jerico noticed the foul taste of iron, rust and sweat had formed in his mouth.

"Ithane Veilwalker you say," the woman said like it was a joke. "My forces tell me she's just arrived in orbit with her entire fleet,"

Jerico had no idea who the hell this Ithane woman was but he wasn't sure about her. It wasn't exactly easy to get a fleet of your own these days between the human-Keres war, the evil control of Rex's Imperium and limited resources everyone had during wartime.

Jerico just hoped beyond hope this Ithane person wasn't a criminal, pirate or a servant of the Rex. If that happened then he might even have to break his oath to his dead friend, something he wanted to avoid at all costs.

An explosion overhead made Jerico jump and he looked and saw five white pods scream towards the valley next to him. The annihilated pods smashed into the sides of the valley's cliff and they exploded.

The battle was getting worse.

Jerico looked at the woman. "We have to find Ithane Veilwalker. Can you take me to her?"

"Maybe," the woman said. "My name is Piper by the way. A forced name your Rex gave me when he enslaved my homeworld during the First Human-Keres war,"

"Jerico Nelson is my name and I don't serve the Rex anymore. I stopped serving him a long time ago,"

Jerico wasn't sure if Piper believed him but as more explosions roared overhead she gestured him to follow her.

And Jerico just hoped beyond hope he wasn't trusting the wrong Keres. Sometimes it was impossible to tell Light from Dark Keres.

A possible mistake Jerico hoped wouldn't cost him his life.

CHAPTER 3

In both my lives, including my human life before I became Genetrix's will incarnate, I have never ever heard anything as scary as an entire bridge full of humans and Keres go deadly silent leaving only the roaring, humming and vibrating bangs of a ship in the background as it's under attack.

I don't know even think I had meant to say it out loud but I had, and now the awful foul aromas of death, burnt ozone and gunpowder filled my senses even more and left the disgusting taste of raw meat form on my tongue.

The situation was definitely getting worse by the minute.

I frowned as I saw everyone step away from their terminals, scanners and battle stations and they focused on me. The humans looked scared and concerned but the Keres looked outraged and like I was almost as bad as the Dark Keres themselves.

"The Motherworld cannot be lost," a male Keres said. "That world is a shrine to our past and it is a reminder that the Keres once ruled the stars. We once had the mightiest empire in Galactic history,"

"Exactly," someone else said.

"And that is why we have to save it," a human woman said.

The entire ship roared as our gun turrets unleashed a volley of shots. We were running out of time and the enemy was well aware of our presence by now.

"Negative," I said. "Genetrix brought me back to life because everything I do is about preserving and protecting life. That is what we have to do now,"

Everyone nodded.

"The Goddess of Life brought us here to find the human with the Soulstone belonging to Spero, God of Hope. We find him, get the Soulstone and get out," I said channelling as much as Genetrix's influence as I could.

A Keres female shook her head. "What about the people on the planet? Don't their lives matter?"

I nodded for a brief moment because this was the problem about being in charge of the Daughters of Genetrix. I was our leader and our Goddess' Will incarnate. I had to make the impossible decisions.

"Better to let them sacrifice themselves for the Goddess then annihilate our entire fraction trying to save them. Because if we die then who will stop the Dark Keres from resurrecting Geneitor and him devouring all life?"

The Keres female backed down and I hated myself as I tapped into the psychic echo of the battle around me. And I heard those Keres scream out in agony as some of their souls were thankfully saved but others had their own devoured and tortured by Geneitor.

I didn't want to stay here any longer than needed.

I clicked my fingers and the air crackled with magical energy as a map of the situation appeared and I gestured over two of my most senior Captains, one Keres, one human woman. Everyone else went back to their battle stations.

I hissed as the smell of death, burnt ozone and gunpowder grew even more.

"My Lady," one of the captains said, "Imperial and Dark Keres forces have touched down on Genesis. They seem to be torturing, taking prisoners and obliterating our monuments,"

"Where is the human?" I asked surprised that I sounded almost fully Keres then instead of a strange mixture of the two.

"Unknown," the woman said. "Can't you just tap into the psychic stuff and just pinpoint him?"

I laughed and gestured towards the battle outside. "There are thousands of people dying and their souls screaming out in the void every minute of this battle. This battle alone stretches across an entire planet and the space surrounding it. Do you really think I can just pluck a non-magical mind out of all that psychic noise easily?"

"Maybe?" she asked.

I saluted her because I really did like her attitude. It was good she wasn't scared to ask questions.

The damn ship roared as a volley of missiles slammed into us. I grabbed one of the captains as the ship jerked so hard she fell over.

"Status!" I shouted.

"Sheilds will last for another ten minutes. Everyone is starting to turn their attention on us. We're already lost 10% of the fleet," a man said but I couldn't see him.

I looked at my Captains and I knew I was going to have to do this alone and I wasn't going to have that much time to do it.

"My lady we have to make a move now," the woman said.

"Agreed," I said going over to the back of my command throne and picking up my two swords. "If our target is anywhere he would have made it to the planet and I suspect he would be in the thickest of the fighting,"

"Why?" a woman asked as another volley smashed into the ship.

I clicked my fingers and an immense golden portal appeared in front of me. "Because our Odysseys are converging Genetrix and Geneitor want me and this man to find each other. I don't know why but the Gods want me and him to be united,"

"And that's what scares me," a number of people said as one.

"Just buy me as much time as you can," I said as I stepped through the portal.

And I had to admit this divine game I was stepping into was terrifying me a lot more than I ever wanted to admit.

CHAPTER 4

The thick aromas of incredibly juicy steak, freshly roasted garlic and deep fried pork filled Jerico's senses as he followed Piper through an immense Keres city. This had to be one of the biggest he had ever had the pleasure of seeing. Jerico had always liked how the large purple-crystal towers that rose up like daggers from the ground were formed so seamlessly that each tower was a work of art in itself.

Jerico really doubted any human could create something so breathtaking, but as he followed Piper between two large towers, he saw that this city had already been attacked.

He saw the scorched marks on the top of the towers and the streams of blood that flooded through the city. Jerico hated seeing the Keres, they were only innocent aliens trying to live in a galaxy they had once owned. It was only because the Rex in his stupidity had been terrified by their peaceful magic that he had decided to wipe them out.

Jerico tried to smile at the small groups of tall extremely thin Keres in blue robes as he went past them. They didn't react, they didn't smile, they only watched him like he was the biggest threat to their lives.

Maybe he was. Back when he had served with the Imperial Army, Jerico had fought, killed and burnt more Keres cities than he ever cared to admit.

He just hoped he could save or do something, anything for this one.

"In here," Piper said without turning around.

Jerico followed her inside one of the purple towers and suddenly found himself on the top floor overlooking the entire city. He was surprised there was only a purple crystal floor, there were no walls or windows that his human mind could see. He supposed this was probably some kind of Keres magic because he could still feel the warm breeze against his cheeks but he had a 360-degree view of his surroundings.

Piper smiled next to him and then Jerico noticed there were six other Keres standing in the middle of the floor. He recognised five of them in their thin golden metal armour as some kind of guards, but the central figure was brand-new in her crimson red robes of office.

Jerico didn't recognise the golden chain she wore around her neck and the bronze staff barely looked strong enough to hold, let alone support any weight. Jerico doubted it had a practical use.

"Great Mother," Piper said, "tell me some good news,"

Jerico had never heard of a Great Mother before, he had no idea what she did in Keres society but she looked important and Jerico really hoped she wasn't going to be an obstacle. He had to get to Ithane.

"Excuse me," Jerico said.

"I know who you are before you say anything human," the Great Mother said. "You are Commander Jerico Nelson, murderer of Keres and a servant of the Rex,"

The five guards instantly whipped swords out of nothing and pointed them at Jerico.

"I am no such thing anymore," Jerico said knowing he couldn't survive a fight. "I am sorry for what I did for the Rex before I knew any better but I want to help you. I really do,"

Jerico gestured them towards the necklace and the Great Mother grinned and clapped her hands.

The guards put away their swords and Jerico cocked his head as he blinked and found the guards were sitting in front of five very human-looking computers.

Piper went straight over to them like the guards were working on an impossible computer problem.

"What's wrong?" Jerico asked joining them.

"The clocks have stopped. The magic has stopped. Everything has stopped," the Great Mother said. "As soon as the Dark Keres and Imperial forces arrived all the clocks on Genesis stopped working and even our magic is spotty,"

Jerico had no idea what the hell was happening. He knew the Keres weren't stupid for their technology to not work, and as far as he knew all the Keres's technology was tied to the universe itself similar to the Atomic Clock back on Earth. This made no sense.

"We've tried to contact the Keres homeworlds but we can't reach them," a guard said.

"Maybe there's interference," Jerico said.

The Great Mother laughed. "No human.

You don't understand. We cannot get any messages out using our technology, our magic, our faith. Something extremely powerful is making sure we don't exist in the universe. It's almost like…"

"What?" Jerico asked looking straight at her.

The Great Mother shook her head and Jerico knew this was bad. He supposed Great Mothers were some kind of ancient leadership role in the Keres and given how long the Keres lived, Jerico was sure this one was ancient.

But she looked scared. In his experience people with lots of years of experience don't get scared unless it's truly warranted.

"What?" Jerico asked coldly.

It's almost like," the Great Mother said looking around, "something is trying to take us out of Reality. Reality is where time is, magic is and everything the Keres rely on,"

Jerico shook his head. He sort of understood what that meant. He had seen a lot of impressive stuff over his military career and he knew the Keres were capable of doing some crazy, impossible things but taking an entire planet out of existence that seemed impossible even for the Keres.

Maybe not a God.

Jerico shook the stupid idea away because there were no such things as Gods or Goddesses. It was simply Keres' stories to give them hope in the face of extinction.

"This human needs to find something called Ithane Veilwalker," Piper said.

"I felt the presence of her fleet arrive," the Great Mother said, "but she isn't there anymore. Not in orbit and there is too much psychic interference but she searches for you too,"

Jerico had no idea why a possibly dangerous woman with her own fleet would be hunting him. He knew nothing of this woman and yet he was meant to handover a so-called powerful necklace. As much as Jerico wanted to honour his dead friend, he had to admit this was seeming more and more dangerous.

"Imperial Forces!" a guard shouted looking at his computer screen.

"Bastards," Jerico said taking out his machine gun.

"We don't have the soldiers to protect everyone," the Great Mother said. "Sound the alarm. Get everyone into the tunnels,"

"It will take too long to save everyone," Piper said.

Jerico pointed his machine gun away from the guards. "Where are they? How much time do you need?"

The Great Mother grinned. "As much time as you and Genetrix can give me,"

"Then you will have it," Jerico said storming off towards the coordinates Piper had given him.

Jerico just hoped he could save some innocent lives.

CHAPTER 5

Something was extremely wrong as I stepped out of my golden portal and the deafening screams of men, women and Keres alike filled my ears like a choir of the dead was right next to me. I tried to cover my ears but the screams of the death only got louder and louder as my magic struggled to adjust to the sheer amount of death happening on Genesis.

I collapsed to my knees and barely felt the cold rough roots in the ground as images of the faces of the dead flashed across my mind. I knew Genetrix was trying to sweep up their souls as best she could before Geneitor grabbed them and devoured and them forever.

I couldn't believe sometimes what Genetrix had to go through daily just to protect and preserve life as much as possible. I know she's a Goddess but I would never tell another soul this but I do feel her pain at times. Sometimes when I try to use magic I get hit by crippling pain and sadness and I realise Genetrix's suffering.

And that puts the fear in the Goddess into me. If a Goddess like Genetrix can despair at the state of the galaxy then I seriously question what the hell I can do about it.

Silence.

I forced myself to take a wonderfully sweet, fruity breath of the cool Genesis air as I stood up and placed my hands firmly on the hilts of my swords. I had to be alert here and I couldn't afford to make a single mistake.

Genesis had to be one of the most beautiful, stunning worlds I've ever had the privilege of seeing. I had to be standing on some kind of beautiful clifftop with a valley thousands of metres below me.

The valley itself was stunning with large straight trees with little boat-shaped copper leaves that shone in the dying light of Genesis. They gently hit each other as a warm gust of wind travelled past me and down into the valley, it made the light sparkle and even sang a little like windchimes.

It was so beautiful.

I didn't know how far away I was from the nearest battle but I could feel the psychic pressures of thousands of unclaimed souls starting to press against my mind again. I wanted so badly to help Genetrix collect them to spare the souls from being devoured, but I had to get out of here.

I couldn't risk the lives of my forces any longer than absolutely necessary.

I started into the forest away from the clifftop. I couldn't help but smile as these trees were even more beautiful than the others below me. Their tall trunks were crimson red like metal with blood red diamond-shaped leaves that sparkled in the sunlight.

And the smell was great. The senses of maple syrup, strawberries and chocolate overwhelmed my nose. It was some of the best smells I had ever walked through before.

"My Lady," my Ship mistress said into my mind. "We have a problem onboard,"

I have to admit that April might have lived, slept and worked down in the very heart of the *Lady of Light* and she might have been a figure of myth amongst the crew because she made a point of never seeing them. But she always knew when to bother me.

"What?" I asked.

"There is something closing in on us in Ultraspace. Something like a massive shadow that is swimming towards us," April said.

I rolled my eyes. This seriously wasn't what we needed because if something was in Ultraspace, the intergalactic network humans used to travel faster than light, then I really didn't want to know how this would affect our escape.

But I knew I was going to have to find out.

"What are you saying?" I asked.

"Someone or something is trying to cut off our escape into Ultraspace. I doubt the Imperial forces will notice it but I am watching it. We might have to go into the Nexus,"

"Make the preparations," I said a lot harsher than I meant to. "Be careful and the Goddess Protects,"

"May she guide our hand like she guides mine," April said cutting off the mental link.

I shook my head at the very idea of having to go into the Nexus, the Keres version of Ultraspace which was actually a lot faster, safer and less infected with Geneitor's taint, considering the reports I've had lately.

It turned out some Dark Keres had managed to tap into the Nexus recently so it wasn't as much as of a safe haven for the Keres anymore. Instead thousands of Dark Keres followers had taken to storming, pirating and obliterating all vessels they came across.

I had a feeling we were going to have enough casualties in this battle over Genesis. I didn't want to get involved in any more battles than I had to. And the Nexus was hopefully one I could avoid.

I had to focus on my mission.

"Guide me to my target Mother of Life," I said as I closed my eyes and allowed my magic to tap into the psychic nightmare that had been generated by the battle.

All I had to do was pick out a single human mind out of this entire nightmare of war.

I hissed as I tapped into the screams, explosions and cries for help that filled Genesis and its orbit. So many thousands of people were dying and killing in each passing minute and each action created an echo in the psychic field I was tapping into.

I hated how this wasn't going to work. There were simply too many minds, too many deaths, too many incidents of Geneitor trying to seek me out to so he could send his forces to kill me.

Maybe I was going to have to focus on the so-called Soulstone this mere man was meant to be carrying. I was going to be so pissed if this was a ruse but I doubted it. And the least I could do was save this man's life and protect his soul like Genetrix wanted.

I shifted my psychic focus and searched for any magical signatures or souls that were too bright to be a death or a Keres. I didn't bother looking for human souls because theirs were simply too dim in the grand scheme of things.

I saw it.

I wasn't sure how many kilometres away it was but there was a massive bright white beacon in the psychic nightmare. It could have been a massacre and a mass release of souls but I didn't want to believe it.

As much as I wanted to teleport there I knew Geneitor could see my teleportations and if the man was there, I was not going to lead the enemy to him.

I had to find, protect and save this man no matter the cost.

As I went towards my target through the crimson red forest, I couldn't help but feel like I was taking one step closer to something far darker and more terrifying than I ever thought possible.

Later on I wish I had listened to myself at this moment.

CHAPTER 6

As much as Jerico appreciated Piper's offer of a hundred Keres soldiers, he made her send them deeper into the city so they could protect the innocent Keres running for the tunnel network.

Jerico lay down on his stomach with Piper doing the same to his left as he aimed his sniper scope at the Imperial forces below them. Jerico liked being on top of a cliff with a charred blackened valley below him.

Another benefit of the position, which was all that Jerico cared about, was how there was a lot of crimson red tree cover behind them. He hoped he didn't wouldn't need it but Jerico wanted that to be a good escape route in case they got caught.

He had chosen this position to attack the hundreds of Imperial army forces in their foul sterile white armour because the valley narrowed behind them. So the Imperial forces would have to slow and that would make them easy to shoot.

Jerico didn't like the awful black smoke and hints of charred flesh that invaded his lungs but he was a commander. He knew exactly how to snipe the enemy into submission. The key was to find the enemy's leadership and kill them before the enemy knew what was going on.

Then it was a simple task of destroying the enemy before they recovered from the crippling loss.

"I don't see a captain," Piper said.

Jerico kept searching the hundreds upon hundreds of white-armoured humans for any sign of a commander or captain. He was a sniper and snipers were always patient.

And if push came to shuff then he would simply get Piper to blow up the sides of the valley near where it narrowed.

"What's your real name?" Jerico asked.

Piper laughed. "After the First Human-Keres war and the Keres leader signed the Treaty of Defeat the Keres language was erased. You could only speak Imperial and so our names became Imperial,"

Jerico felt his throat dry and his stomach twist into a painful knot. He hated that he had been apart of that evil war.

"I'm sorry," Jerico said knowing it was meaningless.

"It's okay, really. You were just following rules and believing the Rex's lies like the rest of your race. You're here now and that's what matters,"

Jerico nodded and he kept searching. As far as he was concerned all the Imperial soldiers looked the same in their sterile white armour and none of them had any medals or symbols on them.

"I'm starting to search towards the back of the battle force," Jerico said.

"Why are you really here?" Piper asked searching the battle force with some weird Keres rifle.

"I told you. A dead friend wanted me to find Ithane Veilwalker, give her this so-called God and make sure she's okay,"

"You really don't believe do you?"

Jerico just looked at her. "You actually believe the Keres's Gods and Goddesses are real?"

"Of course. The Keres get their magic from Geneitor or Genetrix. And they guide our actions, and they protect us in their own way. I was a young adult when a human first tried to kill me because I was starving and I wanted a loaf of bread. That adult would have snapped my neck but he flexed his muscles and his own neck broke,"

"Okay?"

"That had to be the work of Genetrix. A

human snapping their own neck instead of mine," Piper said like this was all true.

Jerico just wasn't sure. It sounded so made-up and fake but she was helping him so Jerico smiled and went back to finding his target.

He found her.

There was a woman towards the very back of the Imperial Forces wearing much thicker white metal armour with a bright red cross over her chest breast. It was the symbol of the Rex, maybe one of his chosen, maybe one of his Hand.

If that was true then Jerico had no idea what was going on here. A Hand of The Rex did not leave Earth or enter a battlefield without any extremely good reasons and even their mere presence normally showed the Imperium had already won.

Jerico looked into Piper's eyes. "Do your people have any ships or shuttles to help them get off world?"

"No. The Treaty of Defeat meant this planet couldn't have any so-called advance technology,"

"Bastards," Jerico said lining up the woman in his sights. "We need to kill that woman with the cross on her chest,"

"Got her,"

"On three," Jerico said having a really bad feeling about this.

"One. Two,"

"Three,"

Jerico and Piper fired. The bullets silently zoomed towards the woman then nothing.

The woman was alive, smiling and looking directly at Jerico.

Something screamed overhead.

Jerico looked up.

An immense fireball was flying right towards them.

"Run!" Piper shouted.

Jerico ran into the crimson forest and just hoped when that fireball hit it wouldn't kill them both.

CHAPTER 7

Something was definitely wrong with this entire planet as I went through a forest with crimson red trees. They were sort of beautiful but there wasn't a doubt in my mind that there was some kind of corruption was going on here.

It was the small things that gave it away really. As I went through the forest, I noticed how the closer I (hopefully) got to my target, the more the trees bent to one side and the roots cracked the soft ground like they were wanting to attack or something.

It certainly didn't relax me that I could have sworn the roots were turning in my direction as I passed. I didn't dare get too close to them in case they grabbed me or something, and I couldn't tell the time at all.

Normally I was a pretty good judge of time and how long I had been doing something for, even before Genetrix had rebirth me, I was pretty good at it. But all I felt was confusion, coldness and like my connection to the Goddess of Life was being dampened.

I might have had my connection cut from her before, I might have been filled with her divine power on other occasions but this time, it felt odd. My skin was chilling more with each passing minute (I guessed) and my magical senses were weakening.

I just had no idea why.

I shook the silly idea away and I just kept going towards my target in the forest. The trees were definitely bending more now and their little leaves just fell off their branches instead of creating sweet music.

Then they turned to ash.

The foul smell of death, gunpowder and sweat filled my senses as I continued. I was almost tempted to try and connect to Genetrix to ask her a question or two but I couldn't afford to brighten my soul in case Geneitor was watching for me closely. My soul would already be bright enough because of my magic, I didn't need to brighten it even more.

He and his servants would find me quickly enough. I had no doubt about that.

The air crackled with black magical energy as five black portals opened around me and I just stopped in my tracks as five Dark Keres stepped out.

I almost shivered in disgust of their twisted forms of their cousins. I had always liked how artfully, beautifully and humanoid the Keres were, but the Dark Keres around me looked awful with black veins pulsing black light across their skin.

Their faces looked beaten, sliced and scarred. They looked monstrous and even their black armour looked twisted and corrupted.

A black flaming sword appeared in their right hand.

I whipped out my two swords and with a thought I made them become engulfed in white cleansing flames.

"Why are the Dark Keres here?" I asked wanting to know why the enemy was actually here.

"It is the Will of the Death God," one of them said psychically so I couldn't tell who it was.

"Then why bring the Imperium?" I asked. "Geneitor wants a fight with the Daughter of Genetrix. It makes no sense for him to bring in another fraction, much less a human fraction,"

All the Dark Keres laughed around me and I realised I had made a mistake. In the original battle between Geneitor and Genetrix, it had been the Goddess of Life that had created the Keres as her army. Yet Geneitor had created humanity to kill in his name, so I just shook my head.

Geneitor could influence the humans a lot more than the Keres. I wasn't sure Geneitor actually believed the Keres could win against my Daughter of Genetrix, much less me.

So he twisted the fate of the Imperium to bring them to this moment, this battle, this point of convergence.

A single point in history where the three greatest forces of the galaxy met and fought. I still didn't understand why or what Geneitor was planning.

The Dark Keres charged at me.

I leapt up.

I felt the Goddess's power fill me.

I swung my sword.

Two Dark Keres swung too.

I slashed their chests.

They exploded.

The other three leapt into the air.

Their supernatural agility guiding their actions.

They swung their swords supernaturally fast.

I ducked.

They kicked.

They punched.

They swung.

I dodged.

Again.

Again.

They swung.

Their swords a blur of motion.

I couldn't see their swords.

They kicked me.

Knocking me forward.

A Dark Keres appeared in front of me.

She swung her sword.

Torrents of flame shot out my fingers.

She screamed in agony.

I spun around.

Swinging my swords.

I beheaded the last two remaining Dark Keres.

Their corpses turned to ash and I just frowned as I felt the cold isolating presence of Geneitor as he devoured their souls. But I couldn't mess around anymore the Death God had known exactly where I was and I knew April was busy preparing for us to go into the Nexus back on the *Lady Of Light*.

I had to get to my target now and get us off this forsaken planet before all was lost.

Because something was coming. I didn't know what it was but something was coming for all of us and I had no idea what Geneitor was planning but this felt like a trap.

A massive trap and that utterly terrified me.

CHAPTER 8

The fireball smashed into the clifftop.

Jerico hissed as he ran as fast as he could into the crimson forest. He kept running. Maybe he could survive.

Moments later he felt the immense shockwave grab him and threw him forward like he was made from paper. Jerico hated the extreme heat that covered him as he zoomed past the crimson trees.

He couldn't see Piper. He tried to move but the force of the shockwave made that impossible. He was shocked he didn't hit anything.

The screaming roaring sound of wind passing him made him feel sick and like he was lost but then he noticed there was only pure white golden light ahead.

He bent his arms and tried to throw his weight forward as he guessed he was about to hit the ground or something.

He couldn't. It wasn't working.

His necklace glowed bright white and Jerico felt something wrap around him like a blanket.

He started running out of instinct and he felt the soft ground under his feet. He ran for about ten metres before rolling onto the ground.

A strange warmth gripped him and Jerico couldn't help but smile in relieve. He doubted the Gods were real but that necklace definitely was amazing and Jerico loved that so-called magic.

Jerico got up and his mouth dropped as he saw in the distance a hurricane of crimson trees swirling, twirling and whirling around where the shockwave had ripped them out of the ground.

Jerico just shook his head. This wasn't natural. This was making little sense but he knew there had to be some kind of foul magic at play here because that fireball should have killed them.

"Jerico," Piper said weakly.

Jerico looked around and rushed across the wide opening in the forest the hurricane had created. He saw her lying on the ground holding her stomach tight.

Then Jerico knelt down next to her and gasped. There was a large branch into her stomach and dark red rich blood was dripping out of the wound.

"I saved you," Piper said, her eyes not able to focus on him.

Jerico nodded his thanks but he had to save her. He didn't care he had only just met her, she was an innocent person and she had to be saved. Her life mattered to someone and that was all Jerico cared about.

He padded down his armour but he didn't have anything to heal her with. He was a fighter not a medic.

A loud whooshing filled the air and Jerico grabbed his machine gun that had landed a few metres from Piper. A large white pod-like shuttle was zooming towards them.

"I'll protect you," Jerico said as he prepared for the white pod to land.

"Go," Piper said. "Get to the Great Mother. You have to save the others. Leave me,"

Jerico shook his head as the white pod banked a little and it started to land ten metres in front of him. Jerico aimed his machine gun at the doors.

"Please Jerico. My life is not worth you dying. The Goddess has plans for you. She never would have allowed Spero to fall into your hands if you were unimportant,"

"Shut up about your Gods for one minute. I am going to save you," Jerico said.

A small white walkway came out of the white pod and Jerico opened fired but his bullets smashed into a purple shield of some kind as five men in sterile white armour came out.

Jerico recognised their weapons instantly. These were special forces and their long blades functioned as guns and swords with equal deadliness.

Jerico hated this position. It was too open, too vulnerable and too deadly. He never would have picked this if he could help it. But he was determined to save Piper somehow.

"In the name of the holy Rex you Commander Jerico Nelson are a heretic and traitor to the Imperium," they all said as one. "We are ordered to kill you and bring back the Spero,"

Jerico couldn't believe all that anyone was interested in was this damn necklace. It couldn't even be that important.

The necklace glowed a little like it was laughing at him.

Jerico fired.

Bullets screamed through the air.

They smashed into the Imperial armour but Jerico gasped as the armour didn't even dent.

The men looked at each other and they nodded.

They smashed their swords on the ground. They cracked with blue electrical energy. They thrusted out their weapons towards Jerico.

Electrical energy shot towards him.

Again.

Again.

Jerico rolled to one side.

He rolled again.

The electrical energy kept coming out.

Jerico jumped.

He rolled.

He leapt.

The ground exploded in front of him.

Next to him.

Behind him.

Jerico just stopped.

He fired his machine gun.

Bullets screamed towards the enemy.

The bullets melted as electrical energy hit them.

The enemy fired.

Bullets smashed into Jerico.

Throwing him backwards.

His armour cracked and flew off him.

Jerico landed with a cold thud and he tried to move but his body ached and crippling pain filled his entire body.

He watched as one man stormed out to him whipping out a blood red dagger that he was fairly sure was meant to kill him.

Jerico tried to move. He tried to fire his machine gun. He tried everything to move.

He couldn't. His body protested with every movement. He was going to die.

The man knelt on Jerico's chest and Jerico screamed in agony as something broke inside him. Agony filled him and Jerico couldn't help but scream louder and louder as the man pressed the dagger against his throat.

A deafening whoosh echoed around him and out of the corner of his eye Jerico could have sworn a golden portal had opened.

And a very human-looking woman was stepping out of it.

Jerico just hoped whoever this woman was wasn't going to kill him. Something he seriously doubted.

CHAPTER 9

As soon as I stepped out of the golden portal I just knew this was the moment everything had been leading up to. My rebirth, my fight and my odyssey across the stars had led me to this damn moment.

I looked with utter rage at the stupid Imperial special force operatives in their pathetic white armour as they stood there staring at me like I was a mystery. They didn't know whether to kill me or save me or even protect me.

I was going to show them the error of their ways for sure. I was going to slaughter them in this large unnaturally empty clearing.

There was one operative pressing a blade against the throat of a man. I didn't know him but I noticed the pure divine energy radiating out of this necklace. He was my target. He was my divine mission and these foul Imperials were going to die.

A female Keres screamed out in pain.

I glared at her. I couldn't believe the enemy had injured her and thrusted a branch through her stomach.

I had had it with these Imperial scum.

I whipped out my swords engulfing them in golden crackling flames.

I flew at the enemy.

They raised their guns.

They fired.

Bullets screamed towards me.

I melted them with a thought.

I swung my sword in the air.

Torrents of white cleansing flame launched themselves at the enemy.

Three operatives screamed in crippling pain as they melted.

I charged towards my holy mission.

The operative went to split the man's throat.

I thrusted a hand out in his direction.

The man hissed as he couldn't move his arm.

I charged at him.

I leapt into the air.

I spun myself and my swords.

Beheading the man instantly.

His corpse collapsed and my target stood up and wearily pointed his machine gun at me.

I ignored him and I looked at the last remaining Imperial operative. I burrowed into his mind. I saw his past, his family, his homeworld.

He collapsed to the ground and I could feel his fear wash over me again and again. I didn't care. I was here to save lives and if he had any information that might help me then I was going to find it.

Sadness washed over me and I hesitated giving the stupid operative the chance he needed to slip free of my control and snap his own neck.

As his corpse fell to the ground I shook my head and as much as I wanted to go over to my target who was still pointing his machine gun at me. I went over to the Keres woman.

I knelt down next to her and was a little surprised by the sheer icy coldness of the soft mud. The mud was part water, part blood and her skin was ghostly white. The evil branch was large and I was sure it had raptured a lot of organs.

I placed my hands over the branch and I closed my hands.

"Please Goddess of Life let me heal her so she may fight in your name once more," I said as I forced my magic into her body.

The woman didn't resist which was a relief. My mind filled with images of cells, her muscle fibres and her organs being destroyed by the dark magic inside the branch. I had no idea how it had gotten there but the dark magic was killing her even more than the branch itself.

I poured bright white cleansing light into her body and the woman screamed out in pain. She never begged me to stop and I wouldn't have listened anyway.

I had to save her.

The images in my mind showed the cells, muscle fibres and her organs were healing. The branch was dissolving and within a minute she was healed.

"Who are you?" the Keres woman asked.

I opened my eyes and just grinned as I saw she was perfectly healed.

"At least Geneitor will not have your soul today," I said smiling. "I am Lady Ithane Veilwalker of the Daughters of Genetrix,"

"Ithane?" the man asked behind me.

I turned around and I just smiled at the most beautiful man I had ever seen. I hadn't had a chance to look at the man before but… he was sensational.

My heart pounded in my chest. My swords were slippery in my hands because of the sweat and my mouth went dry for a few seconds before my magic forced my body to return to normal.

I couldn't help but focus on how cute, beautiful and insanely hot this man was with his large biceps, strong jawline and those deep emerald eyes. He was stunning to look at and I seriously wanted to kiss him but I had a mission to do.

And I had lives to save.

His necklace glowed bright white and I laughed as I knew Spero was saying hello to me. He recognised a servant of his Mother and I could feel so much warmth fill my body (some of it was from being in the presence of this stunner) as Genetrix was pleased to see her child again.

"Are you really Ithane Veilwalker?" the man asked.

I nodded and I felt like my life had just changed forever.

CHAPTER 10

Jerico flat out couldn't believe this was the woman he had travelled all over the galaxy for. She had to be the most beautiful woman he had ever seen. Her eyes were so kind, life-filled and her long golden hair was just divine and he so badly wanted to run his hands through it.

He had been expecting Ithane to be a Keres woman or some kind of evil, monstrous servant of the so-called Death God. But he was amazed at how kind she was, she had focused on healing Piper above all else and he just had to respect her for that.

And Ithane was a stunner in that golden armour of hers. Jerico liked how it highlighted her fit, sexy body and Jerico really wanted to know how hard her body was and what it would feel against his own. He couldn't help but grin like a schoolboy. Jerico really liked this woman.

"I am Ithane Veilwalker," the hot woman said, "and I think fate brought our Odysseys together,"

Jerico rolled his eyes and Ithane had suddenly gotten a lot less attractive. She was clearly just a religious nutter like the rest of the Keres at times. He understood the appeal of believing in the Genetrix rubbish but he wanted everyone to focus on what was really happening instead of believing in Gods and Goddesses that wouldn't save them.

"He doesn't believe in the Mother," Piper said.

Ithane smiled. "I can sense that and Spero is telling me that you're a good man. But I don't understand why Genetrix and Geneitor have brought us together on this planet,"

"Does it matter?" Jerico asked. "I'm only here because a dying friend made me promise to find you, make sure you're okay and give you this,"

Jerico took off the necklace and he was surprised how sad he felt that he was giving up the necklace. But he was a soldier, a fighter and a survivor. He had done his mission and he was done, he didn't need to get involved in this battle.

Jerico went to past the necklace to Ithane when she shook her head and whipped out her swords.

"What?" Piper asked.

"Dark Keres incoming," Ithane said.

Jerico had no idea how this woman could possibly know that but moments later three black portals opened.

Nothing came out.

Jerico aimed his machine gun at the portals but then they closed.

"What was that?" Jerico asked.

"They were watching us," Piper said.

"No," Ithane said shaking her head and Jerico had to admit she was hot as hell when she looked all serious and wise. "Geneitor wanted to see the three of us. I felt his cold stare look at us but I don't understand any of this,"

Jerico looked around and thankfully the smoky black sky was clear of enemies for now. He just didn't know how long that would last.

"What the hell is going on here?" Jerico asked.

Ithane smiled. "I think Genetrix and Geneitor have somehow twisted the fates of millions to bring us all here,"

"Why?" Jerico asked hating this damn divine game and rubbish. "Why bring together Dark Keres, whatever you are and Imperials together? What could a Great Mother and the thousands of Keres on this planet bring this so-called Death God?"

Jerico noticed Ithane was staring right at him like he had said something extremely serious.

"Oh Genetrix," Piper said. "I was so stupid. Why didn't I see it earlier,"

"We're seeing it now," Ithane said.

"What?" Jerico asked hearing the roaring of Imperial engines in the distance.

"When the Treaty of Defeat was signed," Ithane said, "the Keres split into four fractions shortly afterwards. The Dark Keres were Keres and humans that fell to the worship of Geneitor and they want to bring around the resurrection,"

"So he can apparently bring around the end of all life," Jerico said.

"Then there are the Daughters of Genetrix," Ithane said. "That want to protect all life. But there are the *normal* Keres that live in Keres society under the extreme oppression of Imperial rule in all but name,"

"So?" Jerico asked knowing the enemy were getting a lot closer.

"So," Piper said, "there is a final fraction.

A fraction no one talks about and everyone thought they were dead. I've lived with them so hundreds of years so I had forgotten how mysterious we were to the rest of you,"

"The Protectors," Ithane said," were some of the most important Keres in the entire galaxy. They all left for the Mother World of Genesis and they are so powerful their souls burn brightest in the entire species and they were guarding two Soulstones,"

Jerico nodded. He didn't believe in the Soulstone crap but clearly the Imperium and the Dark Keres did. And he was willing to bet these so-called Soulstones were in the tunnels, exactly where thousands of innocent Keres were hiding.

Thousands of innocents that were about to get killed.

"I saw the Soulstones once," Piper said.

Ithane glared at her and Jerico had no idea why that was so important.

"Describe them quickly. I might be able to identify them," Ithane said.

"Um they were both black. One had a red swirl in and another one had a sickly green swirl that was laughing at me constantly," Piper said.

"Shit. Shit. Shit," Ithane said. "Those Soulstones belong to Geneitor. He birthed the Gods of Plague and the God of Rage. If his followers get their hands on them then they are two steps closer to resurrecting him,"

Jerico wasn't sure if that was true but as he saw three enemy bombers heading straight for them he didn't care.

"We have to get to the tunnels now!" Jerico shouted.

Ithane nodded and she waved her sexy arms in the air and another portal opened. Jerico wasn't sure about going inside but the roar of a bomb dropping towards them made him decide.

He leapt through the portal and just hoped beyond hope he wasn't going to die.

CHAPTER 11

I was surprised as hell when I appeared on top of a massive purple crystal tower in the middle of some impressive Keres city. I had always loved Keres cities because like this one, they were so artful, massive and stunning.

But I could sense the fear, desperation and death that was sweeping over the city. I noticed there was some kind of cloaking magic in effect so with a thought I switched it off and just grinned as I saw the Great Mother.

I immediately bowed as I saw the kind cheerful-looking Keres woman in her robes and staff. She waved me to stop me and instead she bowed.

Then I noticed the five dead guards around her and the blood dripping from her staff.

"What happened?" beautiful Jerico said and I couldn't blame him. This was serious.

"Geneitor got to them," the Great Mother said. "He tried to corrupt me too but I resisted him. He promised me wonders, entire planets and entire slave armies to myself but I declined,"

I nodded and I couldn't believe any of this. I knew Geneitor was more conscious than Genetrix and his followers had more power but I had never seen him *this* focused on a planet before.

And as much as I didn't want to, I didn't believe it was all because of the Soulstones. There was something larger going on here and I needed to know what.

"How long has this battle been going on for?" I asked.

"No idea," Jerico said. "All the clocks have stopped. Communications don't work and even the Keres' magic has been spotty. Speaking of which I didn't think humans could use magic,"

I smiled. "Genetrix resurrected me so I'm a mixture of Keres and human. That isn't important now,"

I paced around and that was serious. I presumed the Keres were using their clocks that were connected to reality itself. No one could stop them unless they were being disconnected from reality.

I didn't know that was possible. Maybe it wasn't but something was making this world warped and twisted and strange like I had never seen it before.

Then it hit me.

"The souls. The fucking souls!" I shouted understanding everything that was going on here.

"What?" Jerico asked checking the skies for any enemy aircraft.

I paced around a little. "Geneitor made the Dark Keres, the Imperial and the Protectors all come to this planet at this moment together so he could create a war like no other,"

A deafening explosion echoed all around me and I saw the screams of a thousand souls echo all around me.

"And think about the types of Souls Geneitor made come here," Piper said. "Human souls are like tealights but he brought a Hand Of the Rex and her special forces,"

I nodded. That made perfect sense. Even if millions of humans died here, their souls would only be worth the power of a hundred or a thousand Keres souls. But if Geneitor brought more powerful souls here like a Hand of the Rex then that would be a feast for him.

"Okay," Jerico said. "So he wants to create a massive war. To what end?"

I shut off the sound of the screaming souls that filled my senses and I just laughed at that handsome man. He was so cute in his naivety about the divine chess game he was entering.

"Why else would a Death God want as many souls as he could get?" I asked. "He wants to feast and he wants to unleash his two children on this planet."

Everyone went silent and I felt the purple tower shake underneath us.

Piper swallowed hard. "Are you telling me that if enough souls are devoured here than Geneitor can resurrect two of his Demi-Gods?"

"Yes," I said. "And they will walk the stars once more as they did back in the Old War,"

I shivered. I couldn't believe this was happening but it was true. It was all damn true and I had been so stupid as to fall for it.

"I've brought the entirety of the Daughters Of Genetrix. Two million Keres and humans on my fleet just sitting there waiting to die,"

My hands formed fists. I was meant to protect them. I was meant to save them. And I hated to imagine how many thousands of them had died already for my mistake.

Jerico gently rubbed my shoulder and I loved his warm skin against my armour.

"We can fix this," Jerico said holding up his necklace. "Can this Spero thing help us?"

I grinned as I stared into the bright golden light of Spero God of Hope. I felt a great sense of wonderfully warm hope fill my soul and images filled my mind. Spero was showing me images of life, death and the tunnels. He showed me an image of a massive golden portal and the Keres leaving through it.

He had to be telling me about portalling the Keres off the planet and onto my ships. I didn't even know if my ships could escape but I had to try.

Every life spared was a life Geneitor couldn't use to fuel his foul demi-gods.

I looked at the Great Mother and the horrible aroma of blood, death and decay filled my nose. Something was happening so I was going to have to be quick.

"You said your magic was affected. How?" I asked the Great Mother and Piper.

"I don't know," Piper said, "but I feel cutoff from Genetrix. I feel like her magical presence is through a dense fog and every time I try to reach out to her I get lost in the fog,"

"That would work," I said grinning because I knew exactly how I was going to save everyone but I needed Jerico's help.

I smiled at Jerico and for some reason he smiled back. His grin was beautiful and I was so looking forward to getting to know him better if he survived this.

"What you thinking?" Jerico asked.

"I'm going to break the fog for everyone and save their lives," I said.

Pure happiness filled me and I just hoped I could save everyone.

Little did I realise just how impossible that was going to be.

CHAPTER 12

"You need to buy me as much time as possible," Ithane said.

Jerico just nodded as he checked his machine gun and liked the sheer weight of it in his hands. He was going to light up the immense cavern they were in and he was going to make the enemy pay whenever they showed up.

"My Lady," the Great Mother said to Ithane, "everyone is here,"

Jerico looked behind him and just gasped as he realised just how immense the cavern truly was. There were thousands upon thousands of male and female Keres here in thin robes. They were all lined up in neat rows and Jerico felt sorry for them as he saw fear, pain and terror on their faces.

They believed they were going to die here.

Jerico was surprised the cavern was large enough to fit everyone inside but it was. The smell of death, decay and rotting flesh filled the air and Jerico supposed that could have been caused by the so-called Plague God hiding down here.

"Jerico," Ithane said and Jerico's heart skipped a few beats, "when I start the ritual and the Keres start portalling away the enemy will come. Geneitor will know exactly where we are and he will send his followers to kill me,"

Jerico nodded at Ithane and weakly smiled at Piper and a group of ten Keres warriors came over to him.

"Your job is to keep the enemy back as long as you can," Ithane said.

"Of course," Jerico said. "I've fought in enough wars to know how to defend people,"

"I fear sooner or later won't be fighting Keres or humans," Ithane said.

The entire cavern jerked violently and immense chunks of rock collapsed from the ceiling. Smashing down and killing some Keres below.

"They're here," the Great Mother said taking out her staff.

Jerico watched as Ithane rushed over to a large opening at the edge of the cavern next to the massive staircase they had all entered from.

He was tempted to move over there and protect the staircase but he didn't believe for a second the enemy were going to use stairs to enter the cavern. He hated magic.

Ithane raised her arms and hands and her long beautiful hair flowed all around her like some angel.

The entire cavern shook violently again. Jerico's fingers tightened around the trigger. He looked at Piper and her warriors and they nodded back at him.

They were ready for whatever was coming.

"Brothers and sisters," Ithane said as the air crackled with white magical energy, "reach out into the void and seek the magical touch of the Goddess of Life, our most holy mother,"

Jerico noticed no one looked convinced and he really didn't like the icy cold sensation coming from Spero. Maybe it was a warning.

"The Mother is not lost beyond the fog," Ithane said. "She is there and she is ready to give us her strength. I am here with you, her Will Incarnate, on Genesis. The brightness of my soul will create a bridge to her divine touch,"

Jerico wasn't convinced but he saw most of the Keres were smiling and they were closing their eyes and concentrating.

"We cannot allow the Keres to lose that focus," Jerico said to Piper as the air started crackling with black energy.

"Reach out brothers and sisters! See the Mother in the void. Let her touch your soul and give you the magic you were destined to have!" Ithane shouted.

A loud bang filled the cavern and humming and vibrating echoed all around Jerico. Golden portals opened in front of some of the Keres then more and more. They stepped through.

And Jerico realised it was going to take a while to evacuate the thousands of Keres to the Daughter of Genetrix ships.

Time they didn't have.

"They're coming!" Ithane shouted.

Jerico spun around as black portals opened on the ceiling.

He aimed his machine gun. He fired.

Bullets screamed through the air.

Corrupted humans with charred skin rained down on the cavern.

Jerico fired.

Exploding heads.

Exploding chests.

Demonic blood rained down upon them.

Jerico hissed as the blood burnt his skin.

Jerico kept firing.

He had to protect everyone here. He had to fire to the last.

He had to make sure as many Keres survived this attack.

He had a feeling the fate of the galaxy depended on it.

CHAPTER 13

The thick foul aromas of death, rotting flesh and disease filled my senses as Geneitor tried to corrupt me and make me lose focus. How dare the bastard threaten to stop me from my holy mission. I hope all his servants got slaughtered by Jerico, Piper and their noble warriors.

I had to close my eyes from the battle in the cavern as I focused on what was happening in the magical realm. The magical reflection of reality that all magic played in.

I could see Genesis burn, crack and smoke veil its once beautiful blue sky. I wanted to shout, scream and vow revenge on Geneitor for despoiling the most precious planet in the galaxy, but I had to focus.

To my left I could see a thick cloud of magical fog with thousands upon thousands of screaming, laughing and singing faces with teeth just slashing at me. Geneitor had cut off the Keres from Genetrix's touch and those demons in the fog wanted souls to eat.

I had already purged enough of the demons to create a small tunnel for the Keres to reach out through and Genetrix could gift them her magic again. But I could feel the pressure of Geneitor's corruption pressing against my mind.

A headache corkscrewed across my forehead and I wasn't sure how long I could keep this up for. Geneitor was pissed as hell and he wanted me dead.

My skin grew colder and small shards of ice started to cover my skin. Genetrix couldn't protect me much longer from Geneitor's focus and I knew he would find my exact location in this magical realm very soon.

"Go Mother," I said, "save your children and let me deal with the Father of Death,"

I felt Genetrix pulse cold and then warmth into me like she was struggling to decide but a moment later I felt the warmth leave me. I was alone for a little bit and I just had to make sure

I was still alive when Genetrix refocused on me.

If I died now she wouldn't be able to find my soul and resurrect me again.

"Show yourself Geneitor," I said and smiled as the demons in the fogs stopped slashing their teeth.

Hopefully that would give the Keres more time to escape and I would be able to focus on the Death God instead of protecting the Keres'.

"You look different my Child," a deep booming voice said.

I looked around for the voice but I couldn't see anything. My headache got a thousand times worse and it took everything I had not to collapse to my knees.

"Do you like my handy work Child?" Geneitor asked. "Do you like how I twisted the fate of millions to bring them all here so I can get revenge?"

"Don't you mean resurrect your children?"

The entire magical realm went silent for a moment and I was shocked. My headache got a lot better and I couldn't understand this.

"You didn't know?" I asked. "How can the Death God not know when his demi-gods are on the world he is burning?"

Then I realised that was the least of my problems. I had been working on the assumption that Geneitor was only doing all of this to bring back two of his children so they could burn the galaxy and kill in his name once more as they walked the stars.

If he didn't do all of this for those reasons then why the hell was he burning a planet to ash?

"That is most interesting Child. Are you sure you work for the Mother of Life? You have been most helpful to me as well so I thank you,"

"You are nothing," I said as I managed to feel his presence behind me.

I whipped out my two swords. I spun around.

I smashed into the swords of a giant with four arms with a double-ended sword in each hand. The air around him crackled with black energy and I knew I was looking at one of the major forms of Geneitor.

He wasn't hiding from me this time. This was what he actually looked like.

He wore an immensely long robe that looked a thousand years old judging by the holes and how shredded it was. His face was covered by a black hood but I could feel his piercing glaze look into my soul.

"Such a tasty looking soul you have there. How many Demi-gods do you think you are worth? A hundred? A thousand? A million? Let me taste you and find out!"

He swung at me.

I tried to block. I couldn't.

He smashed his swords into me.

Throwing me back tens of metres.

He ran after me.

Slamming his legs into me.

He kicked me to the ground.

I smashed onto a ground that wasn't there.

Black magical rope wrapped itself around my neck.

It tightened. I gasped. He laughed.

I shot out my hand.

No magic came out.

Geneitor went to kiss me.

I screamed out in terror.

I swung my sword.

Slicing his cheek.

He hissed.

He released me.

I thrusted out my hands.

White fire shot out of them.

Geneitor absorbed it all and charged at me.

I tried to block.

I couldn't.

He kicked me.

Pinning me against a ground that wasn't there.

"Do you think you are the first incarnate of Genetrix's Will? Do you think you are so special that you will even be the last,"

I laughed. "I don't care if I was the thousandth or millionth Incarnate. I serve Genetrix and your time is done,"

"How Child? I am burning this planet, freeing my children and I will devour your soul before I am done with you,"

"No you won't," I said grinning, "because you forget unlike you I am not bound to this realm so I just have to open my eyes and I am free of this place,"

Geneitor roared. He swung his swords.

I opened my eyes.

CHAPTER 14

Jerico flat out hated these damn abominations as he fired his machine gun endlessly inside the immense cavern. Corrupted humans with black veiny rotting flesh kept coming down from the ceiling.

He fired again and again.

Jerico hated how the smell of death, rotting flesh and blood filled his senses and the taste of iron formed on his tongue. He kept firing.

He wasn't allowing the enemy to win here.

Jerico smiled as he kept purging the enemy as Piper and her warriors howled like wolves. They charged around the caverns running like the steep walls of the cavern was flat ground.

They swirled, twirled and slaughtered the enemy as they poured out of the portals.

Click went the trigger. Click. Click. Click.

Jerico hissed as he threw his machine gun at the head of a corrupted human as it landed in front of him.

The black portals crackled and Jerico's eyes widened as tens upon tens of Dark Keres stormed out of them. The humans had only attacked to get rid of his weapons and his ammo.

Jerico looked around.

He rushed over to a Keres sword on the floor. He grabbed it.

The Great Mother rushed over. White fire shooting out of her hands.

Jerico spun around. There were tens of Dark Keres landing on the ground now. They fired at the escaping Keres.

Jerico flew forward.

Swinging his sword.

Hacking the enemy apart.

Blood sprayed up walls. Brain matter exploded out. Flesh burnt.

There were too many.

A Dark Keres landed on top of Jerico. Knocking his sword away.

Jerico fell to the ground. He punched the Dark Keres. He kicked. He struggled.

It was useless.

The Dark Keres pinned his arms with evil magic. Jerico tried to move. He couldn't.

His necklace glowed bright white.

The Dark Keres screamed in terror.

Jerico grabbed the Keres's neck and snapped it.

He leapt up and used the Dark Keres's gun to slaughter three more enemies descending on the escaping Keres.

They were simply too many foes.

Three corpses of Piper's warriors landed around him.

This battle was lost. It was always lost. And Jerico just wanted to protect Ithane.

He rushed over to her. Her eyes were closed and the air was still crackling white light around her. Whatever she was doing he really hoped she was going to hurry the hell up.

A roar came from behind him.

Jerico swung around.

Beheading a Dark Keres.

Then the Dark Keres just stopped and Jerico prepared to strike as three of the enemy dropped down in front of him.

Jerico didn't understand why the enemy were stopping and they were simply allowing the Keres to escape through their golden portals.

The cavern shook violently.

Then it stopped.

Jerico hated the strange silence that washed over the cavern like a wave. He tried to stomp his feet on the ground but no sound came from it.

Then Jerico just looked at the Dark Keres in front of him and they just grinned as they snapped their own necks and laughed as they died.

"What the hell is going on?" Jerico asked surprised his words formed sounds.

The Great Mother was about to speak when the ground collapsed from under her and she screamed in agony as she was murdered.

Jerico moved away and really hoped Ithane would snap out of it soon. He needed her. He needed that beautiful woman back.

"Commander! The hole," Piper shouted still on the walls of the cavern.

Jerico pointed his sword at the hole where the Great Mother had been as four long hands with claw-like fingers appeared and then a humanoid person pulled themselves up.

Jerico's eyes widened as he looked at the extremely tall Keres male (maybe four metres tall) in thick green rotting, rusty armour with flies, maggots and puss oozing from him.

The man grinned at Jerico and Jerico wanted to scream at the man's black teeth, rotting tongue and sheer corruption. This wasn't natural at all and Jerico hated it.

"It is good to walk once more," the man said with flies pouring out of his mouth as he spoke.

Jerico wanted to be sick.

"Yes little human. Be sick, vomit, let me bathe in your sickness," the man said.

"Oh shit," Jerico said as he realised this was the God of Plague. It couldn't be and Jerico didn't want to believe it but he couldn't deny what he was seeing.

He was actually seeing a Keres God in front of him.

The God Of Plague grinned as he looked at all the escaping Keres and he clicked his fingers.

All the golden portals turned sickly green and the Keres screamed in agony as they entered by mistake. Jerico had no doubt they were becoming twisted, diseased and corrupted beyond recognition.

The God Of Plague shivered like he had

just had the best sex in the universe.

Jerico pointed his sword at the God's throat. "Stop this,"

"I will not little human. I am a God and I am the creator of disease and I am giving these Keres a chance to live and serve the True God once more,"

Jerico charged at the God.

Piper tackled Jerico to the ground.

The Plague God thrusted out his hands.

Millions of flies zoomed towards the remaining Keres besides Piper and devoured their flesh. Then the flies disappeared.

Thousands of Keres dead in a single moment.

"Don't worry human and Keres," the Plague God said. "I will turn you into my Greatest Disease Spreaders ever!"

"No you will not!" Ithane shouted.

And Jerico just grinned because he couldn't help but believe shit was about to go down.

That both excited and terrified him way more than he ever wanted to admit.

CHAPTER 15

This was bad. This was so bloody bad. This was the worst thing ever.

I just glared at the twisted, diseased, rotting corpse of the Plague God as I pointed my swords at his chest. I couldn't fight a God. This wasn't my domain and my wheelhouse. All I wanted to do was survive and help Jerico and Piper escape from this damn planet and this cavern.

The cavern was charred and wrecked and I noticed there were thousands of flies and maggots starting to pour down from the ceiling.

The Plague God was actually starting to corrupt the very planet itself. I didn't want Piper or Jerico here any longer than they had to be because sooner or later he would start to corrupt their souls. Something I couldn't allow.

I flew at the Plague God.

I swung my swords.

I slashed at him.

I lashed.

He laughed.

He dodged.

He kicked me.

I charged at him.

He screamed.

Unleashing swarms upon swarms of flies at me.

Fire shot out of my hands.

The Plague God charged at Jerico.

Jerico slashed his sword.

Slicing into the Plague God's face.

Slugs and snails poured out of the wound and then it healed itself.

The Plague God clapped his hands and slugs covered our skin.

I burnt them away and then Jerico and Piper collapsed to the ground and started vomiting.

"Stop this!" I shouted.

"Never," the Plague God said. "I want them to throw up their organs. I want them to give me something warm to wipe on my skin,"

"You're disgusting,"

"I am the Plague God. I am the beginning and the end of all life. I am the killer that lurks in the air you breathe, the water you drink and the food you eat,"

I charged him.

The Plague God clicked his fingers.

I was smashed against a maggot-covered wall.

I burnt the maggots away and I felt a headache form in my mind. The temperature dropped so much that my breath formed vapour.

Something was coming.

We had to escape now but I couldn't open a portal with the Plague God here in case he corrupted it or followed us to my ship.

I just grinned because there was only one hope for our survival. I had to summon Vita, the avatar of Genetrix.

"You look hopeful for a change," the Plague God said. "What happened?"

The entire planet shook and jerked and cracked.

Immense chunks of rock collapsed from the ceiling. Something was happening to the planet.

"I'm hijacking the souls of the dead. Come to me Vita, avatar of the Goddess of Life," I said.

The Plague God laughed. "Genetrix has no avatar,"

"You have been banished way too long to realise what Her power truly is,"

The Plague God clicked his fingers and all the millions of flies and maggots on the walls laughed as they formed into humanoid creatures with puss and disease oozing from their pores.

"Kill her," the Plague God said.

I just grinned as a bright white portal appeared. The Plague God tried to corrupt it but he couldn't. This was a portal made by the souls of the dead and the damned.

A massive Keres female stepped out of the portal with bright white light shining from her. Choirs of angels echoed around the cavern and I just grinned as her long golden hair burnt bright with righteousness.

Vita looked at the Plague God and she screamed in rage.

She flew at the God.

Swords swung.

Swords clashed.

Earthquakes boomed from the fighting.

I rushed over to Jerico and Piper who were vomiting and gasping for air.

I shone white healing light from my hands and purified them and their mind and their souls.

"We have to get out of here," Jerico said.

The planet cracked and jerked and shook. The cavern's floor started to collapse.

I grabbed Jerico's and Piper's arm and I teleported us out of there.

I just hoped beyond hope we could escape the orbit in time.

CHAPTER 16

Jerico flat out hated the foul taste of bile, rot and disease that filled his mouth as he materialised on a large oval bridge of some spaceship he didn't recognise. He liked how beautiful Ithane threw him and Piper onto the same large metal command throne but that was where everything went to hell.

The entire bridge was a hive of activity. Ithane was pointing and shouting and barking orders like their lives depended on it.

It probably did.

Jerico watched as Genesis was glowing bright black and the ground looked like it was ripping itself apart. Even the Imperial and Dark Keres warships around the planet looked like they were trying to flee but they were exploding.

Whatever ship Jerico was on shook, vibrated and popped.

Jerico fell to one side as he tried to get up but Piper grabbed him and forced him to sit down on the command throne. He wanted to start reading the data outputs that were probably in the command throne but he didn't know how to work this tech.

"Fucking hell!" a human woman shouted.

Jerico looked at Genesis as an immense black portal with bright white edges opened to the left of the planet and Genesis just shattered.

The entire planet cracked like an egg and the entire world turned to ash.

The portal sucked the planet inside and then Jerico was forced off the command throne as the ship jerked.

"It's pulling us inside," someone said.

"Get us into Ultraspace now!" Ithane shouted.

"Negative," a human woman said with a nametag saying April.

"Look," Piper said.

Jerico looked out into the coldness of the void and his eyes just widened as the Imperial ships opened Ultraspace portals and as they went into Ultraspace. They exploded.

Ithane gripped her head and Jerico had no idea what this was like for her. He didn't know if she was hearing the screaming souls of the dying but this had to be overwhelming for her.

The ship banged and spun as something smashed into it.

Jerico gripped the command throne as the entire bridge spun around them.

"Get us into the Nexus now!" Ithane shouted.

The ship's engines hummed violently. They sounded like they were about to explode.

Jerico couldn't see anything but splashes of explosions, fires and death outside.

Something exploded on the ship. Screams filled the bridge. Warning alarms filled Jerico's head. He didn't know what was happening.

The ship jerked a final time and Jerico's world went black as something smashed into the side of his head.

CHAPTER 17

The loud deafening beeping of warning alarms, the sound of crying and people in pain filled Jerico's ears as he woke up moments later. His vision was a blur of bright white light with some black lines as he assumed some people were moving around him.

The smell of vapourised blood and burning rubber and ozone filled his senses and Jerico wanted to be sick. But he didn't dare allow himself, he didn't want the awful taste of bile in his mouth ever again.

After a few moments Jerico's vision cleared and he partly wished it hadn't when he saw what had happened. The bridge was covered in the twisted bodies of humans and Keres with their dark rich red blood painting the floor, command consoles and computers.

He saw Ithane sitting on the floor, tears pouring down her beautiful cheeks and he just wanted to hug her. Ithane was holding her head and trying to cover her ears with her arms but Jerico could tell it wasn't working.

Jerico forced himself up and he was relieved to see Piper was alive and talking to a human man behind them. Piper had blood all over her and he really hoped she was going to be okay.

"Ithane," Jerico said going over to her and sitting in front of her. "Are you okay?"

"It won't stop. The screams won't stop. I can hear them. Every single person that died on Genesis and around it. I can hear them all,"

Jerico felt a wave of emotion wash over him. He couldn't even begin to know what it was like and he was fairly sure he didn't want to know. So he took off the necklace and placed it on Ithane's lap and was relieved when she smiled a little. Spero glowed a little brighter so hopefully he was taking some of the burden away from her.

Jerico hated seeing such a beautiful, strong and amazing warrior in pain.

"How many did we lose?" Jerico asked.

Ithane stopped crying immediately and frowned. "Everyone. This is the only ship that survived the attack. We have a crew of five thousand and we managed to take two thousand refugees from the planet,"

"Out of twenty thousand," April said who was sitting down next to them.

Jerico nodded his hellos to her but April didn't look interested.

"My Lady," April said, "there was a problem when you were away. There was a plague that was unleashed on the entire fleet. We fought it and won but the mortality rate was extreme,"

Jerico could see Ithane couldn't take much more bad news but she was trying to be strong for her forces. Jerico could see how much everyone loved her, worshipped her and wanted to please her. But he could see none of this was easy for her.

He didn't want to be here and he didn't want to be in her shoes, but he was involved now. He had seen some Plague God brought back from the dead and he wanted revenge. He didn't wish that vomiting trick on anyone.

"What happened out there?" Jerico asked.

"Please excuse me my Lady," April said. "I need to double-check my calculations. The Nexus isn't as safe as it once was to traverse,"

"Thank you April I mean it," Ithane said giving her friend a weak smile before turning back to Jerico. "This was a mistake,"

"What happened out there? How the hell does an entire planet just shatter like glass?" Jerico asked.

Jerico noticed Ithane didn't say anything until a group of engineers had finished walking past.

Ithane leant in closer. "Geneitor isn't an idiot. He didn't know about the two Soulstones on Genesis. He got the Imperium there, he got us there and he got his servants there just to weaken us all,"

Jerico nodded. That made perfect sense and he loved military strategy as much as the next commander but this was extreme. Geneitor had clearly wanted to destroy the Imperium and the Daughters of Genetrix, but why do it this way?

So Jerico asked Ithane.

"Because when mainstream Keres society learn of this. They will be angry as hell and they will put a lot of pressure on their Sovereign to rip up the Treaty of Defeat,"

"Geneitor wants another Human-Keres war," Jerico said. "So more people will die and he gets more souls to feast on. What happened to the Soulstones?"

Ithane laughed. "You really think the destruction of a planet by Geneitor stops the Soulstones. He has them both now and his

Plague God can walk amongst the stars sowing death, disease and plague wherever he goes,"

Ithane stood up and Jerico followed her to the large circular door that led away from the bridge.

"I'm sorry you got caught up in all this," Ithane said smiling. "If you tell me where you want to be dropped off, I'll make it happen,"

"What?" Jerico asked not understanding why Ithane thought he wouldn't want to fight alongside her (and spend even more time with this beautiful woman).

"This isn't your fight and the chances of you surviving this are basically nothing," Ithane said grabbing his hand. "You gave me Spero and he will be a massive help,"

Jerico loved the smooth warmth of her small hand in his. He loved the flow of electricity between them. He couldn't leave her just yet, if ever.

"Will me joining this fight save lives?" Jerico asked knowing the answer.

"Of course,"

"Then I am staying. I fought in the Imperial army to protect humanity and that is why I came to find you. I might not have believed in this God rubbish until an hour ago but I want to fight now,"

Ithane passed Jerico his Spero necklace again. "The God of Hope chose you to be his wearer, let us not dishonour the will of the Gods,"

Jerico gasped as Ithane kissed his cheek and his wayward parts exploded to life at the sheer chemistry that flowed between them. Jerico seriously wanted to get to know her better.

And he was joining this fight and ship of humans and Keres, he was finally going to get the chance to make a difference, be with the woman he seriously liked and hopefully help to make the galaxy a safer place.

A perfect end to a weird odyssey.

CHAPTER 18

When I went into my large office in the deepest sections of the *Lady of Light*, I couldn't help but frown at the sheer destruction of my once beautiful office. There used to be wonderful purple crystals that covered the dirty walls of the office in their millions, and each one represented a small soul of an agent or spy or servant of Genetrix out in the galaxy.

But they were all mostly shattered and the foul smell of death, burnt flesh and strawberries overwhelmed me. I hated what Geneitor had done to my office and I almost couldn't believe what had happened today.

I was glad my old wooden desk had survived so I sat on top of it, and I simply laid down. I allowed the warmth of the desk to pulse into my body and I almost smiled at the nice comfort the warmth provided, because today had been a mistake and a half.

The ceiling was still covered a good enough amount of purple crystals that pulsed warmly and if I focused on a crystal I could weakly hear the mutterings and talking of my spies across the galaxy.

Everyone was starting to learn about the annihilation of Genesis, and I had little doubt I would get thousands of messages in the next few days begging me for new orders. My spies would want to help and maybe I would get new recruits for my network and fleet, but I had no idea if I could protect them.

I had come here with every single ship I had and now I only had one left. That was a stupid mistake.

I wasn't even sure what my next moves were because I was out of ideas. Genesis was dead, the Plague God had returned and Geneitor himself had another Soulstone and I only had one single stone. It wasn't like I could use Spero as much as I wanted to because I was still human at heart. I didn't live and breathe the ancient myths and texts about the Gods and Goddesses.

But I had to learn sooner or later or everyone would be killed by Geneitor.

Someone knocked on my door.

With a thought I opened the door to my office and I smiled when Piper and April came in. I had wanted Jerico to join us but the rest of the crew were enjoying learning from him and his tactical knowledge. He was a beautiful man and I was so happy he had decided to stay with us.

I was so, so looking forward to spending more time with him.

Piper and April were both in the light blue robes of the Navigators and I was happy that Piper had found a role for herself so soon.

"How's our course through the Nexus?" I asked.

"We aren't being followed and the entire Nexus might be shifting in ways I've never seen before but I've plotted a safe course for us. I still need a destination," April said.

I laughed. "Where the hell can we go? We cannot go to the Imperium because we're traitors and extremists to them. We cannot go to the Keres because they believe in the Treaty of Defeat more than the truth of the situation. And our list of friends are short,"

Piper nodded. "Then we go to the Enlightened Republic and hope they can protect us for a while,"

I had to admit that wasn't a bad idea. The Enlightened Republic was a small group of breakaway systems that believed in freedom, democracy and goodness unlike the Imperium. They had been good to my network before so I nodded.

April went to turn away but I gently grabbed her arm.

"What happened today requires power I have never seen before," I said. "Geneitor is growing more powerful by the day and I think we have to accept that his resurrection is an extremely real possibility in the next few years,"

"I thought that wouldn't be a possibility for centuries," April said.

"I would have agreed with you yesterday," I said coldly, "but today… today was a turning point in the web of fate. Geneitor twisted the odyssey of millions so he would get them to converge on Genesis at the same time,"

"But," Piper said stretching her arms, "my question is, why did he allow your odyssey and Jerico's odyssey to converge? Together you two are extremely dangerous to him, but allow you two to cross paths,"

After a minute of me not replying the two women bowed slightly and left my office, and I went back to lying on my wonderfully warm desk. I had a small theory about that but I wasn't going to tell them because it was dangerous as hell.

I strongly believe that Geneitor wanted me and Jerico to meet because I think he's arrogant enough to want a real challenger. Him and Genetrix could play their little game for a thousand years and not really damage or hurt each other, but I think Geneitor's growing bored in Ultraspace and I think he wants to play.

But he could easily wipe us out and resurrect himself if he allowed himself to deny his servants even the smallest fraction of free will. I think he wanted me and Jerico to meet so he could prolong the game a little longer and make it a little more fun.

A costly mistake for him because I fully intended to save my forces, rally my supporters and we were going to find all five Soulstones belonging to Genetrix so she can kick his ass once and for all.

And that wasn't a threat, it was a promise.

AVAILABLE NOW AT ALL MAJOR BOOKSELLERS!

AUTHOR OF ENGLISH GAY SWEET CONTEMPORARY ROMANCE SERIES

CONNOR WHITELEY

DAMAGE, HEALING, LOVE

A SWEET GAY UNIVERSITY ROMANCE NOVELLA

DAMAGE, HEALING, LOVE
A Sweet Gay University Romance Novella

CHAPTER 1
23rd January 2024
Canterbury, England

"Why are we going to this Fair thing?"

Zach James just laughed and pulled his best friend, Lora, in the entire world in for a massive hug as they went up a long terribly tarmacked path with thick oak, pine and beech trees lining it. He shivered a little as he watched his breathe condense and formed thick columns of vapour.

He sort of felt like a dragon. He breathed heavily and just smiled as the thick columns shot out his nose. The air was great with hints of grass, damp and freshly cut wood that only helped to make the day even better.

Zach had always really liked the smell of cut wood. It reminded him of being home with his Mum, Dad and two brothers who helped their Dad on their tree farm. Zach had never actually cared too much about the farm but it was sustainably done so he supposed he shouldn't have minded that much.

The sky above was grey but at least it wasn't going to rain and it wasn't wet. Zach really didn't like going out when it was wet and cold, it was so draining and there was nothing better than being in-doors with friends and a boyfriend.

Not that Zach actually had a boyfriend even more because of… an old friend called Jayden. Zach shook the thought away because thinking about Jayden, what they had done to each other and how innocent Jayden was, was never a good idea.

"Why?" Lora asked like a small child.

Zach shook his head and just smiled at his best friend. She always did look great with her long blond hair that ran down to the top of her legs, her green jacket showed off her thin body and she was really fun to be around.

She was brilliant, but she clearly didn't see the benefit of going to the Big Fair.

"Because I want to look at the Societies, which before you ask because I know you're a big kid at heart. They are what the university calls adult social clubs and no I do not know, why they are called Societies," Zach said.

They both smiled and Zach focused back on the tarmacked path. It was rather nice not seeing any other students on it, normally when he went to his lectures the path was packed full of students and it was a free for all.

It was even worse when it was raining or had just rained. And the wide stretches of grass to the side of the path turned into mud baths and sadly the trees provided little to no cover.

The sound of birds, cars and students in the far distance made Zach realise they were coming up to the university campus. The last time he had been up this path was before Winter Break so he hadn't realised how far and close everything was at different points.

"Why do you want us to do a society together?" Lora asked. "We already spent so much time together, so why don't you admit the real reason you want me to come along?"

Zach forced himself not to stop in his tracks, so he kept on walking. He didn't want to tell Lora how he had been spending so much time with her and still wanted to be with her constantly just so he didn't have to think about Ryan. Ryan had left him, shattered his heart and just wrecked him because of what Jayden had innocently done.

Zach shook his head. He couldn't start thinking about Jayden and what had happened last August. It wasn't healthy. It wasn't good and he would only start getting depressed again.

He couldn't go back to that place, so he lied.

"The real reason is because we have both been living in my flat and talking with my flatmates for the past four months. We need to get out and see people," Zach said.

"Sure, sure," Lora said smiling.

"It's the truth and I know we both have other friends, and once a week we go out to Q-Bar with six people. But I want to actually *do* something more,"

Lora laughed. "Darling, you haven't *done* anyone for two months,"

Zach flinched a little and tried to grin and

smile. It didn't really work and he was going to have to tell Lora that he didn't want reminders of Ryan. It was true him and Ryan had been very active in the bedroom and Ryan had left him in November after struggling for months.

He just didn't need to be reminders of it.

"I am sorry you know. I really am and I won't mention it again," Lora said knowing he didn't like reminders of Ryan. "How about we look at a baking society? We both like baking, right?"

Zach laughed as they went towards a little black path that shot away from the one they were currently on. It was a shortcut towards the Sports Hall where the Big Fair was happening.

Zach had no idea if he actually liked Baking or not because he had never tried it. But if it meant meeting new people, making new friends and getting out back into the world then he was certainly up for it.

And that excited him a lot more than he ever wanted to admit.

CHAPTER 2
23rd January 2024
Canterbury, England

University student Jayden Baker was so excited as he laid on his back on his soft, warm, cosy single bed in his university flat. He couldn't wait for his friends to knock on his door so they could go to The Big Fair together at the university. An event that Jayden really hoped would allow him to join new social groups, new activities and meet new people.

Maybe even a boyfriend.

Jayden sat up a little on his bed and hissed a little as the icy coldness of the flat's white walls chilled him a lot more than he wanted to admit. He had only gotten back to Kent University last week but he was still getting used to the cold winters. And how the university's apartment buildings failed to keep out much of the cold.

Jayden really liked the flat though. It might have been a bit pricey (which was why his parents were thankfully paying for it), but it was great and it was home. He was so glad the university had allowed him to put up some of his favourite landscape photos that he had taken. He had loved the trips from the hilly landscapes of Wales and the rough coastline of Cornwall and the stunning sunsets he had gotten in the Lake District.

He flat out loved photography and managing to actually capture a moment like the viewer was really there. That was the whole point of taking a photo.

Jayden heard a hiss as his automatic air fresher (a little Christmas gift from his mother) was activated. He still needed to find out how to turn the silly thing off but he liked the calming notes of fig and amber and there were some hints there that he wasn't too sure about. They were probably violet and jasmine but he wasn't sure, but they did smell great.

He could almost taste the great fig pie his grandmother used to make. Jayden had always loved that as a kid with whipped cream, strawberries and the most intense vanilla ice cream he had ever tasted.

A buzzing sound filled the flat.

Jayden leant across the tiny gap that was between his bed and his wooden "desk". That was actually nothing more than a very nice sheet of walnut wood that stretched the entire length of the flat (all five metres of it) with a desk chair. Not a traditional desk but Jayden didn't mind.

Jayden picked up his phone and took out the charger. He grinned as his best friends in the entire world Caroline, Kate and Jackie were coming to his flat now. Jayden was glad he was going to see them because he hadn't seen them since they went up North for the winter break.

Jayden wasn't exactly sure why he wanted to go to the Big Fair. It was a massive event where all the social group or Societies as they preferred to be called, got to advertise themselves again and students could see them.

He had gone to Freshers' fair back in September, but Jayden tensed a little because that really wasn't the best time to look for new, stressful and scary events.

Jayden hated how he had just recovered from his breakdown, how he had just lost all his friends and how he had needed to see a therapist intensely for a month. She was brilliant and Jayden couldn't thank her enough for all the amazing things she had said and done for him.

But he hadn't wanted to do many societies. He had been happy enough when he met Caroline, Kate and Jackie at an Art Social for all the Art students at the university. That had been bad enough.

Jayden hissed as his heart rate increased. His ears rang and he simply forced himself to count out of order. He was still surprised it worked, but apparently the brain couldn't focus on panicking and counting at the same time.

Three women laughed outside and Jayden just grinned as he leapt off his bed and opened it for them.

Jayden was so happy to see Caroline in her thick winter coat (she was always cold even in the height of summer) and Kate in her blue shorts and summer shirt (she was always too hot). And Jayden just hugged Jackie and really liked her sweet coconut perfume.

He felt a little underdressed compared to his friends. He was only wearing blue jeans, black trainers and a black hoody that wasn't even a designer one. Compared to the women that all looked great, wonderful and almost seductive.

"Come on Jayden," Caroline said. "Let's go and see the Societies. There might be that baking one or LGBT+ society you wanted to visit,"

"Watch out Caroline," Kate said grinning. "It might be too cold for you,"

Caroline stuck her tongue out. "No, watch out yourself Kate. It might be too hot for you with all those university students. That's a lot of body heat,"

Jayden smiled. He really had missed his friends.

Jackie hugged Jayden again. "Let's just see if Baking society is on,"

Jayden pretended to roll his eyes out of boredom. There was nothing he would like more than to go to Baking society because he loved cooking. It was so relaxing, fun and the best part was he could eat it.

Jayden was so excited as he left his flat and he was looking forward to putting his past behind him and making new friends. Friends that he wouldn't hurt and friends that wouldn't hurt him almost as badly.

At least he ever had to see anyone from that part of his life again.

Little did know Jayden realise the exact opposite was about to happen.

CHAPTER 3

23rd January 2024
Canterbury, England

Zach seriously supposed he should have realised the reason why the Big Fair was called the Big Fair, but it was absolutely massive. He had been in the Sports Hall before and he was always shocked the central hall alone was the size of a football pitch and then there were two other halls that were only slightly smaller than a football pitch on each side.

The Big Fair made use of all the different halls and even some of the small rooms where the University's sports teams met, had their training meetings and teaching stuff.

Zach stood to one side of the massive blue doors to the Sports Hall and he was amazed at the scale of it. He had his back pressed against the perfectly warm green block walls and to his left a river of students washed into the fair.

He had never seen so many students of all shapes, sizes and ages come together. There were a lot of students in blue, black and even white jeans. A lot of them were designer ones along with the matching designer shirt but Zach didn't mind too much.

Some of the men were seriously hot.

Zach focused on one group of friends in particular as they came in. He couldn't help but focus on their sexy large asses in their black jeans as they stood near him and Lora and decided where to start. They were all wearing designer shirts that highlighted their fit bodies and long black curly hair.

They all looked identical but they were all hot.

"Someone's enjoying themselves," Lora said smiling. "You're grinning like a teenager,"

Zach tried to frown but those men were hot, and it was only now he was realising just how long it had been since he had been out and about and allowed himself to check out men.

He had really missed the feeling.

"What row do you want to start in?" Lora asked.

Zach rolled his eyes as he actually looked for the first time at where the river of students were flowing to. It was a nightmare and there were so many societies to cover.

He realised the Big Fair in the central hall was split out into three rows with different stalls lining each one. Zach couldn't see that much because of the sheer amount of students there but there were things on each stall including swag and other freebies. Zach loved freebies.

There were different things on often for each stall and some of them looked a lot more interesting than others. Like there was marketing society with two large women standing behind it offering people free mugs, but the stall next to it was only offering pens.

Zach still wanted to see both.

"Come on," Lora said.

Zach allowed her to drag him into the massive group of students and they slowly shuffled towards the first row of stalls. He could barely see what the stalls were because there were so many students with the smells of sweat, perfume and manly musk filling the hall. Zach seriously didn't mind the scent of manly musk.

He wanted to roll his eyes because he was only realising now how long it had truly been since he had allowed himself to focus on men. And men were beautiful people.

Zach gently guided Lora forward through a small gap between two different friendship groups, who in their divine wisdom, had just decided to stand in the middle of the row making it hard for others to get round them.

He hated people like that.

Zach pushed Lora forward and they glided through a large group of students until he accidentally found himself at the University Football Society. Zach just grinned like a schoolboy at the rich aroma of manly musk and sweat as he looked at the blue and black football kit the three striking men were wearing behind the little bench.

Zach had no idea why the men felt the need to wear their "used" kit to get new members, but he was hardly complaining.

The man with the words "Team Captain" on the front of his football shirt smiled. "You're Zach, right?"

"Yeah," Zach said wanting to take a step back but he couldn't because of the wall of students behind him.

"I'm Colin. I'm Ryan's new boyfriend. I've heard a lot about you. Do you want to join?"

The words struck Zach like bullets and stab wounds and the entire world just fell away from him. He could see Colin's lips move and he didn't doubt other people were talking about him but he just couldn't hear a word.

This couldn't be happening. He had wanted to move on from Ryan and that part of his life. He couldn't be doing this. He didn't want to be reminded of Ryan and what he had lost.

Zach shook his head and pushed his way through the other students and when his hearing returned he simply kept on gliding through the crowd.

"Talk to me," Lora said.

Zach shook his head and he was glad when he spotted the Baking Society up ahead. He could just focus on that, he was safe and he could deal with Colin and Ryan later on. Right now he could pretend he was fine and nothing bad was happening.

"Excuse me please," Zach said as he made his way through the crowd with Lora close behind him.

After a few moments of passing art students in long red, colourful dresses, he found himself right next to the Baking stall and he was so happy it was filled with little samples of cookies.

Exactly what he needed after that awful encounter.

"So how much is it for the rest of the year?" Jayden asked.

Zach looked to see who was standing right next to him and as much as he wanted to frown or panic, he couldn't believe he was standing right next to the most striking, stunning man he had ever met.

But also the man that had damaged, hurt and wrecked him because of an innocent mistake.

CHAPTER 4
23rd January 2024
Canterbury, England

Jayden flat out couldn't believe how packed the Big Fair was as he went into the Sports Hall. He had never been interested in Sports, he actually hated them but the hall was massive. He supposed it could have been the size of a football pitch but he had no idea what the size of them were. It was an expression that he fully intended to use.

He followed Jackie, Caroline and Katie around through the sea of students up and down the long rows of little stalls. He had wanted to make a little more progress than they currently were but there were simply too many students in all their different clothes, ages and heights walking about.

Jayden rolled his eyes as Caroline pulled them all towards a little wooden table where the Knitting Society (of all things) had set up shop. He had never ever seen the point in knitting, because it was something that old ladies did and Caroline was not an old lady.

But the stall looked nice enough. There were all sorts of red, purple and blue balls of wool on the wooden table. Jayden didn't like the look of the long grey knitting needles but he supposed he could have positioned them in a way that would make the moment come alive.

The vivid colours of the wool mixed with the Sports Hall lighting (which wasn't actually that bad) and the monotone knitting needles were all things he could work with. Jayden nodded to himself because he would have really liked to do that.

The rich, fruity, citrus smells of oranges, lime and lemons filled the stall as a group of young women in tank tops, skirts and little tiny handbags came over. Jayden wanted to cough but he forced himself not too, he didn't want to be rude.

But that aroma was way too strong for his liking.

"And if I knit something how warm would that keep me?" Caroline asked. "The problem is I am always cold,"

Jayden just laughed, because he really did love Caroline as a friend. She was hopeless, always concerned about keeping warm and she was just funny.

Jayden looked at some of the other stalls but it was hard with the wall of other students in his way. He could see a football Society on the other side and Jayden shook his head.

He couldn't imagine him playing football or any sport to be honest. He loved masculine and sporty men but he wasn't into it himself. It was just so damn pointless grown men running around after a ball for 90 minutes. What was the point? They were going to get tired and sweaty and it just didn't achieve anything. Sure it might have been entertaining for some people but to Jayden it was just so, so pointless.

"Oh Jayden," Kate said. "There's baking society over there. Come on,"

"But I haven't finished with knitting Society," Caroline said.

Jayden shrugged. "Join us when you're done, because I have a feeling Katie's getting hot just looking and thinking about wool,"

"Awh you do get me," Katie said giving Jayden a mocking hug and a kiss on the cheek.

Jayden gently took his best friend's hand and they fought through the immense crowd of students. This crowd all mainly seemed to be made up of hot fit sporty men in tight jeans, shirts and their aftershave was so overwhelming with hints of aromantic apple and rose that Jayden was rather turned-on.

Jayden made his way over to the Baking Society stall that was a lot busier than he expected. He stood to one side as the two smiling, clearly happy women in their blue t-shirts were talking to a bunch of other students.

The stall itself was great and Jayden so badly wanted to help himself to the different samples of chocolate, vanilla and maybe chilli cookies that were on the wooden table. There were pictures of the society's events, their social media details and Jayden had to admit this all looked great.

He couldn't help but smile to himself because he felt like him joining baking society might be a good idea. It would be fun, he would get to meet people and he would get to do tons of fun stuff in the long-term.

The other students moved away and Jayden went with Katie over to the two women who looked really happy to see them. Jayden noticed there was someone else standing next to him, a blond man, but Jayden didn't pay him any attention even though the smell was very familiar.

And very nice.

"So how much is the society for the rest of the year?" Jayden asked.

Out of the corner of his eye he noticed the blond man had turned to look at him and Jayden turned to see who the hell this blond man was.

Fucking hell. He was stunning and he was the man that Jayden had hurt so, so badly.

Jayden's heart pounded in his chest. His chest felt like it was going to explode. His ears rang.

Cold sweat ran down his back. His mouth turned dry. His stomach filled with butterflies and churned and then it felt like an angry cat was inside his stomach.

And then he realise Zach really was beautiful and so damn attractive and striking. He looked as great now as he had back in July and August.

Jayden really loved how Zach was still so insanely fit, sexy and his black t-shirt highlighted how Zach didn't have any body fat, he was so lean and toned without having any muscles. His face was still so perfect and lovely to look at, with his slightly pointy chin, his light blue eyes and his smooth perfect skin. Yet Jayden was so glad Zach was still a hot, seductive blond with his hair parted to the right so it covered his forehead and Zach just looked so strikingly masculine and perfect.

Zach moved a little on the spot and Jayden realised that was the smell he had missed. There was always the subtle smell of manly musk about Zach that had always turned on and made him horny around Zach, but he had fallen in love (toxic love but love nonetheless) in August not because of Zach's perfectly seductive twink body, but because he was one of the nicest people Jayden had ever met.

Now he just needed to know if Zach was still angry at him for all the damage he had caused.

CHAPTER 5
23rd January 2024
Canterbury, England

As much as Zach wanted to say, believe and shout that it was bad seeing Jayden again, he just couldn't. He didn't really know what it was but as his heart rate calmed down and some of the dryness of his mouth went away, he realised that Jayden was still a really good-looking guy.

He might not have had much brown hair but his cute face was all lines and angles and Zach had always liked Jayden's deep hazelnut eyes. They were so alert, so full of life and Jayden had always looked at him in a really caring way. Zach had always liked that about him because they both cared so much about each other last August.

Zach couldn't help but smile as he subtly checked out Jayden's rather fit body again.

Zach didn't mind that he had some meat on his bones as his mother used to say but Jayden was still fit, cute and he looked so good.

It was only then that Zach realised he had sort of wanted this chance to meet again. Sure they had seen each other around campus, they had walked past each other and Jayden had tried to say hello. But Zach always stayed silent and kept on walking because he wasn't sure what he would say.

He certainly didn't know what he was meant to say now. He didn't know what Jayden was like, if he had changed or anything. Zach didn't want to talk to Jayden if he was still the same intense, obsessive and overwhelming person he had been in August.

Zach shook at the idea. He couldn't go back but he wanted to see if Jayden was okay, and it wouldn't be a bad thing to see if this cute man was okay.

"How are you?" Jayden asked.

Zach forced himself to take a deep breath and he got an interesting hint of some kind of aromantic apple and rose aftershave.

"Let's go," Lora said pulling at Zach's arm a little.

Zach pulled away from her touch because he was a grown man and he did want to talk to cute Jayden.

"How are you?" Zach asked knowing full well he was dodging the question.

"Yeah I'm good thanks, a lot has changed since August. Therapy went really well, I've met a lot of new friends and life is great. I came out to my parents and my wider family and everyone has been so nice at home,"

Zach just grinned and forced himself not to hug Jayden. That was amazing news that he had come out to his family, it was all Zach had ever wanted for him because Jayden was such a nice guy and his family had taken such a toll on his mental health that it was brilliant to know Jayden had changed.

Zach frowned a little. He was surprised more than anything else because the last time he had seen Jayden, the idea of coming out to his family had been awful, like a death sentence so it must had taken a hell of lot of courage to do that.

"That's brilliant. I am so please for you," Zach said. "I hope things continue to go well and yeah,"

Jayden looked like he was about to reply when a large group of students slightly knocked into him. Zach went to moan at them but he forced himself not to. Jayden wasn't his friend anymore and Jayden could look after himself.

"Thanks, that really does mean a lot coming from you. I know it was something that you always wanted for me, so I'm really glad I did it. How about you? How's Ryan?"

Zach frowned. Jayden didn't know, he didn't know anything because that was how Zach had done their last messages and the ending of their relationship. He had blocked and partly ghosted Jayden on Instagram because it was better for everyone that way.

Zach couldn't believe Jayden didn't know the pain, the trouble and the consequences he had caused Ryan when he had messaged him to find out more about dealing with bad family members. Zach knew it was all his fault because he had told Jayden about Ryan's family when they started to be friends back in July, he hadn't realised Jayden would actually ask Ryan about it. Not that Zach told him it was an off-limit subject.

Zach had seriously screwed up.

"Me and Ryan broke up," Zach said forcing the fakest smile he had ever done. "It was for the best and yeah, Ryan has a new boyfriend after only two months,"

"Who's this?" a woman asked in a t-shirt and shorts.

Zach was a little annoyed that someone would interrupt him and Jayden, but over the sheer deafening noise of the other students he supposed that was bound to happen at some point.

"This is Zach," Jayden said, "and Zach, this is my new friend Katie,"

"Oh *that* Zach,"

Zach felt really cold all of a sudden and he had no idea what he wanted to do, he wanted to run, hide and just scream a little.

"What do you mean *that* Zach?" Zach asked wanting to know.

"Um, just that you hurt him and you wrecked Jayden," Katie said.

"No," Jayden said the panic clear in his voice. "Honestly I only told them at I hurt you badly and what happened between us is why I struggle with friendships,"

Zach shook his head. "I have to go. I have a thing. It was good seeing you and I'm glad you're okay,"

Before cute Jayden could say another word Zach went away and glided through all the different students again with Lora close behind him. He was annoyed with himself because as much as he didn't know how to handle the idea that Jayden had told others about what had happened, he only wanted to spend more and more time with Jayden.

He was so cute, so pretty and so fit but Zach just felt like there was more to it than that. He just had no idea why.

No idea at all.

CHAPTER 6
23rd January 2024
Canterbury, England

"I'm sorry Jayden,"

Jayden just waved Katie silent as they all sat around the little white chipboard table in Katie's university kitchen. He certainly didn't like Katie's cheaper accommodation compared to his own because the kitchen was rather awful. It was so small and clinical with its dirty white walls, white cabinets and white kitchen table that was so clearly made of chipboard that it just looked so cheap.

Jayden didn't like to be a snob but it was the truth. There was nothing luxurious or even that nice about the kitchen and it was even worse that some of Katie's flatmates had left a small takeaway container filled with mash potatoes, a steak and gravy. Yet judging by the cracked surface of the gravy, it had been uncovered for ages and that was just disgusting.

The only thing Jayden did like about the kitchen was the fact that Katie, Caroline and Jackie were with him. They all had their bags of freebies and swag arranged on the table, and some of it looked really cool.

Jayden was so impressed that Caroline had gotten a whole bunch of free knitwear including a blue scarf, two red jumpers and some green gloves. She was wearing the scarf now and like always she complained that she was too cold.

Maybe Jackie had gotten the most useful freebies and swag at the Big Fair, because Jayden really liked the three mugs she had "borrowed" from different stalls, and the pens, notepads and other free things were impressive.

Katie had managed to grab some freebies but there was barely anything. And Jayden didn't have anything.

After what had happened with Zach and Katie's wonderful little bombshell, Jayden had sort of walked around the Big Fair like a zombie. He felt so numb, so cold and so emotionless that he didn't know what to feel.

Katie passed Jayden a piping hot mug of coffee, and Jayden really liked the bitter, rich aromas that hit his nose.

"You've told us the story in various ways," Jackie said, "but what actually happened between you, Zach and Ryan?"

Jayden laughed. "God that really is a story and a half but I think I need to tell you,"

"Definitely," all three women said leaning closer like this was the start of a child's story time.

"So I first met Zach about a year ago, he was fucking beautiful and he stood out to me immediately. He was cute, funny and he was just amazing with his blond hair. And we spoke a little but we didn't really do anything else because we didn't really talk, talk,"

"Okay that sounds fine so far," Katie said fanning herself like she was still too hot.

Jayden nodded. "Then back in May we got talking a lot more, we exchanged information on Instagram and then May to July we spoke a fair bit. We made each other laugh, smile and we spoke about Ryan, his boyfriend. It was the start of a good friendship,"

"Okay," Jackie said a little tense.

"Then in July, Zach messaged me saying how he wanted to meet up so we went out.

And over the course of the next four weeks we developed a very fast, very caring and very intense friendship. Like we loved spending time together, but I developed a problem,"

"You fell in love?" Caroline asked wrapping her arms around herself because she was still cold. "And you mentioned before you developed Emotional Dependency on him?"

"Exactly," Jayden said, "because my family was so bad towards me being gay and Jayden accepted me without question, I sort of *needed* him to feel loved, safe and secure in myself so that made our friendship very toxic in the end. But he always wanted to support me no matter what happened and no matter how intense I got,"

"He did care about you," Katie said.

"Absolutely," Jayden said. "Like Zach is one of the most caring people I have ever met and he is amazing. And honestly... I did love him truly because he was everything I wanted in a man,"

Jayden didn't like it how his friends didn't look convinced and he couldn't blame them at all. He knew how it sounded, he knew it sounded like he didn't love Zach he was only using Zach for his validation and had a minor obsession with Zach.

An obsession he did not have any more.

"So you had an intense and toxic friendship," Caroline said, "so what broke it?"

Jayden laughed nervously and he just focused on his coffee mug.

"Oh this is going to be good," Caroline said.

"Well," Jayden said, "the problem was I met Ryan. I had been wanting to meet Ryan for ages because I knew Zach really loved him and I honestly wanted to see a gay relationship. But seeing Zach so happy, so in love and so great with someone else, that in itself didn't bother me. But what scared me was the fact that I didn't believe I could ever have that happiness,"

"Why not?" Jackie asked.

"Because of my past and my family. I just didn't think I could have that level of happiness so I just sort of spiralled from there. I was so scared of losing Zach that I tried to become friends with Ryan, but I was way too intense. And I asked him about his own family, the family they don't talk too anymore,"

"And you upset him," Caroline said rubbing her hands together to keep warm.

"Yeah because then Zach messaged me that he didn't want to be friends anymore. Zach was wrong to have shared something so personal and delicate about Ryan's life without his permission and I was being too intense,"

"And that's what led to your breakdown," Katie said not asking but knowing.

Jayden nodded and he took a large sip of the wonderfully bitter and rich coffee.

"How are you feeling now after seeing and talking to Zach again?" Katie asked.

Jayden was about to answer when his phone buzzed and he realised he had a message on Instagram.

Zach had messaged him and that both scared and excited Jayden a lot more than he ever wanted to admit.

CHAPTER 7
23rd January 2024
Canterbury, England

Zach didn't exactly know why he had contacted Jayden but as he looked at his phone just waiting for that annoyingly cute man to reply, he couldn't help but feel so excited and also a little nervous. It was clear that Jayden had changed, he was healthier and he wasn't as intense or needy when they had spoken earlier, but Zach really didn't want to rush into anything.

Zach laid on Lora's bright pink bed, that looked rather horrible in a way, as him and Lora watched a comedy film she raved about. Zach didn't exactly see the appeal and given how much time he had spent in this flat over the past four months, he supposed he should have been used to it by now.

But he looked over to her little desk and there was a wide rack of shelves above it, and there was a row of three large teddies that somehow managed to look elegant and rather adult. Zach just didn't like the one in the middle with the dark eyes that felt like it was staring into his soul.

It was so off-putting.

Lora moved around on the bed and Zach looked up at her as she was laughing, smiling and really enjoying the comedy. She had pulled her long blond hair up into a pony tail and he so badly wanted to talk about today with her, but she had shared her feelings earlier.

She wasn't happy and she did nothing but berate, talk and just complain about Jayden. He understood why she had done it because she had seen how badly Jayden had hurt Ryan and him and their relationship, but the thing was Jayden was never a bad person. He was just really traumatised and he didn't know how things worked and he struggled a lot with friends. Especially gay ones.

It was why Zach had put up with Jayden for so long, but he always felt great, happy and light around Jayden because Jayden was a great guy. And he was so sweet and nice, but it was intense at times.

"Who are you texting?" Lora asked as she stopped the film as it ended.

Zach smiled because he really couldn't tell her that he was messaging Jayden. She wouldn't like that and he would never hear the end of it.

He had only sent Jayden, a message of *Hi, it was nice seeing you today. I'm glad your life's getting better.*

It wasn't too nice, leading or anything it was just a matter of facts. A good healthy way to start a conversation.

Zach smiled as Jayden replied. *Yes, it was nice seeing you today and life is really good thanks. My friends are nice. What you up to?*

Zach took a deep breath of the creamy pumpkin-spiced latte aroma with a rich splash of vanilla and toffee filled Lora's flat. He almost panicked at the idea of maybe Jayden was being intense again, but he was being silly. It was normal to ask people what they're up to.

Zach texted back. *Nothing much. Just watching a comedy with Lora. What about you?*

He was surprised he actually didn't want Jayden to text back saying that he was with a boyfriend or something. And Zach just rolled his eyes as his stomach filled with butterflies, it was annoying as hell he was finding Jayden cute, fit and he couldn't stop thinking about Jayden's sweet eyes that were so full of life.

"Who are you texting?" Lora asked coming over.

Zach hid his phone so she couldn't look, and he just knew he was going to have to lie to her. Not because he wanted to but because he wanted to save himself from an evening of being told "don't you remember how much he hurt you and you're making a massive mistake,"

"I'm texting a guy," Zach said, "and it hurt like hell knowing that Ryan's moved on and dating someone like Colin, so I wanted to meet someone,"

Lora folded her arms. "And you just happened to have someone ready to talk to just like that,"

Zach nodded like he was a player and he had a million hot sexy men he could contact for some fun at the drop of a pin.

"Of course, I am very hot according to a lot of men," Zach said, "and why do you care so much?"

Lora went over to her desk and took a long sip of her latte. "Because I don't want you contacting Jayden. He hurt you and it was awful seeing you go through that,"

Zach nodded but he didn't like it. When him and Jayden had gone out a few times, Jayden had talked a lot about how his mother and family controlled who he could see and whatnot, apparently Jayden's parents thought the two of them were dating for those months.

An idea that made Zach smile, because Jayden was a cute, caring guy that just wanted the best for the people in his life. Zach supposed it wouldn't be a terrible idea to see about dating, but he had to know Jayden was different before he committed to anything.

He was not going back to the way things were in August. Lora was right, that was hell for him too.

"I'm not talking to Jayden because you're right. He really hurt me, he caused me and Ryan to break up by mistake and he just isn't the right guy for me," Zach said knowing he was lying because he actually wanted to meet up with Jayden so badly.

"Okay good," Lora said. "I'm going to the kitchen. Do you want anything?"

"No thanks," Zach said looking back at his phone.

I'm in my friend's kitchen talking about what happened today. I did like seeing you and I am sorry about Ryan. He was a great guy.

Zach couldn't help but smile. Jayden was always so sweet, so caring and such a great guy.

It's okay. Zach said not knowing if that was true or not. *I'm actually curious to see how much you're changed and um, what else you've been up to lately. Want to hang out sometime?*

As soon as Zach hit send he couldn't believe what the hell he had just done. He wanted this badly and it would be good if him and Jayden could be friends again and maybe even boyfriends, but he was nervous. Jayden was amazingly sweet but he could be so intense with his feelings. Zach didn't want to hurt him and he really didn't want Jayden to hurt him in return.

Sure I'm busy for the next few days with lectures and assignments but Saturday sounds good.

Zach was shocked and grinned like a schoolboy. The old Jayden would have said something like *any time is great* or Jayden would imply that he was prepared to drop everything he was doing or had planned to spend time with Zach.

But he wasn't like that anymore, Jayden was actually going to wait four days to see him.

And that was brilliant and Zach was so excited about Saturday. It could be brilliant or it could be awful.

CHAPTER 8
27th January 2024
Canterbury, England

Jayden flat out couldn't believe how brilliant, wonderful and lovely it had been just talking to Zach over the past few days. They hadn't spoken for very long or very deeply but it was nice just talking about university and whatnot. Jayden was glad that Zach was enjoying his course, he had made a bunch of friends that he sometimes hung out with and he was thinking about joining the Fencing Society.

Jayden seriously couldn't have cared less about Fencing or any sort of sports, but he couldn't deny the idea of Zach wearing sportswear was a massive turn-on. It would be good to see Zach's fit, sexy body without a gram of body fat covered in sportswear. Jayden just grinned to himself.

He was sitting on a rather cold wooden chair inside of one of the university's many little cafes and restaurants that were spread out all over campus. Jayden rather liked this one because it was sort of an Italian joint with its warm cream colours, little photographs of Italy and the wonderful aromas of basil, tomatoes and garlic filled the café.

It was brilliant.

Jayden rested his arms on the slightly cold plastic table and really wanted Zach to hurry up so they could see each other. There were a lot of other students in the café because it was lunchtime and most of them were having a working lunch.

The table in front of Jayden was filled with a group of young women in hoodies, jeans and they all had their laptops out. Some of them had yellow legal pads and they were debating some kind of group project that at least two of the women hated with a passion. A rather cute waiter went over to them with a tray full of pizza and that managed to make the two women smile a lot more.

Jayden smiled weakly at the waiter as he went pass and he looked at his own half-empty cup of coffee. The Italians (even fake ones like this café) really did know how to do great coffee with just the right amounts of sugar, milk and bitterness that left a good aftertaste on the tongue.

"Hey," Zach said.

Jayden looked over and just grinned like a little schoolboy as the most beautiful man he had ever seen came over to him. Zach looked so striking in his black t-shirt that highlighted how fit he was, how he didn't have any muscles but he was so lean and fit and Jayden just wanted to hug him. And Zach's thin legs looked good in his black jeans and he was so stunningly perfect.

"Hi," Jayden said as he watched Zach take a seat and they sort of looked at each other and smiled.

Jayden had really missed Zach's smile because he was so cute and attractive when he did smile.

"I have no idea where to start," Jayden said. "All I know is a lot has happened and I respect you enough to let you decide what you want,"

Jayden was a bit surprised that Zach looked a little shocked. He supposed it was fair considering part of emotional dependency and Jayden making their friendship toxic was he had made it very one-sided by mistake. So maybe Zach was surprised he wanted a more equal one.

"Oh okay," Zach said. "Well hey, I contacted you because I want to see what happened to you and how your life is now, because I did care about you a lot. And I think I might still care about you but I don't know,"

"Okay, let's see how today goes and *you* can decide if you want a friendship or not and we can go really slow," Jayden said.

He was actually rather impressed with himself, because he had played out this situation a thousand times over the past few months in his head. Like what would he say or do if Zach ever wanted to get back together as friends and hopefully more now that he wasn't with Ryan.

And in some of the situations in his head, Jayden was sadly intense and said his feelings too soon, but he hadn't today. Something he was so glad about.

"Katie seems nice, how did you meet?"

Jayden laughed because that was sort of connected to his breakdown, so that was going to be interesting for sure.

"So after you and me stopped being friends and after everything I did to get you back, I realised I needed more friends,"

"More friends besides me," Zach said smiling.

Jayden was glad Zach felt comfortable enough to make a small dig in his wonderfully caring voice that Jayden had missed.

"Yeah, because my breakdown was about gay stuff and my abuse and trauma. I found a little social club for gay young adults, like you said I should find, and that's how I met Katie. She's bi,"

"That's great and I'm glad you did take onboard what I said. That's why I told you and gave you those resources,"

Jayden really liked just talking, reconnecting and spending some time with such an attractive, fit and stunning man. And Jayden was surprised he wasn't anxious, scared and his ears weren't ringing like he had always expected them to if he had seen Zach again.

"Want to order some food?" Zach asked.

Jayden had been waiting for him to ask that because he wanted today to last as long as possible but he couldn't say it. Because the key to building a friendship first and maybe a relationship was to go slowly and that was exactly what Jayden intended to do.

Little did Jayden realise just how large the difference between *intending* and *doing* actually was and messing up that difference had massive consequences.

CHAPTER 9
27th January 2024
Canterbury, England

Zach had been in this particular café plenty of times with Ryan and Lora and some of their other friends, and he had always liked it. The chefs here did the best pizza ever because it was so fresh, so flavourful and the pesto here was to die for. Zach was really glad he had suggested it because after an hour of talking, laughing and smiling about everything and nothing, he was realising why he had been friends with Jayden in the first place.

Zach watched as Jayden finished off his pasta dish with a name he wasn't even going to try to pronounce. It looked cheesy and really nice with chunks of tomatoes, basil and little bowtie pasta shapes. Zach's own dish of Neapolitan pizza had been really delicious with the rich, creamy cheese, rich garlicy tomato sauce and the little touch of basil at the end was a nice touch.

Zach just couldn't believe he was enjoying his time with Jayden so much. He had always been interesting, he had always been caring and he had always been such a nice, wonderful guy that Zach was sort of expecting he was into him a lot more than he wanted to admit.

"Do you mind if I ask you a question about Ryan?" Jayden asked.

Zach froze for a moment so he wrapped his hands round his pint glass of diet coke so it looked like he had been thinking about if he wanted a drink or not.

"Sure," Zach said really not wanting this question to ruin their lunch together.

"What happened? And please know how sorry, so sorry I am for what I did to him," Jayden said.

Zach smiled a little. That was typical Jayden being caring enough to say sorry even though he didn't really know what had happened. Zach had never revealed how much Jayden's question had hurt his ex-boyfriend. Zach had just stopped talking to Jayden before anything else could happen.

Something he was starting to regret.

"What happened?" Jayden asked in a caring and slightly seductive tone that surprised Zach.

Zach was about to answer when a group of students behind him with yellow legal pads started arguing about something. And they had packed up and thankfully left.

That was why Zach hated group projects.

"When you asked Ryan about how he dealt with his parents and family, you freaked him out. It was even worse that you told him I told you about that so he shouted, screamed and he was so mad at me," Zach said.

Zach focused on the bubbles in his Diet Coke as he talked. He didn't want to look at cute Jayden, this was his fault and he should have handled everything better.

"I tried to explain that I had told you a month before and I didn't even expect you to remember. I certainly didn't remember telling you and then he was so mad at me. He actually stayed with Lora for two weeks,"

"Oh shit," Jayden said. "Then what happened because I started to try to get you back after three weeks,"

Zach sighed. He actually wasn't sure what was the worst bit about August and the very early chunk of September. When Jayden had asked the question that had been the first chip in Zach's and Ryan's relationship, or the messages and even a letter trying to get Zach back as his friend.

Zach wasn't sure but that was an intense time.

Zach smiled as he got a whiff of a waiter's apple and rose aftershave with a slight undertone of musk.

"It was okay to be honest for the first week after he came back. We had a lot of sex, he smelt amazing as always with his manly musk and it was nice. Then you started to try to get me back, I tried to hide everything about that from him but he found your letter,"

Zach looked up and he hated seeing how pained Jayden was as he placed his face in his hands with only his sweet eyes visible.

"It was a nice letter by the way, a little long but it was nice hearing what had happened in therapy and why you were the way you were," Zach said.

"But I was silly and intense trying to get you back,"

Zach nodded. "Then me and Ryan had another fight because, I know you are such a cute and nice person. I know you are capable of caring about people so much and you don't know how to process those feelings at times,"

Jayden nodded.

"But Ryan and Lora and everyone doesn't believe me when I say how nice you are and how… I just like you for a reason I don't know or even understand. I just want to be your friend," Zach said.

Zach realised that might have been a little forward but he was really enjoying having lunch with Jayden, a great, cute, attractive man that cared about him. And he had clearly changed for the better.

"I would like to be friends again," Jayden said.

Zach made himself look away for a moment and he focused on the long line of lecturers in their business suits, white shirts and black shoes near the counter. He wanted to be friends again with this cutie.

Zach nodded. "Okay great. But remember, go slow. We're different people now, you're cute and let's just keep things slow for now,"

"Of course," Jayden said. "But you find me cute?"

Zach just grinned and shook his head because he couldn't confirm that. He found Jayden really cute, attractive and he wanted to do some things to Jayden but he had to protect himself first.

He wanted things to go slow but Zach couldn't deny he wasn't sure he could wait that long. And that was a feeling he hadn't had for a long long time. Maybe since him and Ryan had first met all those long great years ago.

CHAPTER 10
8th February 2024
Canterbury, England

Jayden had absolutely loved the past two weeks with sexy, fit Zach because they had been texting every single day for at least an hour talking about their day, what had happened in the past and just normal friend stuff. Jayden had loved talking with his old best friend and it sort of felt like this was a lot better and healthier than it had been before.

And he flat out loved how light, wonderful and cared for Zach made him feel, but Jayden couldn't deny he was scared as hell about making a mistake. He was always double-checking his messages because he just couldn't afford to sound too intense, too invested and too damaged to Zach.

He couldn't do that again.

"Pass me the eggs please," Caroline said.

Jayden grabbed the six-pack of large eggs on the black chipboard kitchen table that was in Jackie's block of flats. He had never been here before but he rather liked it. The kitchen was massive and Jayden had no idea how many people shared this kitchen, it had to be at least ten or twelve, and everything was black.

Jayden rather liked the smooth black cabinets that were almost posh for university accommodation, the black oven hummed a little louder than he would have liked but he wasn't too concerned, and the bright yellow lights in the ceiling lit up everything perfectly.

The only bad thing about his own flat kitchen was how the lights flickered from time to time. It wasn't meant to but Jayden was just glad modern phones had a torch on them.

He liked the sweet aroma of vanilla, chocolate and mixed spice that filled the kitchen from the cookies and cakes they were baking. He had no idea how the conversation had popped up at first, but he was cooking and that was what he loved doing. Well, he loved it now the girls had strong-armed him into helping out.

"How many cookies are we making?" Jayden asked mixing his own bowl of butter, sugar and flour together.

"I don't know. The University Sports Collective want people to help fundraise for new kit so we are helping," Jackie said.

"It is a little cold in here, don't you think?" Caroline asked adding some vanilla extract to her bowl.

"No, if anything it is way too hot with these ovens on," Katie said.

Jayden just laughed. He had actually been missing his friends lately because instead of spending most evenings with them, he had been texting Zach and he had been working on a bunch of art assignments. He was so glad his drawing was getting better.

"So how's it going with Zach?" Caroline asked readjusting her knitted scarf.

"Really good thanks, but I am a little scared. You know how bad I am with friendships," Jayden said.

"Rubbish," Katie said. "Just because your first friendship with Zach ended in a rather impressive way doesn't mean you're bad at friendships,"

"Sure you can be intense at times," Jackie said. "But we learnt how you work and you learnt how we worked in turn and we love having you as a friend,"

Jayden nodded and he finished mixing up his ingredients and added some mixed spice. He flat out loved the great, rich depth of flavour the brown powder gave his cookies.

He couldn't disagree with his friends though. They were right and he had almost had a fight with Caroline and Katie in the first two months of their friendship because they had accused him of being too intense. And Jayden had argued that he was only being nice, something they agreed to in theory but all the *nice* things Jayden said came out as way too intense.

To the point he made them uncomfortable.

"Why don't you just talk to Zach about your fears?" Katie asked fanning herself with a baking tray.

"Because that's scary and we've only been talking again for another three weeks. It was about this time I started the series of unfortunate events that fucked us up the first time," Jayden said.

He mixed his bowl a little more as his heart rate increased, sweat poured down his back and his ears started ringing.

He forced himself to quietly count out of order but he was tense. He didn't like that fact and now he was just scared he was going to mess everything up like last time.

"Jayden? You okay?" Jackie asked.

Jayden nodded but he was lying. He was not okay. All he wanted in the entire world was to be with, talk to and hug and kiss sexy Zach, but he couldn't. It didn't matter how much he seriously liked Zach, they just couldn't be together because he would mess it up and hurt Zach again and again.

Something he simply could never ever allow.

CHAPTER 11
9th February 2024
Canterbury, England

As much as Zach flat out didn't want to admit it, he couldn't get the idea of Jayden covered in flour, mixed spice and other sweeter things had out of his head. He had no idea he was turned on by the idea of Jayden cooking, but he just wanted to see Jayden again.

And Zach was so impressed that Jayden really had changed because 99% of their messages and conversations were fine. Of course some of Jayden's messages were borderline intense, like how much Jayden cared about him considering they had only reconnected three weeks ago but it was milder than they used to be.

"When am I going to meet your boyfriend?" Lora asked.

Zach laughed to himself as him and Lora went into the bread isle of their local supermarket. He had never been to this one before but it seemed okay, the prices were good, the staff were all fit young men including two Zach had slept with, and the food looked good.

The current isle had a rather interesting (tasteless) black and white diamond tile pattern on it, and the left hand side was lined with some great artisan breads, some commercial ones and some pastries. Zach so badly wanted to buy tons of croissants. They looked great.

Yet Zach was way more interested in the right hand side filled with cakes, cupcakes and an entire range of delicious, creamy, sweet coffee cakes.

"I thought you would like the coffee cakes," Lora said.

Zach stood in front of them and studied them. They looked amazing and the rich aromas of yeast, freshly baked bread and buttery pastries hit his nose, and Zach just knew he was going to be spending a lot of money in this one isle.

"Your new boyfriend when do I get to meet him," Lora said like a child.

"Soon and I think you'll really like him," Zach said.

He wasn't exactly happy he had been lying to Lora for weeks about him texting Jayden, and the one time they had gone out. Yet Jayden was so cute, so funny and just so careful. All Zach wanted to do was look into his strikingly sweet blue eyes again.

Jayden was so, so cute and Zach always felt brilliant around him.

"Why don't you just tell me who it is?" Lora asked picking up a commercial coffee cake.

"Because I don't want you to scare him off. You're very intense in your protection of me," Zach said knowing the irony there.

"That's only because you let some traumatised loser in your life, he wrecked it and caused you to lose the best relationship you ever had,"

Zach subtly looked at Lora and bit his lip. That wasn't fair, that wasn't right and she was wrong. Jayden was not a loser, he was not a traumatised wreck and he did not ruin anything.

Zach wasn't even sure that Ryan was the love of his life anymore. Sure Ryan was amazing, beautiful and just a God amongst men but he wasn't Jayden. Jayden was so sweet, so caring and so intimate in the non-sexual ways that he didn't actually believe for a moment Ryan was capable of the same.

"Don't you agree?" Lora asked pointing to a more artisan coffee cake.

Zach picked up the smaller but more decorative coffee cake filled with caramelised coated walnuts, and he didn't doubt it was going to bite him in the ass, because this wasn't how he felt but he nodded.

"Yes Jayden did ruin a lot of stuff in my life but he isn't a bad person," Zach said glad he didn't have to lie about the last part.

Lora laughed. "I love you as a friend Zach and I will always protect you,"

Zach smiled his thanks to her and he placed the artisan coffee cake in Lora's basket and they moved onto the bread section. He wasn't exactly a massive fan of bread but he liked sandwiches so they were a necessary evil.

He was really impressed as he looked at the rows upon rows of white, brown and seeded loaves that covered the shelves. It was going to be a nightmare to choose.

"Why don't you like Jayden though?" Zach asked. "Like I know he hurt me so badly and he wrecked Ryan too, but is there anything else?"

"Yeah," Lora said. "I met him once and he's a nice guy but he's just… I don't know. He's pathetic. Like if your life really is as bad as he made out to you then why didn't he fix it sooner?"

Zach tensed a little. That was not a fair question and that was something he always liked about straight people that had lived perfect lives. Lora was a classic straight girl who had had good relationships, had a perfectly supportive family and had never ever been told that being straight was wrong.

Zach hated it how it was pointless trying to tell her about homophobia and how tough life and families could be for queer people. She just believed that because she was really supportive that everyone else was too.

So he went with a classic line that he knew was wasted breath.

"You can only help yourself when you're ready and you might find me ending the friendship with Jayden gave him the kick he needed to change," Zach said.

"Maybe but he should have done it sooner,"

Zach didn't even comment as he picked up two large packs of croissants and him and Lora went to the checkout.

As much as he loved Lora as a friend, he just wanted to be with Jayden so he was going to invite him out today for a little light lunch.

And that excited Zach way more than he ever wanted to admit.

Little did he realise things were about to start changing. Some good. Some bad.

CHAPTER 12
11th February 2024
Canterbury, England

Jayden was so excited that sexy, attractive, fit Zach had asked him out again for a little bit of lunch. He really didn't care what it was, he was just glad to be getting another chance to spend time with him, because texting was great but he just wanted to be with him.

Jayden had to admit as he sat down on the little wooden picnic table that had certainly seen better days (some of the wood had rotten away around the edges) that a picnic lunch might not have been the best idea for February. It was wet, a little chilly and damp.

It might have been right next to a narrow road with a few red, black and green cars parked on one side, but it was private and small. Which Jayden really liked, he loved these small private moments with the man he was falling for, and he never wanted to stop having these moments.

Jayden shivered a little as he got comfortable on the bench of the picnic table but he just couldn't stop looking at Zach as he sat down with a little white tote bag filled with food. Jayden still couldn't believe how artful, fit and divine he looked, and how perfect his body was even with Zach wearing a thin little blue coat.

"Do you remember when we last did this?" Zach asked.

Jayden laughed. "Yeah, me and you were talking one day and Ryan had gone to visit a friend up North so you wanted something to do. And then you of all people convinced me to go painting. I haven't touched watercolours since,"

"You were good though," Zach said getting out a whole host of different picnic pieces.

Jayden smiled to himself. He really liked the croissants, vegan sandwiches, little chocolate eclairs and other things that Zach had brought. It was going to take a while for them to finish this, which was hardly a problem because that just meant he got to spend even more time with the man he was seriously falling for.

"Do you still paint much? And didn't you do puzzles or something?" Jayden asked knowing the answer was yes.

Zach's face lit up and Jayden loved seeing his beautiful, perfect smile that reached all the way up to his eyes.

"Of course, I really like doing puzzles and now I'm back at my uni flat I can spread out on the kitchen table. I have this really beautiful one at the moment that's sort of an abstract photo with stunning, bright colours,"

Jayden reached over and picked up a vegan turkey and stuffing sandwich. He really liked knowing that Zach was still doing what he enjoyed, he was still passionate and he was still excited about a lot of things. And it was so great to hear him talk about his hobbies.

"I would like to see it at some point," Jayden said.

Then he bit his lip because he realised what he was basically asking. He was asking Zach to come to his apartment block, where he lived, studied and slept and that might be a little too soon.

"Relax," Zach said going for Jayden's hand but stopping himself.

Jayden smiled because he so badly wanted Zach to touch him, hold his hand and for something more to happen. And it was a little weird that Zach had gone to touch him, even during their first friendship Zach had never ever done that before.

It was strange and Jayden realised that Zach might actually like him a little more than a friend. It might explain why both of them had been texting each other every single day without fail, and there was interest on both sides. He was wanting to know the ins and outs of Zach's day and Zach would want to know the same for him.

But it was time to stop being a little too cautious.

"Do you like me?" Jayden asked.

His heart pounded in his chest. He didn't want this to be the fuck up moment again. He couldn't keep fucking up friends around the three-week mark.

Zach grinned. "What do you mean *like*? As a friend or more,"

"More," Jayden said.

Zach grabbed a vegan ham and cheese sandwich and Jayden opened his sandwich and he seriously enjoyed the rich, spicy aromas of the vegan turkey and the stuffing that he just knew would be an incredible explosion of flavour on the tongue.

"I think… I think yes I might be into you romantically," Zach said, "because you do make me feel good, I know you're really caring and I have never thought you're a bad guy,"

Jayden didn't know how to take the last part because he wasn't a bad person. He never had been and never ever would be.

"Do you like me?" Zach asked grinning.

"You know I do. I never spoke to you about it when we were friends because you were with Ryan and I respected the hell out of that relationship,"

"And that's why I like you," Zach said liking how Jayden respected his past relationship, "because you're so caring, you're so good and you are really nice,"

Jayden took out the sandwich, surprised by how incredibly soft the white bread was in his hand.

"So," Jayden said, "do you want to try us dating?"

"Aren't we already?" Zach asked grinning. "We text daily, we go out and we both like each other's company,"

"Maybe we are," Jayden said but he so

badly wanted to say so much more and he couldn't believe how brilliant this lunch was.

All he wanted to do was hug, kiss and hold Zach's hand, but he forced himself not to. Zach had only agreed to date and this was the start of a new relationship. They had technically only been dating ten seconds, but Jayden felt like he had been dating and being with Zach in his mind for weeks.

Jayden was about to say something when he saw someone out of the corner of his eye.

"What the hell are you two doing?" Ryan asked.

Jayden's stomach churned up a storm as he realised his nice peaceful lunch was going to end badly.

CHAPTER 13
11th February 2024
Canterbury, England

Zach flat out didn't understand what was happening as he watched Ryan with his sensational body storm over to him and Jayden as they sat at the picnic table. He had picked this spot at the university because it was isolated, private and perfect for a date in all but name.

Zach just looked at how great Ryan looked with his sensational biceps, six-pack abs and insanely fit body as his tight-fitting black hoody and jeans left little to the imagination.

"What the hell are you two doing?" Ryan asked.

Zach didn't need this. He had only wanted to have a nice lunch with a friend who he really, really liked. He didn't want any drama, any pain or trouble, and he certainly didn't want to see his ex-boyfriend.

He placed the vegan ham and cheese sandwich back in the packet because as much as he wanted to enjoy the extreme creaminess of the cheese, he simply had to deal with this first.

"We're having lunch together and it isn't any of your business who I spend time with," Zach said knowing it was a complete and utter lie because of who Jayden was.

Ryan stopped right next to Zach and Zach forced himself not to smile as Ryan's thick manly musk hit his nose and made his wayward parts spring to life. Ryan must have just finished football practice or something so he would be hot, sweaty and horny as always.

"Do you not know what *that* boy did to me? To us? He is a hurtful, self-fish, intense idiot. They are your words, not mine and you are spending time with him," Ryan said.

Zach didn't dare look at Jayden. He didn't know what he would say because Ryan was right, he had said a lot of nasty stuff about Jayden in the weeks after he had ended their friendship.

"And how long has this been happening? And most importantly why the hell would you let that loser back into your life after what he did to you, to me and our relationship? Did you ever end the friendship?"

Zach just looked straight into Ryan's eyes. "Of course I bloody did. I ended my friendship with him, because he was too intense, he was a nightmare and he was toxic back then. He's better now and healthier,"

Ryan laughed and looked at Jayden. Zach had no idea what either one of them were thinking, he wanted to spare Jayden some pain and make up some half-truth about what had happened behind closed doors but he couldn't.

Ryan wanted to have this fight and he was going to have it now of all times.

"You called you every word under the sun you know," Ryan said grinning. "You called you pathetic, weak, a wreck and everything else. He doesn't care about you. You're a charity case, a nothing and you never will be anything,"

Zach was about to say something when Ryan walked away and Zach found some strength to stand up.

"You ended you and me you know. And I only started talking to Jayden three weeks ago. That's the truth,"

He never had expected Ryan to turn around and respond but it still hurt that he didn't. Zach had never wanted to hurt anyone and Ryan had been a great boyfriend who cared and treasured Zach a lot, but Zach couldn't really understand why Ryan had never forgiven Zach for telling Jayden things about his life.

Zach could understand the things he had told Jayden in an effort to help him were never his things to share, but that wasn't a reason to hate him for months and then dump him. Not after Zach had done a million things to make it up to him.

"Are you okay?" Jayden asked.

Zach laughed as he looked at the cute, innocent man that he had always cared so much about. It was why he had listened and allowed Jayden to basically shit all over him about his mental health, how bad his life was and how bad his family was.

Because Zach really, really cared about Jayden. He was so cute, so sweet and so perfect in every way and even now, Jayden was still focusing on others.

He was so amazing.

"No not really," Zach said. "I didn't want to hurt Ryan and I didn't want to hurt you,"

Jayden gestured he wanted to reach across the table and hold Zach's hand, which Zach allowed. They both grinned like schoolboys as they enjoyed the warmth, attraction and sexual chemistry that flowed between them.

Zach gently rubbed Jayden's hand. "I am sorry you know about what I said,"

Jayden tensed. "You didn't have to confirm it,"

"I didn't want to lie to you. It all mattered but I was so angry and mad at myself, Ryan and what had happened to our relationship that… I regret a lot of things I said about you,"

"Do you still think of me like that?"

"Never," Zach said picking up his ham and cheese sandwich again. "I like you a lot so let's try to move on. Let's focus on the future, do you want that?"

"I really would," Jayden said as he finished off his own sandwich and moaned in pleasure at the taste.

Zach just hoped beyond hope Jayden would one day moan at him in utter pleasure because he loved that sound and he really wanted to hear it over and over again.

CHAPTER 14
11th February 2024
Canterbury, England

As much as Jayden didn't want to admit it, he couldn't help but have Ryan's cold, hard words replay constantly in his head. He was helping Caroline (who was now wearing three scarves because it was apparently too damn cold), Jackie and Katie (who was wearing blue shorts and a tank top because it was too warm on an icy cold February late afternoon).

Jayden really didn't understand his friends' temperature sensitivities at times, but he loved them, supported them and considering he had ditched them to hang out with Zach, he sort of owed them.

Jayden had two large plastic boxes filled with about a hundred largeish chocolate chip cookies. The rich butter, sugar and dark chocolate hints that filled his senses made Jayden really want to chomp into the box himself, but Jackie had made a plate of cookies for the four of them so sadly he was going to have to wait.

Even though he seriously didn't want to.

Jayden really liked the main plaza of the campus, where the Sports Guild wanted everyone to leave their donations. Jayden had always liked how large it was so three rows of exotic food trucks could line up and serve students. Today it seemed like the local Indian, Chinese and Japanese food trucks dominated the scene.

Jayden had always preferred when the middle eastern trucks were there but hopefully they would be back tomorrow or sometime soon.

"What is that smell?" Caroline asked loudly.

Jayden laughed as he looked over to the coffee shop next to university bookshop with beautiful, breath-taking displays of the latest bestsellers and the local corner shop on the very end.

He coughed a few times as the coffee shop had clearly burnt their coffee beans yet again. It was so overwhelming, so awful and so strange that Jayden was definitely going to get out of here as soon as possible.

"That coffee shop's always burning their bean," Jackie said as she carried three boxes of cookies.

Jayden followed the women as they all made their way towards the large white tent in the middle of the plaza with a long line of students with their own donations.

Something he had no intention of waiting for.

"Hey," Katie said, "didn't you say you saw Ryan earlier?"

"Yeah why?" Jayden asked.

"Isn't that his boyfriend Colin?" Katie asked gesturing with her head to the white tent.

Jayden just rolled his eyes and frowned. Of course it was bloody Colin up ahead taking all the donations, writing up what was what and smiling and being all friendly when in reality he was a dickhead.

Zach had only told him what had happened at the Big Fair about a week into them restarting their friendships. Jayden had wanted to say some strong words but he behaved himself.

He flat out couldn't believe that Colin would actually shoved the fact he was Ryan's new boyfriend in Zach's face. Who did that? Especially considering how much Zach had been hurting at the time.

"You alright?" Caroline asked.

Jayden smiled at her. "I don't know,"

And then Jayden told them all about what Ryan had said to him about Zach's choice words when their friendship had ended.

"He was angry," Jackie said flicking the plastic boxes up because they were clearly getting too heavy for her.

"I guess so but if he really cared about me back then, why would he say it?" Jayden asked.

"Dearest," Caroline said shivering slightly,

"you know how much we love you but you ever think, you and Zach are living too much in the past,"

Jayden shrugged. He had no idea what the hell she was talking about, but Jayden couldn't help himself when he realised how great the light was with the cold grey sky above with but small rays of golden sunlight still managed to light up the sky.

It was only now Jayden was realising just how much he had been neglecting his passion, his favourite hobby and the thing that had gotten him through so much. He definitely needed to go on an "artist date" again to just take photos.

And enjoy his favourite artform.

Jayden stepped out the way of a student as a large group of them walked past.

"Answer the question," Jackie said smiling.

"I don't know Jackie," Jayden said. "You have no idea what it was like to have a breakdown, lose someone who you had a toxic and very unhealthy relationship with and then have to recover from that,"

The women went silent and then Caroline wrapped her scarves a little tighter and smiled.

"I'm sorry, we don't know what it was like," Caroline said. "We only know the aftermath and how much you struggled during those four months when you were trying to get back on your feet,"

"But," Jackie said, "we also know how great you are, how caring you are and how much Zach means to you now. Maybe just see if you can let go of the past, hurt and anything that happened between you both,"

Jayden smiled. "If I wasn't holding these boxes I would hug you all,"

"Then let's put down our boxes," Katie said.

Jayden put down his boxes at the same time his friends did and then they all did a massive group hug, because they were right. He should talk to Zach about just forgetting and not worrying about the past.

They were different people now and he was healthier, stronger and he wasn't dependent or intense with Zach anymore. He knew what to say and what not to say to people.

And the very idea of that made Jayden so damn excited because it meant there could be a real wonderful, lovely chance of him and Zach having a relationship that was healthy and not wrapped up in the past.

A past that was extremely hurtful and damaging for both of them.

Little did Jayden realise everything was about to come crashing down.

CHAPTER 15
17th February 2024
Canterbury, England

Now Zach definitely knew how Jayden had felt when he had asked him out that one time to do painting in the woods where both of them lived, the idea of an "artist date" sounded silly, a little weird and a little woo-woo. But if it meant spending time with someone as fit, hot and attractive as Jayden then he was up for it.

Which was probably the exact same reason Jayden had agreed to go painting with him.

"This is beautiful and perfect for painting," Jayden said.

Zach just grinned as him and Jayden walked through Blean Wood. The air was cold, damp and crisp so there might not have been much mud but the ground was lumpy and uneven. Not that Zach minded too much.

He had always wanted to go to Blean Woods near Kent University but he had never had the time to go yet. And now he was here with the man he was seriously falling for, he was so damn happy that he had come here.

Zach was rather impressed with the thin silver birch, pine and oak trees that lined the pathway. Their branches were shooting out in all directions and long blanche vines hung off some of the trees.

"Oh wow. That is so perfect," Jayden said as he knelt down, messed around with angling his professional camera and he took a few shots.

Zach laughed, because Jayden was so damn cute. He had no idea what Jayden saw in the Woods, it was a complete mystery to him but he loved, truly loved seeing Jayden so happy and in his element.

When Jayden came over to him and showed him some of his photos, Zach was amazed at how detailed the photos of a Robin were in the trees. The detail in the photo was only amplified by the lighting, the slight sparkle on the branch because of the frost being hit by the sunlight at just the right angle.

"You're amazing you know," Zach said.

Jayden grinned. "Um, I really want to kiss you,"

Zach smiled and he honestly couldn't have cared less that he was technically in public and Jayden had said back in August that he would never kiss another man in public.

Zach took a step closer and he gently stroked Jayden's cheek with one hand and he ran the other hand down his black coat.

He liked it when Jayden's breath caught and Zach went closer.

When their lips met, Zach moaned in pleasure as Jayden did the same. The kiss was electric, intense and so tender and filled with so much passion that Zach never ever wanted this kiss to end.

This was so much better than anything Ryan had ever given him because this was a deep, intense, caring kiss. It wasn't a hot, I-want-to-fuck-you kiss, this was a you-matter-so-much-to-me kiss.

And Zach loved it.

"Wow," Jayden said. "Thank you,"

Zach playfully hit him on the arm and he took Jayden's hand in his as they went along the pathway. Whilst trying not to twist an ankle on the uneven ground.

"You know when I see something picture worthy I'm going to let go," Jayden said grinning.

Zach ignored it. "You don't have to thank me for kissing you. I like you a lot and, I meant what I said about wanting to give us a try now you're better and healthier,"

Jayden looked around. "Thanks, and you know I am so sorry for what happened before,"

"I know," Zach said meaning it. "You were just trying to deal with a bad situation at home, you were trying to do it all alone and you just developed an unhealthy attachment to me because I was the only person that accepted you,"

"And you're beautiful," Jayden said.

"Getting intense again," Zach said with a small smile.

"Sorry," Jayden said as he let go and knelt down to take another photo of something in the trees.

"See but I like this, this is what we need to do. Just be open, talk and just you make a mistake I'll correct you and you can do the same with me,"

"Now that I would like. Definitely going to make talking to you less stressful for me," Jayden said.

"And that's what boyfriends are for,"

Zach stopped dead in his tracks as soon as the words left his mouth. The term *boyfriend* felt strange, awkward and a little weird to say out loud. He had called Ryan his boyfriend for more years than he cared to admit so it felt a little weird calling Jayden of all people his boyfriend.

But he couldn't help but smile because it felt good, right and lovely to call him his boyfriend.

"One of my friends mentioned something a few days ago," Jayden said. "She thinks both of us are living too much in the past,"

Zach nodded and he jogged a little to catch up with Jayden who was already taking more photos of something up ahead.

He supposed that was sort of fair. Both of them had been concerned about how the other would react because of what had happened before, so maybe they should forget the past and just live in the moment. And if something connected to the past popped up then they would deal with it.

So that's exactly what Zach told him.

Jayden hugged him and Zach liked the feeling of his hard body against his.

"Actually," Jayden said. "When we went painting that time I really wanted a photo of us together. Can I… I don't know, have one now?"

"Sure but how can you take a selfie on that pro cam of yours. Does it have a secret selfie setting?" Zach asked failing to stop himself from laughing.

Jayden playfully hit Zach on the head. "No I have a phone for that,"

Zach went over to Jayden and they both placed a tight, caring arm around each other, they grinned and they both took some pictures.

Zach poked his tongue out on some of them. They both pulled silly faces and then there were nice ones and happy ones and photos that just made Zach want to cry in happiness. He loved this. He loved these small precious moments where they could be a real couple without worrying what others would say about them.

Lora was still banging on about how he was hiding something and Ryan had been messaging him on social media. Ryan was threatening him, telling him he was making a big mistake and Zach had tried blocking him but Ryan just had a new account.

"Want to think about going back?" Jayden asked after they took a final couple's photo together. "It's early, we can catch a film or something at my flat,"

Zach laughed and he was about to respond when he heard a twig snap in the distance.

"Seriously!" Lora shouted. "This is your boyfriend. What the fuck!"

Zach's eyes widened as he realised shit was about to hit the fan.

CHAPTER 16
17th February 2024
Canterbury, England

Jayden flat out couldn't believe what was happening here. It couldn't be her, not Lora. Anything but that woman with her long angelic blond hair that had made his life hell back in September and October when he had seen her a few times.

Not Lora. She was evil, harsh and an awful person who hated him.

Jayden felt his heart pound in his chest, cold sweat ran back down his back and his ears rang slightly as he watched as her and Ryan come down the path towards them. The uneven frozen ground didn't even seem to slow them or bother them in the slightest.

The pine, oaks and silver birches moved slightly and their branches banged into each other as an icy cold breeze flew through the woodlands. And Jayden just knew that this was going to end badly.

"So this is your boyfriend?" Lora asked frowning.

"I wasn't lying to you," Zach said. "I just sort of bent the truth because Jayden wasn't my boyfriend when we first started talking,"

"How bloody long has this been happening?" Lora asked.

Jayden shivered at the rage and anger and hate in her voice. He hadn't realised Lora still had so much hate in her after she had cornered him in one of the shops on campus and really bit into him.

Jayden had cried so damn much that evening and he had done everything he could to forget it.

Ryan stepped forward. "See Lora Zach doesn't care about you. You were always a good friend to me after what that loser did to me and Zach, but Zach just doesn't care. He only ever thinks of himself,"

"Shut up," Jayden said. "You're a snake and you just hate me for going what you went through,"

"No," Ryan said taking a few steps closer to him. "I hate you because you are a loser, a charity case and you are nothing,"

Jayden forced back the tears. It was happening all over again but instead of happening over text, it was happening to his face.

"Enough," Zach said. "Me and Jayden are trying to date and I was going to tell you and-"

"He's only going to hurt you or have you actually forgotten what that loser did to you and Ryan back in August?" Lora asked.

Jayden couldn't help but look at Zach. He had always known he had hurt Zach with his intensity, his obsessiveness and his sharp questions about how to cope with his trauma and abuse but he had never wanted to know *just* how much he had hurt him.

The man he seriously liked and cared for and maybe even loved.

The dampness in the air got even thicker as Jayden realised that Zach was looking at the ground. He might have been thinking or remembering and Jayden really wanted to support him.

Surely that was how good relationships were formed, one partner supporting the other partner and then their relationship got even stronger and better. That was how it worked, surely?

Jayden took a few steps forward. "You might not like me but I do love Zach and I genuinely care about him. I won't hurt him again and I'm better now,"

"No you aren't," Zach said looking up at Jayden with watery eyes.

Lora and Ryan laughed and Jayden shivered as he hated the sound of that cackling.

"You have only known me again for three weeks. You can't *love* me," Zach said straining to keep back the tears. "You are so intense, so connected to feelings that it takes others time to develop and you… you are so lovely but I can't keep doing this. Every time you come into my life you cause so much upheaval,"

Jayden's eyes widened. It was happening. He had fucked-up yet again because he had been too intense, he had said those little words too soon and Zach didn't feel the same.

He was an idiot.

"So… so you're siding with them?" Jayden asked pointing to Lora and Ryan.

Zach shook his head. "You all pretend to care about me but Lora you just want to control me. You could have asked and respected my decision to talk to Jayden again. And Ryan stop texting and threatening me,"

Jayden was about to say something and question that but Zach just glared at him.

"You are so caring and kind but, I just can't keep doing this with you," Zach said as he walked away.

Jayden looked at Ryan and Lora as they looked all nice and smug and Jayden stood his ground. He didn't need to be scared of them anymore, he didn't need to be concerned about what they thought of him, he didn't even like them.

When Zach was out of sight Ryan and Lora smiled and bowed and walked away.

"Loser," Ryan said.

Lora turned around. "And you do realise, it was only a week ago Zach said *Jayden ruined a lot of stuff in my life*,"

Jayden didn't dare react until they were out of sight and then he simply fell against an icy cold oak tree and he let everything out.

All his pain. All his anger. All his sadness.

It all came out.

CHAPTER 17
17th February 2024
Canterbury, England

Zach had absolutely no idea if it had been forecasted to rain later in the day but he hadn't checked. He continued along a long road filled with potholes and wonderful little semi-detached houses with white exteriors, perfectly clean driveways and little rose gardens out front as he went back towards the university.

The rain fell down all around him and Zach just smiled for a moment because his coat was thin, so it was good for warmth in the cold but it was useless in the rain. Especially heavy rain like this one.

A black car drove past him with its headlights on as the grey sky started to turn a little black. Even three of the streetlamps turned on as Zach went past because it was so dark like his mood.

Zach was slightly regretting finding a park bench to sit down for a long time (he had no idea how long he had sat there just hating his life and hating everything about Ryan) because now he was caught in the rain and he was going to get soaked.

Zach was surprised how deafening the rain was as it splashed onto the pavement, it hit tin roofs of little outbuildings in people's gardens and cars past him.

This really wasn't how he had wanted today to go but he had sort of always known this was what would happen in the end.

He had always known that Jayden "loved" him and Zach wanted to joke to himself that it was impossible not to. Jayden had always liked blonds and men with fit bodies and Zach supposed he was very good in both departments.

He had just never wanted Jayden to be so intense in that particular moment. Not when Ryan and Lora were there with him or against him as was the case. Zach had really wanted Jayden to be quiet and maybe he could have reasoned with his friend and ex so they would leave him alone.

Zach shivered as his hair was soaking wet, his coat wasn't doing anything anymore to keep the water out and the light cold breeze was starting to chill him. He still had another five, ten minutes easily before he reached the university and then another ten minutes of walking before he reached his shared flat.

It wasn't ideal but nothing about today was.

Zach couldn't really blame Jayden though because he knew he had only been trying to help. Jayden was probably trying to be the same lovely, caring and wonderful person that he always had been. He probably saw the situation with Lora and Ryan as a problem that needed to be fixed and he wanted to try.

He was great like that.

Zach smiled to himself as he kept walking through the rain because he really did like Jayden.

Zach had never really meant something as kind, caring and great as Jayden. Because sure Jayden could be intense as hell at times, it was wrong of him to say he loved Zach after only three weeks, but Jayden had never been a bad person.

And Zach wasn't sure he wanted a repeat of the past.

He had never really given it much thought before now because he had been so focused on Ryan and angry at Jayden. But it had sort of killed him the first time he had put his friendship on pause with Jayden.

He wasn't sure why he felt like someone had ripped out a part of him, but now he supposed it was because Jayden had been such a good, lovely and fun friend for that month.

They had talked a lot, gone out a lot and they were always smiling and laughing and having fun. And Zach had hated putting the friendship on pause because that meant all the "fun" just stopped immediately.

He regretted that now.

Zach shivered again as the rain came down even harder and he was fairly sure he looked like a drowned rat with his blond hair being darkened and awful.

He was so cold and shaking. He just wanted to go home back to his apartment.

Zach tried to get his phone now so he could text one of his flatmates to put the kettle on and make sure the heating in the shared kitchen was on, that radiator was bigger so he could dry more of his clothes, but his hands were shaking too badly to do anything.

He was so cold.

Zach saw a large white SUV drive up next to him before it sped up and drove right through a puddle.

It splashed all over him and Zach just wanted to cry. This day wasn't going right but he wasn't going to let the past repeat itself.

He cared and seriously liked Jayden so he was going to go to his shared university accommodation and get warm there and sort this out.

Mainly because he didn't want to lose Jayden but also because Jayden's accommodation was so much closer than his own.

And right now he only wanted to get warm and he seriously wanted to get warm in Jayden's arms.

CHAPTER 18
17th February 2024
Canterbury, England

Jayden was rather impressed with himself for not spending any more than twenty minutes crying, screaming and just being angry at himself, the world and Lora (with Ryan just being a natural idiot). He was even happier he had managed to make it back to his university accommodation before the rain had started.

"I hope Caroline doesn't melt out there," Katie said fanning herself.

Jayden smiled to himself as he wrapped his hands round the piping hot mug of coffee that Jackie had made him.

They were all sitting in Jayden's shared kitchen and Jayden was just glad it was so clean for a change. He had never seen the black fake-marble countertops so clean, shiny and they smelt of orange-scented bleach. That wasn't a bad smell at all. Jayden was impressed the other flatmates had really been brilliant about their cleaning responsibilities after the university had moaned and officially warned them yesterday.

Even the black chipboard dining table that had more cracks and holes than most UK roads was rather impressive. Jayden could almost see his own reflection in it but Jayden seriously doubted Caroline would melt.

"She isn't a witch you know," Jayden said.

"How do you know? She's always cold and the rain only makes things colder," Katie said grinning. "Maybe she's cold blooded,"

Jayden almost jumped at the deafening sound of the rain hammering into the glass windows of the kitchen that was only amplified by the echoing in the kitchen. He really hoped the rain would lighten up soon.

Jackie took a few sips of her herbal tea and shook her head.

"I'm sorry about what happened," Jackie said before looking at Katie. "Because someone here needs to be supportive,"

"I was going to comfort him but I was more concerned about Caroline and I hate this heating by the way,"

Jayden smiled. He really did love his friends.

"Do you think you'll contact him again?" Jackie asked like how a mother might ask a small child something.

Jayden shrugged. "Yeah probably, but not for a few days. Part of the reason why Zach put our friendship on pause in the first time was because I was contacting Ryan too much in an effort to become friends with him,"

Katie went round the table and hugged Jayden. "I am so proud of you,"

"Why?" Jayden asked.

Jackie looked like it was obvious. "Because that's healthy. It means you can learn from your mistakes and you want to get better at friendships and relationships,"

Jayden nodded. That was fair and he really wanted Zach to know he was different, he was healthy and he was committed to trying to be a good boyfriend.

"But how are you doing?" Katie asked taking a seat at the table.

"I don't know to be honest. It was so… weird seeing Lora again because I hadn't seen her since the start of the year,"

"What happened and why didn't you tell us?" Katie asked. "You've known us all since September,"

Jayden just looked at his steaming coffee. "Because after everything with Zach I convinced myself that talking about how I was wasn't a good thing. I didn't want to burden you and our friendships were way too new for that sort of information,"

Katie looked like she was going to say something but Jackie just glared at her.

"Maybe you're right and me and Katie don't have to think about the same things as you when it comes to friendships,"

Katie nodded like that was what she had always wanted to say.

Jayden was about to say something because he felt great and he had always liked how wonderful Zach made him feel, but the rain got even louder and he could barely hear himself think over the noise of the rain against the window.

Then it went quiet for a moment before the rain continued to hammer down and echo around the kitchen.

"I miss him," Jayden said. "I really miss Zach and I don't want him to be angry with me. I didn't mean to hurt him, and don't, want him to go through what he went through in August,"

Jackie and Katie smiled like they knew something.

Jayden took a sip of his strong bitter coffee and gestured them to say whatever they wanted, he really hoped it was going to be helpful.

"Then you wait a few days, prove you aren't intense and obsessive like before and then you fight for this relationship," Jackie said. "You go slow to continue to prove how much better you are and then you convince Zach through your actions that this relationship matters,"

Jayden nodded. He liked the idea of that because all he wanted in the entire world was to see Zach's fit, sexy body again and amazing smile. Jayden wanted to kiss Zach's soft, wonderful lips again and he really wanted to run his fingers through Zach's delightfully soft blond hair.

Zach was so beautiful and perfect and Jayden's stomach filled with butterflies.

He got what he said was wrong and he shouldn't have said he loved Zach so soon, but he really, really did.

The kitchen door opened and Jayden's mouth dropped and he couldn't help but grin as Caroline came in (soaking wet) with some blond man that looked like a drowned rat.

The most beautiful drowned rat Jayden had ever seen.

CHAPTER 19
17th February 2024
Canterbury, England

Zach was so damn cold and he couldn't stop his shivering as he stood in the doorway to Jayden's shared kitchen. He was glad Jayden had mentioned where to find his flat and accommodation in passing in a random conversation they had been having over text, because he was so damn cold.

He really liked it how Jayden came over to him and hugged him and gently pulled himself inside. Zach just grinned because he knew that Jayden was going to take good care of him and then when he was thawed out Zach really hoped they could sort everything out.

As Jayden focused on getting him out of his soaking wet coat, Zach wanted to cough at the sheer strength of the cloves, oranges and lemon aromas in the air. Maybe it was from bleach or something because the kitchen was so clean but it was strong. Too strong for it to be normal.

The sheer strength of the aromas made Zach's eyes water and his body kept shivering. He had never seen countertops so shiny and clean and black, and the dining table that looked like it was going to fall apart at any moment looked relatively new (from a secondhand store).

"Tea or coffee?" the woman who called herself Caroline asked.

Zach tried to talk but his teeth were chattering too much. He hated being this cold and wet but he loved it when Jayden hugged him tight after putting his coat on the radiator near the window.

Zach hugged Jayden as tight as he could manage as he shook. And he realised if someone walked past they might have thought he was twerking on Jayden, he was shivering so badly.

Zach gasped as Jayden playfully put his wonderfully warm hands under Zach's wet hoody and he grinned like a little schoolboy. He was even happier that Jayden didn't stop and Zach laughed and his wayward parts sprung to life as Jayden explored his body.

"I knew you were fit but I didn't realise you had such a hard body," Jayden said like he was a kid in a candy store.

"Here's your coffee," Caroline said clearly choosing Zach's drink for herself.

Zach clung to Jayden a little as they went over to the dining table with two other women already sitting around it. He had no idea why one of the women were wearing shorts and a tank top on such a cold day so she had to be Katie.

"Are you okay enough to come into my room and change?" Jayden asked. "Just to get you into some new clothes, I promise I can wait outside whilst you change and we don't have to talk or anything until you go back,"

Zach rubbed his hands together and he wrapped them round his wonderfully warm coffee mug. He smiled at Jayden for a moment because Lora was so wrong about Jayden. He had changed, he was different and he was a lot more aware of his intensity at times.

Of course Jayden would make mistakes but Zach knew he wasn't exactly perfect either. But he still wanted him and Jayden to work out so that was why he was here.

"I appreciate it you know," Zach said grinning. "It means a lot that you're trying but I wouldn't mind getting out of my clothes, and you can watch if you want,"

Zach was so glad he was sitting down as his wayward parts were showing as clear as day to see in his soaking wet jeans.

"I wouldn't mind that either," Jayden said as they both got up, took their mugs with them and they both said bye to the girls.

Zach followed Jayden out along a narrow little corridor with dirty white walls and the same blue carpet squares that the university seemed to be obsessed with.

Then Jayden opened a door and they went into his flat. Zach was impressed with it, it was rather lovely, small but lovely. He smiled at the rather beautiful photos hanging on the walls, he knew he shouldn't have been but he was always surprised at how great of a photographer Jayden was.

The bed was small, a little high and Zach wasn't sure if he was going to have to jump up to get on it, but that was definitely a theory to test later on.

Jayden pushed past him to get to a small wardrobe and Zach watched as Jayden expertly picked out a matching black outfit of a black hoody, jogging bottoms and a black t-shirt. Zach had wanted to ask for some boxer briefs so he could get out of his soaking wet underwear but he supposed he wanted to keep Jayden guessing about some stuff in their relationship.

"Here you go," Jayden said weakly smiling as he passed the clothes to Zach. "I am sorry you know,"

Zach nodded. "I know you are and that's why I'm here. Stand over there, watch me get changed if you want and we'll talk because I think there's a lot we need to fix before we can be together,"

"Like what?" Jayden asked, "you make it sound like there's more to fix than you and me,"

Zach nodded because as much as he didn't want to admit it, he did want his best friend back.

"I know it sounds stupid but Lora is a great friend and she cares about me a lot. If there's a chance we can still be friends and if she can accept you're a good part of my life then I want to take it. Is that okay?"

Zach wasn't sure what Jayden was going to say for a moment but after a few seconds, he nodded.

"If that helps you to be happy then that's okay and we all need more friends these days,"

Zach hugged him. Jayden really was brilliant, caring and wonderful and he was so glad he had come here to fix everything.

Now he just needed to get out of these soaking clothes and get warm.

CHAPTER 20
17th February 2024
Canterbury, England

Jayden had absolutely no idea what he needed to do in this situation as he leant against a warm white wall of his flat. He watched a very hot, fit and soaking wet Zach place the clothes down on his bed and Zach stood in the narrow gap between his desk and his bed.

Jayden had always wanted to see Zach's fit, attractive and just divine body under his clothes but he had never thought he was actually going to see it. Especially with Zach shaking and shivering so much from the cold.

All Jayden wanted to do was go over to Zach and brush his soaking wet hair to one side and just kiss him and love him.

"You nervous?" Zach asked as he took his drenched hoody and damp t-shirt off.

"Maybe," Jayden said.

Jayden couldn't help but grin like an idiot as he admired Zach's insanely fit body. He had always known there were no muscles and no real definition to Zach's body but it was still amazing to look at. There wasn't an ounce of body fat, Zach had a strong stomach line and his body curved slightly so Jayden was certain if Zach did some ab workouts he would have a six-pack in a short order.

He was that fit.

Jayden was surprised when Zach didn't put on his dry hoody and t-shirt. Instead Zach took off his soaking wet jeans and Jayden gasped in pleasure.

Zach's legs were long, sexy and thin like he had always known. They were hairless and smooth and Jayden really wanted to run a hand up them and Zach's package was hardly a bad side.

And Zach was clearly aroused to say the least.

Then Jayden crossed his own legs as Zach got unchanged into Jayden's favourite black hoody, jogging bottoms and t-shirt.

"That was very nice. Thanks for that," Jayden said.

"You're welcome I want to see your body at some point too,"

Jayden laughed and shook his head because this was why he had always loved him and Zach. Their friendship and relationship was so fun, full of laughter and it was so positive.

"Help me up," Zach said as he tried jumping up on Jayden's bed but he couldn't.

Jayden hugged and lifted up Zach and he accidentally threw him on the bed and then Jayden sat next to him.

"Note to self you throwing me on the bed is hot," Zach said like he was embarrassed.

"So we're okay then?"

"Yeah. I think we always were okay but I was just shocked that you said *I love you* and there was all the grief from Ryan and Lora and I just needed some space,"

Jayden took Zach's hand in his. "I know I can be a lot at times and I know the intensity of emotions isn't normal, but I am trying. Just ask the girls because I have been intense with them before and I am a lot better now,"

Zach nodded. "I know, over the past three weeks I know you've been a lot better and not *as* intense. Sure you're going to make mistakes at times because you are intense and that's partly why I like you so much,"

Jayden smiled. His stomach filled with butterflies at the idea of Zach liking him a lot.

"And I know," Zach said, "I can't change how intense you feel things, but I can tell you and help you come across as less intense. Like if we're talking and you get intense then I'll just tell you and we make a course correction or something. Is that okay?"

Jayden nodded and hugged Zach.

"That was all I ever wanted in the first place," Jayden said. "When you put us on pause and when I was trying to get you back, I know I was super intense and maybe even a little unstable back then, but you only had to talk to me."

"Yeah, um sorry,"

"It's okay," Jayden said breaking the hug and running his hand through Zach's damp hair.

"Let's just promise from now on we'll start talking more, we'll focus on being us and supporting each other. Because I want this relationship to work,"

"Me too," Jayden said.

Jayden loved it how Zach pulled him close and kissed him again. Jayden couldn't believe how great and soft and wonderful Zach's lips felt against his and he never wanted this moment to end.

It was perfect.

"You want to watch something and snuggle?" Zach asked.

Jayden nodded and grinned like a schoolboy as he grabbed his laptop and snuggled with the beautiful man he loved.

He knew that they still needed to fix Zach's and Lora's friendship and deal with Ryan but tonight was about them. And that made Jayden a lot more excited than he had been in his entire life.

And that was a great feeling to have.

CHAPTER 21
24th February 2024
Canterbury, England

Zach was flat out shocked that he had to take a leaf out of Jayden's book when it came to Lora, because Zach had wanted to text her, phone her and fix everything about their friendship the day after she had almost wrecked his relationship with the man he loved. But Zach couldn't believe that Jayden had been right that he should wait a few more days, maybe a week and then approach Lora.

Now Zach knew exactly how Jayden felt when he had paused their friendship, even though this was slightly different.

About a week later, Zach held the hand of the beautiful man he loved as they both sat down in the library café at a small plastic table with a horribly wobbly leg, as they saw Lora coming towards them.

The entire café with its white walls, massive floor-to-ceiling windows and tons upon tons of students revising with their friends made Zach smile a little. He had never liked coming to the library café because he just wasn't comfortable and he had always revised better in his room. If he wanted to see his friends he would go out with them, he seriously wouldn't revise or study with them.

"You okay?" Jayden asked.

Zach laughed. "You're always asking about me. Shouldn't I be asking you about how you're feeling, after all Lora did shout at you a few times?"

As much as Zach had loved spending the past week kissing, hugging and watching films with Jayden, he had hated to find out what Lora had done behind his back. Even when he was so annoyed at Jayden for his intensity and emotional dependency, she never should have shouted or cornered him.

That was wrong.

"Thanks for the coffee," Lora said sitting down on the chair opposite them.

Zach smiled at his old best friend. Lora looked really well and she was sipping the coffee they had brought her so she clearly wasn't *that* angry at them.

Zach squeezed Jayden's wonderfully smooth, soft hand a little. He hated Jayden to start talking but Lora was his friend so this was his problem to solve.

"I'm sorry Zach didn't tell you about us," Jayden said. "I never wanted that and I've actually always liked how good you two are as friends,"

Lora took a sip of her coffee. "Thanks because unlike you I don't hurt Zach and I always look out for him,"

"You're hurting me right now," Zach said.

Zach had never expected to say it but he was only realising how he had been spending the past week, and every waking moment with the man he loved, because he didn't want to be alone so he could think about how badly his friend had treated him.

"What do you mean?" Lora asked. "I am only looking out for you, it's what I have always done,"

"You have done nothing but-" Zach said.

"I think you mean that," Jayden said, "but I think you're going about it the wrong way because you are hurting his feelings,"

Zach was surprised Jayden could speak so calmly, nicely and like Lora actually had a good point. Maybe he didn't need to fix this problem alone.

"I think," Jayden said, "you want to know about me and if there is any chance I am going to hurt Zach again like I did before,"

Lora played with her coffee cup and nodded a little. Zach was glad to see she was calmer now with the rich bitter aroma of the coffee filling the air and she leant forward so she had to be listening to Jayden. There was clearly a first time for everything.

"I have been through therapy, I have been through a lot of personal growth with my friends that I have now and I am a lot better. I've dealt with my past really well and I'm dealing with everything that pops up,"

"Okay," Lora said playing with her coffee cup even more making the aroma of coffee even more intense, "but can you promise without a shadow of a doubt you will never hurt him again?"

Zach looked at the man he loved and smiled, because it was a pointless question. They were a couple in love, they liked each other a lot and Zach just knew there might be arguments or intense moments in the future but it didn't matter. They were two people in love and they would deal with everything that popped up.

"I love him," Zach said grinning like a schoolboy, "and that means I'll take the so-called risk,"

Lora frowned. "You can't love him,"

Zach looked at Jayden and he really did love those light blue eyes, they were perfect.

"Why not?" Zach asked. "He's kind, caring and just so great. And honestly, I want to see where this relationship goes, I'm not scared anymore and if you have a problem with that then I don't need you in my life,"

Jayden kissed Zach on the cheek then Zach kissed Jayden on the lips. They might have been kissing for over a week now but Zach still flat out loved how great of a kisser Jayden was. He never ever wanted to stop kissing this beautiful man.

"You know what," Lora said smiling. "If you're happy then I can be happy for you too. I actually haven't liked the past week very much,"

Zach cocked his head. He had spoken to some of their other friends in his lectures and they had all been spending lots of time with Lora.

"And yes I know I spend a lot of time with the gang at the bar but… they aren't you,"

Zach laughed. "I am pretty great,"

Zach loved hearing Jayden and Lora laugh together and then Zach hugged his best friend.

And for the next three hours, Zach just grinned, laughed and talked with his boyfriend and his best friend for the first time ever. They spoke about their lives, their degrees and everything in-between.

Zach loved every moment of it because it just showed him the power of having honest conversations and standing up for the person he loved.

Now there was only one problem left to deal with and Zach could be with Jayden forever. Something he was definitely looking forward to.

They had to deal with Ryan.

CHAPTER 22
26th February 2024
Canterbury, England

Jayden had never expected to like Lora as much as he did but after spending a few hours with her in the library café, texting her a little and meeting with her and his friends this morning, he couldn't deny that she was actually a great woman with a really interesting life.

But this was the moment they had all been planning for the past two days.

Jayden held Zach's wonderfully soft, smooth hand tight with Lora, Caroline and Jackie close behind them (Katie was already at their destination talking with Ryan to stall him from escaping) as they went through the large brown corridors with gym lockers lining the walls as they went towards the main sports hall.

Jayden couldn't help but grin as he could see that Zach was getting a little turned on because of the slight aroma of sweat that filled the corridor. Maybe Ryan's football team had just finished a practice session and Jayden playfully jabbed his boyfriend.

"Relax I am getting distracted," Zach said, "but I might give you a little reward later,"

Jayden's stomach filled with butterflies at the idea of having sex with the man he loved. He would love that.

They all went through the white doors and then hooked a left and then a right through more gym-locker-lined corridors before they made it to the main sports hall.

Jayden was surprised how massive it was without all the stalls and other students inside. The immense football pitch was all marked out, the block walls of the hall were gigantic and the three other people in the hall looked like ants from this distance.

They all went towards the three people. Jayden could see Katie a mile away with her blue tank-top, short-shorts and black fan that she was still fanning herself with. He was never going to understand her.

Jayden's heart started to pound in his chest. his ears rang slightly. His stomach tightened into a painful knot.

He could see Ryan and Colin talking to Katie. They looked annoyed as hell and Jayden really couldn't have anything bad happen, not today, not any day.

"Babe?" Zach asked. "You alright?"

Jayden kept on walking but he smiled as his body relaxed. He actually was okay, for the first time since August, maybe ever because he truly was okay. He was with his friends, Lora and his boyfriend.

This was everything he had ever wanted and Jayden couldn't believe how great it felt to have friends and a boyfriend that cared, liked and wanted to be with him. He didn't have to panic or be scared about them leaving him because they had all chosen to be friends with him and they liked him for him, and there was no changing that.

Jackie, Caroline and Katie had proved that time and time again, and Jayden had really liked how they had taught him how healthy friendships worked after a few problems. And they were still here today and wanted to help him.

And Zach was still here and loved him and was an amazing boyfriend because… he just was. Jayden was never going to question that because it didn't need to be questioned. Jayden loved him too.

"That wasn't a foul in the last minute!" Colin shouted at Katie.

"Don't you dare shout at her," Jayden said a lot harsher than he normally would.

"Oh my god the loser and the dumbass are still together. And what?" Ryan asked with a massive grin. "Lora, I thought you were better than that, he lied to you,"

Lora shook her head. "You are nothing but a liar that manipulates people to make them miserable,"

Ryan shrugged like that was nothing.

"I might have loved you once," Zach said, "but I will never love you again. I don't even know what I saw in you,"

Jayden smiled even more as Ryan's grin disappeared. Jayden had no idea that would hurt Ryan, maybe Ryan still loved Zach and was only trying to get him back.

"Come on babe let's go," Colin said. "Let's leave these losers alone,"

Ryan shook his head. "But… but I don't understand how *this* happened?"

Jayden laughed as Ryan shook his head around and highlighted how him and Zach were holding hands like a true couple.

"Because," Jayden said, "you will never understand true love. Love doesn't have to be explained, logical or make that much sense. Love is about respect, joy and that strange feeling you have inside you whenever you see that person,"

Jayden so badly wanted to kiss Zach but he didn't want to go out of his way to annoy Ryan. Jayden was annoyed at him, he didn't want to be cruel to the idiot.

"And Jayden's amazing," Caroline said pulling on her knitted scarf.

Ryan frowned and Jayden was surprised when his shoulders slumped forward and he looked really down.

"Babe come on," Colin said starting to walk away.

Ryan took a step towards Zach and everyone except Colin took two steps closer to Zach. Jayden was not letting Ryan anywhere near his boyfriend.

"We really aren't getting back together are we?"

"No," Zach said. "You were lovely once and I think when you aren't being a dick, you might still be lovely. But no I don't love you anymore and I haven't since August. Since I met Jayden here, what he did to you back then was awful and he triggered so much for you. I get that but you could have handled a lot of stuff differently,"

"We all could have," Lora said.

Jayden felt a lump form in his throat.

"Yeah you're right," Ryan said and he looked at Jayden. "I forgive you and I'm really sorry for what you went through,"

"And you," Jayden said stepping forward and hugging Ryan.

When Jayden broke the hug, Ryan gave Zach a little kiss on the cheek for old time's sake and Jayden just grinned as Ryan and Colin walked away hand in hand.

He wasn't really sure why he was smiling so much, or why his stomach filled with a swarm of butterflies or why he felt so damn amazing. But he had a feeling that it was because everything was settled and perfect. He had a wonderful boyfriend that loved him more than anything, he had so many friends that he really liked and they were so much fun to be around, and Ryan wasn't going to bother them anymore.

That was the great thing about dealing with the past. It could be dealt with, overcome and everyone could move on in the end.

And as Jayden kissed Zach's wonderfully soft, full lips again, he had to admit he was the luckiest man in the world. And he couldn't help but appreciate that he had sorted everything out in the sports hall where him and Zach had reconnected and ultimately started their journey of falling in love.

A journey that had to be the best journey in the world.

CHAPTER 23
24th April 2024
Canterbury, England

About two months later, Zach really enjoyed how warm and light the evenings were starting to get now it was April, and it might have been the Easter Break away from the university, but Zach still loved spending every minute of every day with stunning Jayden.

Over the past three months, they had spent every day together and kissed and done more adult things almost as often. Zach really liked hanging out with Jayden alone with all their friends and he didn't even consider Lora his friend or Caroline, Jackie and Katie Jayden's friends anymore.

They were all their friends and he really liked that.

Zach still didn't want to admit how much he was enjoying photography with Jayden, and he was so damn proud of Jayden for starting to sell photos to magazines, on his own online store and he was making good money from it.

And the past three months were the best ones of his life.

"I love you," Jayden said.

Zach brushed Jayden's smooth hair as they both sat on top of the warm grass hill at the university that overlooked the striking city of Canterbury. There were so many treetops standing up like soldiers but beyond that there were tons of ancient rooftops, the Cathedral spire and so many other landmarks showing off Canterbury's impressive history.

Zach had always loved sitting here in the evenings and talking with his friends and past boyfriends, but this time it felt extra special. Him and Jayden had sat here a few times but tonight, it just seemed extra romantic and Zach couldn't deny he was really enjoying stroking Jayden's hair. It was so smooth and nice that Zach didn't want to stop for a while.

"Don't forget we're meeting your parents tomorrow?" Jayden asked.

Zach laughed. He was looking forward to that a lot more than he wanted to admit, because it would be fun. His parents would pretend to be tough and interrogating because they were somewhat aware of what had happened back in August, but Zach knew after the first ten minutes they would love Jayden.

They would be able to see he was happy, in love and Jayden was so much better than Ryan. Zach was still surprised Ryan and Colin were together and Zach had seen them together a few times since they had sorted out everything, and he had to admit, Ryan and Colin looked even better than they did when they were dating.

"What you thinking about?" Jayden asked.

"Oh, nothing much," Zach said grinning. "Just how you and me are a great couple, how much I love you and how much better my life is now I know you,"

Jayden laughed and blew Zach a kiss. Zach playfully ran a hand down Jayden's hot, sexy body and nodded at a group of girls in summer dresses as they walked past.

Zach moved over a little as Jayden sat up and pulled him close.

"You know why tonight feels even more romantic than normal," Jayden said more of a statement than a question, "and we've known each other a long time to be honest,"

Zach nodded. They might have only been friends and dating for a total of six months including their first attempt in August, but Zach felt like he knew everything about Jayden, and Jayden had said the same about him.

"Yeah, we've been through more together in a few months than most couples ever have to deal with," Zach said smiling.

"Exactly," Jayden said taking a small black box out of his pocket. "Zach James will you do me the honour of becoming my husband?"

"Yes!" Zach shouted kissing, hugging and making the beautiful man he loved fall backwards onto the grass. Then they rolled over kissing and celebrating the best news in their entire lives.

And that was what happened.

They both went to Zach's parent's house the next day and it was the best time of their lives, because Zach's parents were happy, delighted and they were more enthusiastic about the wedding than they were (something Zach had no idea was possible).

Then 9-months later in the Christmas break from university, they married and Zach flat out loved it, because him and the man he loved more than anything in the entire world were together forever. And neither one of them had a problem with that in the slightest.

And Zach realised on his wedding day that when you truly love someone like how Zach loved Jayden and Jayden loved Zach, it didn't matter who they were before, how bad their life was or their mental health, people could improve, get better and life could be great.

Zach was so proud of Jayden for everything he had accomplished and they had both helped each other be better in ways Zach never thought was possible.

And as Zach and Jayden drove off towards the airport for their honeymoon, Zach felt like the luckiest man alive because him and Jayden had gone through damage, healing and love and that made their love even stronger.

Something Zach would always, always treasure.

Sign Up Bonus

Keep up to date with exclusive deals on Connor Whiteley's Books, as well as the latest news about new releases and so much more!

Sign up for the Grab a Book and Chill Monthly newsletter, and you'll get one **FREE** ebook just for signing up: Agents of The Emperor Collection.

Sign Up Now!

https://dl.bookfunnel.com/f4p5xkprbk

Subscriptions:

Never miss an issue!

3 Month Subscription… $14.99

6 Month Subscription… $29.99

12 Month Subscription… $49.99

Subscribe Up Now!

https://payhip.com/b/aMJyj